GREEN
TRIANGLES

DONALD DEWEY

MILFORD HOUSE

an imprint of Sunbury Press, Inc.
Mechanicsburg, PA USA

MILFORD HOUSE

an imprint of Sunbury Press, Inc.
Mechanicsburg, PA USA

ISBN: 978-1-62006-206-7 (Trade paperback)

Library of Congress Control Number: 2018937204

FIRST MILFRED HOUSE PRESS EDITION: March 2018

Product of the United States of America
0 1 1 2 3 5 8 13 21 34 55

Set in Bookman Old Style
Designed by Crystal Devine
Cover by Lawrence Knorr
Edited by Lawrence Knorr

Continue the Enlightenment!

For my extraordinary godson Kevin and Patty

CHAPTER 1

I like listening to bizarre stories. Not only can they be entertaining, but they test my tolerance for the ludicrous. In theory, I like thinking of myself as being open to any fantasy my clients bring into my office. Oh, the wonderful colored rainbow of the human race, and all that. But as I've gotten older, I've also felt myself gravitating toward the primary colors and wanting to stay there. You want to move me from yellow to cinnamon, it's going to cost you a good dose of skepticism and a bigger dose of crotchetiness.

Phil Caporale was making me feel like every old crab I'd ever seen throwing breadcrumbs to the pigeons in Prospect Park. Every time he added another name or place or official agency, I imagined myself snarling at passersby for getting in the way of my crumbs. ("Can't you see where you're walking, you clown? You haven't got half the sense of these birds.") The trouble was, I knew Caporale wasn't making up anything, at least as far as he saw it. When he wasn't talking about Indian propaganda movies or Peter Lorre-type informers or FBI agents, he was remembering that he had just been hit by a locomotive and still didn't know why. His kind of misadventures were not supposed to happen to middle-aged history teachers on Long Island.

I'd met Caporale once before, at my father-in-law's place in Garden City. Once a week, Joe Carroll hosted a salon for gab, cheese, and wine. Sometimes the gab was about the War of the Roses, sometimes it was about the social significance of Liza Minnelli. It all depended on the people who showed up and their ability to shout over my father-in-law's predilection for talking about the material he had expounded on for 30 years with Adelphi's history department. As I recalled, Caporale had been one of the successful shouters. Joe had wanted to steer the discussion toward Czechoslovakia between the world wars, and Caporale had objected that, believe it or not, continents like Asia and South America had also had a history between the '20s and the '40s and that it was typical of the Joe Carroll Eurocentrics to think nothing of importance had happened outside Europe in that time. I remembered seeing Joe's ultimate tell—a rapid thumping of his lounger armrest with his middle finger—for admitting he was in the wrong.

But the Phil Caporale sitting across my desk didn't seem all that sure even where Asia or South America was. He was a balding, paunchy man around 50 with hooded eyes, not used to asking for things. He was, as my grandmother once would have said, somebody "set in his ways," and had been for a long time. The straight-backed chair I had inherited from a neighbor's discarded dinette set only added to his discomfort, and he held on to a crossed knee as though it was the only thing he could trust in my apartment. "I don't know what else to tell you," he said. "The Professor thought it would be useful talking to you, but I can see from your face, you're not any more convinced of that than I am."

Say one thing for my father-in-law: He could scare up as many dead-end clients for me as I could find on my own. "Everything you've said, Phil, sounds like you need a lawyer more than an investigator."

"I know, I know. Florence, my wife, says the same thing. They walk in with their dime store IDs like they're still working for J. Edgar Hoover. I thought the FBI had become all cuddly and user-friendly?"

I looked down at the three scratches that added up to my note taking while he had been talking. It was a tic I had picked up as a cop on the Island: When somebody said Washington, D.C. was the capital of the United States, you wrote down *Wash DC cap US* to reassure the speaker he was receiving your full attention. "This Neil Kinsey, you haven't seen him since when?"

"A good 25 years. At Harry's Bar."

"On the Left Bank."

"No, Harry's is on the Right Bank."

Sometimes I needed reassurance, too: If Caporale had never been in Paris, little of what he had said would have been worth even my chicken scratches. "Never been. I should go one of these days."

There was a passing suspicion in his eyes, but he let it go. "I'm sure it's Kinsey who started this ball rolling. There's too much self-importance in all this for it not to involve him in some way."

"Going back 25 years."

He threw up his hands in exasperation. "What can I tell you, Paul? As soon as one of these FBI robots mentioned his name, I knew, just *knew*, he'd been telling stories to somebody. That's all the guy ever did."

"Tell stories."

"Tell stories."

"Twenty-five years ago."

"That's what I said." Testier.

"And now they're asking you questions about India and Pakistan."

He finally had enough of the chair. "They belonged on 'Saturday Night Live,' for Christ sake!" he said, clapping his foot down and jumping up. "Was I involved in any way with some Indian or Pakistani group in New York? Did I have Hindu or Islamic beliefs? What did I think of the situation on the Asian subcontinent? A fucking tragedy, that's what!"

"That's what you told them?"

"That's what I told them."

"That's good, Phil."

He stopped in front of the Venetian blinds. "Yeah, I thought so," he grinned. "Got them out of the house. The first time."

"How many times they been back?"

"I told you. The first time was my house, the second time my office. Thank god Florence wasn't around when they knocked on the door, or I'd still be explaining it. Then there were the phone calls and the invitations to go down to their office."

"So if I'm following you here, your guess is this Kinsey is somehow involved in Indian or Pakistani politics, he got himself into a corner, and somehow your name seemed like the easiest way of getting out of it."

"Can you think of something else?"

"Phil, I don't know Kinsey, the only time I've paid attention to the Indians and Pakistanis lately is when they're rattling nuclear bombs at one another, and I don't know why the hell some American egomaniac would seem valuable to either one. I also don't know why your name would pop up if you haven't seen this character in 25 years."

He took that in with a whining ambulance down in the street. He looked so interested in following the ambulance down Fourth Avenue that I smelled his first . . . let's call it omission. "Are we skipping something here, Phil? Some little detail that might've made driving in here all the way from Garden City not such a crazy idea?"

He waited until the ambulance siren had evaporated into the late afternoon. "I've got some old films," he announced finally. "Stuff we shot in Paris in the '90s. Kinsey thought he was going to be Fellini, I was going to be Antonioni. I haven't looked at the stuff in ages. That I remember, it's mostly people going up and down the steps of the Metro or going in and out of *pissoirs*. You know, *cinema verite*?"

"There's another shoe, Phil. Drop it."

One of my favorite kinds of embarrassment is the kind that comes with an energetic shake of the head. Even as the face turns the color of a St. Louis Cardinals uniform insignia, the head is trying to wind up to Linda Blair speed so it can spin off the shoulders across the room and divert attention. "Nothing dramatic," he said. "Just that I have them all, including what Kinsey shot. Real old-time stuff, still in film cans. Some years back—I mean, we're talking when Reagan was still president! —he wrote to me asking for the cans that belonged to him. I ignored the letter."

"And?"

"No and. He never wrote again. And fuck him if he did. I figured for all the crap he pulled in Paris, keeping his masterpieces was little more than a token payment. Your aunt has better stuff in her attic, anyway."

"So you didn't keep them for their value."

"As film, they never had any."

"Then what, Phil?"

The attic was his, not my aunt's. "As revenge, I suppose," he said, trying to look brave about staring at me. "To stick it to the bastard. 'Here, Kinsey, here're these years in Paris you're never going to have a record of because I have it all. You fucked with me, now I'm taking all that time away from you and creating a big hole in your life. Deal with it.'"

I postponed another look at the scratch about Kinsey the Casbah spy who had been informing on his friends in the '90s. I would still have that after Caporale had left. "If you hated him that much, maybe he hated you the same way. Maybe your name didn't come out so accidentally."

He seemed impressed I'd been listening to him so closely. Then he shook his head. "He had nothing to be vindictive about. *We* were the aggrieved parties. He got his 30 pieces of silver passing along our every conversational tidbit to his favorite American Embassy spook."

"You're talking about what, Phil? The hostages in Iran? The Middle East terrorists back then? Plane hijackers? What the hell does any of that have to do with India and Pakistan today?"

I suppose I had asked for the academic's condescending smile and his "we can have that discussion another time." Naturally, that was the moment I asked myself whether I liked Phil Caporale. It was a question I always asked about people who were thinking of giving me retainers, and often it popped up when I had the least reason for liking them. I'm sure a psychologist would find that timing suggestive, perhaps concluding that, at bottom, Paul Finley was more interested in *not* taking on a client than in assuring himself of another week of meals and rent money. What surprised me then and there, though, was the certainty of the answer to myself: *No, I didn't like him.* People had patronized me before, had played cat-and-mouse games on relevant information with me before, had even hinted with their glances around my office/living room that they saw themselves as having fallen pretty low to be confiding their problems to this Brooklyn PI. Misdirection, spoken and unspoken, was part of the game. But watching Caporale's eyes land on my favorite Lamston's print of a raging sea (entitled *Calm*), I heard some faintly ominous movie music in the air. This guy was a 25-year-old treasure chest, I told myself, and even if I ever found out what was buried in it, I knew from the start it wasn't going to be gold ducats.

"Coming here today, you must've had some idea about what you wanted to ask me to do."

He nodded readily. "I want you to find Kinsey. I'm very good on the Internet, but I've found absolutely nothing. My attorney is extremely able when it comes to estate planning, but his idea of tracing somebody is to call a few record bureaus—or worse, hire somebody to do it for him so I end up with a bill that looks like the Pentagon budget. Whatever you may have heard about having tenure, I can't afford that. The Professor said I might be able to afford you."

"That's all very nice, but I don't think you've thought this through."

"Tell me."

The chicken scratches on my pad suddenly looked like bills of indictment. "Number one, he may be impossible to find. The FBI wants to know about your politics? Maybe they've been matching your answers to what Kinsey's been telling them in some safe house. Or maybe some other agency has him registered in a Des Moines hotel under the name of Jimmy Hoffa. Maybe he's not even in this country. Or vice versa, they're looking for Kinsey and they were hoping you'd give them a lead. If their open-ended budget can't help them locate one guy, how am I supposed to? Or we throw away both those possibilities and go at this like a normal missing person's case, no Indians, Pakistanis, or defenders of the Republic in the middle. Here we end up spending your salary, your pension, your Social Security benefits, and the proceeds from the sale of your house. And we still get no further than somebody named Kinsey who maybe once upon a time *might* have lived in a Mesa, Arizona trailer park, present whereabouts unknown. But why stop there? Moving right along. The guy has changed his name to Pradash Singh and he lives in Kashmir stirring up trouble for the wrong religion on the other side of the street. We send him an e-mail: 'Hi, Kinsey, it's your old pal Phil. See how I've tracked you down? You can't hide from the long arm of Finley Investigations.' But Pradash Singh, he's so busy putting together a bomb to throw in the temple or mosque of his religious choice, he never bothers answering you and changes his e-mail so you don't keep pestering him."

He seemed to have heard all those objections before. "I appreciate the warning," he said, not sounding appreciative. "But there are some people you could ask. A few days, a week tops."

"And why exactly am I going to be asking them where Kinsey is? You want to forgive him for being a creep 25 years ago?"

"That I don't think I'll ever be up to," he said. "But I want him to have his films back. I don't want anything more to do with him, even indirectly. And I had this creepy feeling when these FBI guys were there they would never be bothering me if I didn't have those film cans stowed away. I know, I know. I sound like somebody who belongs in a haunted house. But I just want to get rid of the goddamn things."

"How about . . .?"

"No, I can't just throw them out. Would you want somebody throwing out part of your life that you once thought was important?"

I had too many answers to that one, including it was none of his business. "How about a blind ad in the paper or on the web?"

"What paper? I should assume the guy reads the *New York Times* and *Newsday*?"

"So what you're telling me, Phil, is these Feds have given you a conscience crisis after 25 years. All this time you couldn't give a goddamn what was 'important' to Neil Kinsey's life, but now they've made you see the light."

He poked his finger at his Adam's apple almost as though he had to dislodge his reply. "Sorry if that sounds juvenile, but that's where I am with it, yes."

"And suppose these movies aren't so important to him any-more? Reagan was a lot of presidents ago."

He looked at me so blankly I wondered if I'd broken the news Reagan wasn't in the White House anymore. "I don't care what *he* thinks is important, Finley," he said, enunciating like a first-grade teacher. "*I'm* the one who wants to hire you and get rid of them."

It was such a logical comeback my dislike of him shot up the thermometer. "And these people you want to refer me to, why don't you look them up yourself?" That answer I knew; I'd known it as soon as he had started peppering his tale with little com-mercials about how he was seen by many as "a spokesman for more things than the university." What I was supposed to have understood was that Phil Caporale was also a valuable resource for East Coast academe, for the image of third-generation Ital-ian Americans, maybe even for people who wore mustard-colored socks. If only in his own eyes, it had been a long time since he alone had walked into a room. But I also wanted to hear him say it. "Because you don't want to make trouble for them with your Federal friends or because you want them to stay in the past, away from Garden City, Florence, and other present realities?"

"A little of both," he said, conceding nothing. "But if anybody knows where Kinsey might be, they would."

"And you really want to do this now? I mean, if the Feds are so hot on the trail of Kinsey, they could still be watching you. This really the time for you to go looking for him on your own?"

He finally found something else funny. "But I won't be looking for him. You will."

I told myself it was my own fault for trying to get into debates with somebody who had spent his whole life standing in front of a classroom and taking on wise guys. "Okay. What're we talking about here—Yankee Stadium crowds, the number of just men in the world?"

"Four people," he said, removing a slip of paper from his inside jacket pocket and handing it across the desk. "I'm not even sure a couple of them are in the States. But if Kinsey's been in contact with anyone, they're the most likely people. If they're not here, forget it. We'll have tried. If you do get to talk to them and they know where Kinsey is, you don't have to get too specific about me or the film cans. In fact, I'd prefer you not to mention me or the movies. Make up some story about why you're looking for him."

I have nothing against making up stories; I've never been in a bar longer than for making a phone call when I haven't made up one. But there was a flinty taste to having a client propose I have a few on tap. "And assuming I have success in this great hunt, what then? I arrange a meeting between the two of you so you can turn over the movies?"

He went to his Adam's apple with his nail again. "Tell you the truth, I haven't really thought that far ahead. But no, I don't want to talk to him, Finley. I just want him and all his possessions gone. I liked him in the past, I really did. I had my French adventures, I had his little films as payment for stress, and that chapter was over. It was all very neat, and I've come to depend on neatness. I don't want it disturbed again 10 years from now. When the time comes, yes, I'll probably ask you to deliver the damn things to him. How much do you think this will cost me? Just an estimate. I've really got to work this all out so I can explain it to Florence."

Rodin's *Thinker* would have envied the grist I had for a good hour after he had left. Count the items. *Finley* was one. He had given up the pretense of treating me as *Paul,* a fellow salon guest of the Professor's; *Finley* was the employee he had come from Long Island in a panic to hire. The talk about neatness was another. I could believe it. If India and Pakistan had defined their borders as cleanly as Phil Caporale had apparently divided his life, nobody would have been rattling nuclear swords. Caporale was an expert historian not only because he had degrees on his walls and tenure at Adelphi, but because he had also consigned a younger Phil Caporale—the one who had met Neil Kinsey in Paris—to the days of the Goths and Vandals. How dare Neil Kinsey and the FBI mess with all that order!

And what about all the mess on the far side of that frontier, back in Paris a quarter-century ago? I tried imagining the younger Phil Caporale he had described to me. There he was, just out of graduate school, all his cards in order for the academic track his parents had apparently sweated to steer him toward, but also hesitating at the starting block. He was weary, both physically and mentally. He needed a break from showing Italian Americans were good for more than being extras in *The Godfather*. He needed time for himself to think through the options that had been so automatic during all his schooling. He went to Paris. It was supposed to be only the first stop on a European holiday, but he never got past a modest Left Bank hotel. There he fell in with a crowd of actors, models, and writers, some of whom made ends meet by dubbing Indian movies. First, some Frenchmen wrote the scripts for the approval of Calcutta film producers, who proceeded to shoot them back home in Hindi, Urdu, and Bengali. Then the finished pictures were shipped back to Paris for dubbing in English and French for wider distribution around the world. Only some of the movies were about mad Pakistani scientists. For variety, there were others about mad Pakistani serial killers and mad Pakistani child molesters. Caporale was particularly good at dubbing Pakistani villains. ("They even started calling me Ali after a while.")

I thought some of this was pretty nifty. That Phil Caporale I would have invited to dinner to hear more about how the hell Frenchmen got to make Indian propaganda movies and how an American would-be history teacher ended up shouting "Hindi scum!" to a good part of the world before being blasted by New Delhi counterespionage agents. That Phil Caporale had been so unneat he had been tempted to drop all his academic pretensions and live in France permanently, his parents' ideas of social striving be damned. I wasn't *always* cantankerous about being moved from yellow to cinnamon. All I asked was that the trip is entertaining.

But that Phil Caporale, I had to remind myself, wasn't the one who had given me a check for $500 before walking out of my Bay Ridge apartment. The Phil Caporale for whom I'd immediately gotten busy creating a new file was Prig Lite, who, come to think about it, might have needed a few visits from the Feds for shaking up his daily smugness. That Phil Caporale expected not an enthused listener for funny stories, but somebody who would earn his retainer by seriously looking into the four names he had typed out for me on unmarked stationery.

The names were names—not a Jennifer Lopez or a Klinglark Kjkyx among them. The first one was a Jean-Claude Servais, described by Caporale as "the French producer in charge of the dubbing sessions, now working with the French delegation to the UN in some cultural capacity." Second was a Mireille Pouchol ("I have no idea"). Third was an Inge Matson ("she works in the fashion business, maybe an agency or a magazine"). Fourth was a Roberta Weiss ("I have no idea").

I had a couple of them. The first was to wait for the UN guy, Servais, to return to Paris for vacation, then hop a flight across the ocean to do all my investigating along the Seine. Another idea I had—based on absolutely nothing Caporale had said—was that Roberta Weiss was the main reason I was $500 richer, that, more than Neil Kinsey, she was the one he was *really* skittish about seeing again. For all I knew, the story about returning movies to Kinsey was a complete fraud. The FBI had reminded Caporale of how life had been in Paris with Roberta Weiss before wife Florence with the rolling pin had entered the picture and now he wanted to relive it, even if only vicariously through whatever I could find out about her.

Why Roberta Weiss instead of Mireille Pouchol, about whom he also had "no idea?" A flimsy feeling, nothing more. I could say it was because he had listed her last or because he had annotated her exactly as he had Pouchol, all the better for disguising her importance. But I probably would have found equal rationalizations if he had listed her first, second, or third. I'd learned the hard way that trying to legitimize intuitions with profound explanations was counterproductive. You went with them and they turned out to be right or wrong, period. Phil Caporale and Roberta Weiss had balled from the back pews of Notre Dame to the Louvre galleries, he had left her in the lurch with twin daughters, had returned to the Long Island suburban life, had contracted middle-class amnesia, and now wanted nothing to do with children who had grown up to be ninja killers bent on avenging their abandoned mother. That was enough for me to get on with things. Some people were in love; I was in romance.

CHAPTER 2

Not that there wasn't more to Finley Investigations than Phil Caporale. As long as they made white coats, there would always be doctors, dentists, and veterinarians flirting with malpractice suits and somebody like me helping to establish them. Marriages meant divorces, funerals meant contested wills, trials meant background checks on jurors and witnesses—and all of them meant phone calls asking if I could add to my caseload. Financially, I was past the point of replying "Are you nuts? Of course, I can!" but not so far along that I could turn my decisions over to the kind of instinctive dislike I had for Caporale. Put it this way: I was able to toy with the idea of hiring somebody for a few hours every week to come in and digitize my paper file folders, but still a few impulses and comfortable dollars away from actually doing it. I still relied mostly on the peck-peck keyboard system I had learned with the Nassau County police department and on the manila folders that took up the widest shelf of my living room bookcase.

One reason I was in no hurry to move my Caporale notes to the side of the desk after he had left was the alternative of having to return to two other clients. Neither represented Finley at his suavest. The first was an apartment house group in Canarsie trying to round up photographic evidence that a hump named Klaus was bent on driving all his tenants into the street so he could slap on a fresh coat of paint and charge newcomers three and four times more. The problem wasn't the building where the tenants themselves lived; they had already put together an album of rat droppings, water-logged walls and ceilings, broken hall banisters, and the other delights of big city land lording. This had been enough for the Housing Authority to weigh in with some warnings and even deadlines to Klaus. But the tenants had been down that road before, and with little hope, they would gain anything but a few months of peace before Klaus and his sons went back to inviting in rats as squatters. What I had been hired for —through the lawyer for the tenants—was gathering proof Klaus was doing the same thing in three other buildings he owned in Brooklyn and Queens; in short, demonstrate a pattern of deliberate abuse the Housing Authority couldn't shrug off with a couple of visits and official letters. But there were obstacles. The first was the reluctance of the tenants in the other houses—mainly Hispanics with more cots than green cards—to support any action against Klaus. The second was my skills with a camera. I'd never thought of myself as Matthew Brady. To me, a Polaroid was high technology in the same class as the Mars Probe. As a cop, I'd been perfectly content to admire the Crime Scene people who could cover every angle of a homicide or robbery without a second's hesitation over the camera button. Why force things? What need was there for *me* to have to drop by buildings where I wouldn't be welcome in any of several Spanish dialects and start shooting pictures that would probably feature my fingers in tight close-up? It was a question I'd been pondering for almost a week since the attorney's call on behalf of the tenant group.

The other open sore was Sarah Harrah, whose name wasn't quite the palindrome it should have been. As her husband had suspected (*known* was more like it), Sarah had been having weekly afternoon meetings not with the girlfriends and business acquaintances she claimed, but with the owner of an Upper West Side restaurant in Manhattan, usually at his apartment in the Westbeth complex. What Harrah wanted was a detailed record of his wife's doings that would either make the case for his divorce attorney or force him to find another excuse for dumping her.

My attitude toward cheating spouse cases was usually like that of the electrician called in to change a fuse: If somebody wanted to pay me for what he should have been able to handle by himself, I was going to take the money, feel superior, and make as quick a job of it as possible. This left little room for speculating about where I, the cheating spouse, and the cuckolded spouse stood in the moral universe. The trouble with this outlook was that every so often, as with Sarah Harrah, I caught a glimpse of more than a *case*. Sarah Harrah was a tall, slim woman in her mid-thirties, with the kind of hair my old Crayolas had called burnt sienna. She was some kind of clothes buyer who roamed here and there throughout the five boroughs, especially in heavily Asian and Latin neighborhoods, apparently, on the lookout for colors, materials, or styles, she could bring back to her Manhattan employer for some high-class inspiration or theft, whatever the trade called it. After the first few days of following her around, I was convinced Harrah had been paranoid, that Sarah hadn't been seeing anybody on the sly. If she wanted to make excuses for this or that time frame, I'd told myself, her normal daily travels to the edges of Brooklyn and the Bronx should have made unnecessary all the "ladies out to tea" stories she had been passing on to him. But then on the fourth day, she had gone to the Westbeth apartments.

For the first 45 minutes, I'd sat behind the wheel on Bethune Street keeping an eye on the complex door she had entered. Once I had persuaded myself she hadn't gone to the apartment of a sari or kimono dealer, I had spent a fast quarter-hour confirming a fear that West, Washington, and Bank streets also had exits from the complex for anyone wanting to escape detection. Why I had bothered with the confirmation I had no idea since there wasn't much I could have done about it anyway except to do what I had done—get back into the car and resume watching the Bethune Street door. Finally, three hours and five minutes after she had gone in, Sarah had come out again, with the restaurant man. Tall as she was, he had towered over her. Well-combed and -dressed, graceful movements, the kind of guy who gave off expensive aftershave scents even when you couldn't smell them. They had made for a handsome couple on their way to a MOMA cocktail party—except it had been too early in the afternoon for cocktails and they weren't supposed to have been a couple. He had walked her to the corner of Washington, then left her on the sidewalk to step out to find a cab. At that moment Sarah Harrah had stopped being merely a case.

Mr. Westbeth had raised two fingers to the traffic heading his way—a self-assured fins for the city to stop for a second so he could glide back into his place in it. I hadn't been alone in my admiration. From the sidewalk Sarah Harrah had watched him with a smile I would describe as worshipful if it didn't sound like I was making the case for all male restaurant people, even those who just asked for menus. I hadn't seen such sexy affection in ages and hadn't wanted to count the eras involved. I'd also known in that instant that Gerald Harrah had a lot more to worry about than a bored wife in the mood for sheets of a different color every so often. In her expression had been one message only: *Everything* was boring except being with Mr. Westbeth.

He wasn't perfect: He had needed three fins signs before finally stopping a taxi. He had opened the back door, she had stepped down off the sidewalk, he had kissed her while she had given his hip bone a quick circular rub, she had gotten into the back, and the cab had taken off. Then Gerald Harrah had had his second thing to worry about: Mr. Westbeth had stood watching the cab disappear down Washington until he could finally accept the best part of his day was over. They might not have been going to a MOMA opening that night, I had thought, but they would be going to one soon.

I'd done my duty that day. I'd followed Mr. Westbeth's second cab up to a Columbus Avenue restaurant called Tino, had learned his name was David Bale and he was the owner and had put my Bass Ale from Tino's bar on Harrah's bill. I had felt mean every step of the way. I had envied Bale, had wanted to lock up Sarah and her love inside me and had despised Harrah. My favorite analogy of the electrician and the fuse had felt as profound as a summer teenager movie. *I* had felt as profound as one of those gross-outs. Paul Finley, meet a vomit joke.

And then Harrah had gotten me off the hook for a week by leaving a message on my machine saying he was going to a conference in Colorado Springs and would check in with me when he returned. The last I'd heard, Colorado Springs had a telephone system, so I'd given him half a point for wanting to put off what I had discovered for as long as possible. The day Caporale showed up with his Indian-Pakistani tale was the sixth since the machine message, so I was down to counting the hours when I would have to make up my mind about what to say about my Manhattan travels.

One of the nice things about 5:01 every afternoon is that, unlike your natural fury earlier in the day, you can be pleasantly surprised living people aren't at the other end of your calls. In the case of the French Embassy to the UN, I told myself, wasn't it even 11:01 (at least in Europe)? How could I have possibly expected to start looking for Jean-Claude Servais at such an ungodly hour? No, Jean-Claude was going to have to wait until the next day. Since the publishing world was notorious for keeping office lights on beyond five o'clock, I put off my calls to *Elle* and *Harper's Bazaar* for Inge Matson until I could be sure a mechanical operator took over the switchboard. That left Mireille Pouchol and Roberta Weiss for exploratory calls. By happy circumstance, neither of them showed up on the Internet telephone directory, at least in New York, Boston, New Orleans, Montreal, Chicago, and San Francisco. What was a soul to do after such a tiring day if not go down to the Green Fox for a club soda?

The occasional glass of ale or wine aside, I hadn't been doing my part for the booze industry for about five years. I hadn't eaten too many Brussels sprouts over that period, either, and sometimes liked thinking I had given as much thought to one as to the other. The biggest disruption to that fancy came a couple of times a week when I dropped down to the Green Fox on my corner. I admit it: There were no neighborhood Brussels sprouts places that attracted me as regularly. And maybe there *was* more than met my consciousness in simply liking to relax during Happy Hour with Cynthia and the saloon regulars, sipping my club soda while they sought my wisdom on world and domestic affairs in between groggier swallows. But I didn't care if there was or not. I had gone through all the guilt, denial, and repentance stages over my last big booze-up. I had penetrated them so wholly I knew they would always recur at unexpected moments. When I was 110 and they were still shooting me up with turnip preservatives, I had come to accept, some wave of nausea would erupt from my brain to my stomach at the memory of collapsing into my father-in-law's bed while he'd done nothing to stop his daughter and granddaughter from driving home alone on icy Christmas roads. But there was nothing to do about that anymore, and the idea that those images would disappear for good if I kept my eyes glued to the sidewalk every time I passed a saloon, seemed to kill Jenny and Susan all over again with phony piety.

Johnny Yeager was holding forth at the bar's short arm to Miles Harkleroad and Blanche Walsh. There was nobody else in the place. Yeager's topic at the moment seemed to be the Israelis and Arabs—warning enough for me to give him a wave and head directly for Cynthia at the far end of the bar. She was already going for my soda. "You been up to something you shouldn't be, Finley?"

And with that, Phil Caporale stopped being just another ground ball to run out.

Cynthia laughed at my expression. "Nuclear secrets? Chemical weapons? Something like that?"

"What the hell you talking about?"

"Two characters who looked like they were wearing their fathers' suits came in this afternoon," she said, laying down my glass. "Were you a regular in here? What kind of people did you hang with? How much of your bar talk . . . Wait a sec. How did he put it? Right. 'How much of your *argumentative conversation* was about politics?'"

"You gotta be kidding."

She said something else she considered funny. I thought a few dozen things that definitely weren't. Her Fathers' Suits hadn't just improvised their questions after following Caporale to my place; people like that didn't work that way. They must have known where Caporale was heading before he had ever gotten into his car in Garden City and had planned ahead of time how to spend their wait for him to come back down from my apartment. And the most likely way for them to have known that was to have the nitwit's phone bugged. First question: Had he called me the day before to set up our appointment from his home phone or from his office phone at the university? Second question: What the hell difference did it make?

"What's the matter?"

Cynthia was a freckled blonde who liked to wear her hair in the ugly parted fashion of the old New England colonists. She was a couple of years older than I was, but seemed able to erase or widen the difference depending on her mood. Sometimes she could sound like a naive tourist in need of directions to Central Park, other times like the owner of a speakeasy who knew where all the rods, gats, and tommy guns had been stashed. Her uncertain look meant she hadn't decided yet whether to be my baby sister or mother. "I'm thinking of mechanical things. Easiest way to ignore important ones."

She glanced down at Yeager, then leaned over her elbows on the bar; she seemed to be getting closer to the mother. "So tell me."

"A new client, I think. They say they were from the FBI?"

"They didn't have to. I didn't know they made shirts that white anymore."

"Mention a guy named Caporale?"

She shook her head, and seemed tempted to go for the little girl if it meant hearing a good story. "Just wondered if I knew you, asked what I told you. Then they turned around and left. You lucked out. A minute later, Yeager walked in. When they were here, it was just me and old Harkleroad. One of them took one look at him and decided it wasn't worth their trouble. Yeager, he'd still be talking to them."

Look at the bright side of it, I told myself: Caporale hadn't lied about where Harry's Bar was and hadn't lied about who had been visiting him. Didn't that increase the odds he had told me the truth about everything else, too?

"One of them left this."

Cynthia handed me a business card that said nothing more than BRIAN SELDES with a telephone number in the Manhattan area code of 646. No affiliation, fax number, or e-mail address. "In case I could think of anything useful, he said."

Mechanics, again. What had there been to gain by making a display of themselves at the Green Fox? Why waste a business card on somebody likely to tear it up as soon as they had walked back out into the street? Both answers came out of Police Investigation Procedures 101. When we had wanted to flush out somebody helpful on the Island, we had advertised ourselves in some public place to make our target jumpy. Since the target couldn't be sure the wrong person wouldn't hear about our interest, he had often used the phone number we had also left in strategic places. Brian Seldes had expected just one thing from Cynthia: to do exactly what she had done—tell me about their visit and then pass along their card.

"Why not just ring your bell?" she asked.

"Because that would skip their test to see how much I wanted to cooperate with them."

"Cooperate on what?"

"Putting an end to mad Pakistani scientists in Karachi."

"No way!"

"Just the kind in the movies."

"What movies?"

"Indian movies. Did you know they make hundreds and hundreds of them over there every year? Three, four times as many as Hollywood."

She thought about admitting her bafflement one more time. But then Yeager called to her for another beer. "Up yours, Finley," she decided, wandering slowly down toward her Happy Hour trade.

CHAPTER 3

I could have done without the next few hours. Thanks to the business card in my shirt pocket, every minute passed like the squandering of some last chance to pay my taxes on time. The fact that I knew this was part of the business card strategy didn't help much. Pork chops at the Greek's was arguing with myself that I could cut some corners for Caporale by going up against Brian Seldes quickly and directly. Watching a Richard Widmark festival on cable was reassuring myself that whenever Brian Seldes came around (and he *would* eventually), I could more than hold my own with him in any interrogation match. Finishing off the *Times* crossword puzzle in bed was trying to believe all the sidling tactics in invading the Green Fox and leaving business cards meant there was no rush toward anything but self-importance, and not just Neil Kinsey's. The only thing I'd persuaded myself of before dropping off to sleep was that an eft was a salamander.

The next day started off better. The attorney for the Canarsie tenants called not to complain he hadn't yet received his pictures, but to apologize for his effrontery in asking me to deliver them "within a week or two." The morning *Times* featured a big article on the background to the Indian-Pakistani troubles; by the time I'd finished it, I was more convinced than ever that 25-year-old movie dubbers in Paris had nothing to do with Kali or Allah and that Caporale was just using me for a jog down memory lane to Roberta Weiss. Best of all, the French Embassy operator didn't make me feel as if asking for a Jean-Claude Servais was like asking for Napoleon: She put me through to him immediately.

Caporale hadn't specified one way or the other, but Servais didn't sound like a new arrival to the French legation. Once I dropped Caporale's name, his stiffness opened into an easy curiosity that was one-part amiability and one-part possessiveness about the Manhattan he knew and that some Long Island professor, no matter where he had been born, couldn't be expected to know. "I didn't know that was where Ali ended up," he said, his Frenchness more in his rhythms than in an accent. "But maybe he was always a fish out of water in the big city."

"Oh, yeah? How's that?"

"Paris was too big for him. I'm sure New York is, too. People think too many things at the same time in big cities. Ali could pursue only one thought at a time. A teacher in suburbia you say? Yes, that sounds right. If he hadn't been a pedagogue, he might have been a terrorist zealot. He always needed to feel in control."

"You don't think people can change after so long?"

His laugh said he never bothered thinking about things he had made up his mind about—even if he had made it up while talking. "What can I do for you and Ali, Mr. Finley?"

There might or might not have been some unscheduled Verizon repairman playing with my circuits overnight; it might or might not have mattered. But if only to be able to say I'd earned some of Caporale's retainer, I dodged the question in favor of suggesting a meeting. He wasn't all that enthusiastic. If something had happened to somebody he hadn't seen in 25 years, why didn't I just say so? He couldn't imagine how it would have concerned him anyway. No, nothing had happened to Caporale, I assured him, but there was a "project" I was working on with him and he recommended I speak with his one-time producer in Paris. Servais might or might not have heard the feebleness in my voice; the important thing was he trumped my idea for a drink after work with an invitation to lunch. I hung up wondering if, in his place, I would have moved so quickly from wariness to conviviality.

It was also only then I realized I'd broken my instruction about not involving Caporale explicitly with the people from his list. I wondered how I could have ever agreed to something so impractical.

I didn't listen to some of the 500 possible reasons.

Even though it meant taking the R line from Hell, I decided against driving over to Manhattan. Finding a parking space on the East Side in the middle of the day was an Olympic event and having to surrender to some shark's lot or garage was so predictable it was demoralizing for more than money reasons. Besides, I persuaded myself that by taking the subway, I would have no excuse on my way back home not to get off in Sunset Park and survey at least one of the other buildings owned by the scumlord Klaus. The opportunity was so unavoidable I had no choice but to pack my camera and tape recorder in my shoulder bag.

As usual, the ride on the R proved the city was intent on enlarging public transportation: Not only did the damn thing stop every few blocks, but it stopped between stops to await the completion of new stops. This might have made for some extended analysis of the *Times* gallery openings and stock listings if I hadn't been developing an itch about the broker who had gotten on the train with me at 86th Street. A few hours earlier during rush hour, he wouldn't have been noticeable: neat blue suit, shining black shoes, scalp-tight black hair, maybe a little too much red in his face. Near noon, though, he didn't fit any of my What's My Line? guesses comfortably. Senior executives didn't ride subways, junior executives didn't ride them to work in the middle of the day, and office supervisors didn't look so unbothered about the clock. For most of the ride to downtown Brooklyn, I tried to give him the benefit of the doubt. He had taken the morning off for a funeral. He was an undercover cop trying to entrap some serial subway pickpocket. He was an ice cream peddler who had left his cart and Charlie the Cow uniform back up on the street at 86th. It didn't work. When the East River finally washed away all my rationalizations, I did what any healthy paranoid in my situation would have done: I gave him a deliriously happy wave.

Wrong response. The broker frowned at me as though I was the kind of subway moron his parents had always warned him about, then made a show of staring up at some leopards in an ad for the Bronx Zoo. I went back for a closer look at what the *Times* critic thought of the latest neo-neo-conceptualist art show.

Servais had suggested one of those englassed sidewalk restaurants in the East 50s where patrons sat around tiny tables like doll house creatures. He himself turned out to be heavier than I had pictured on the phone—a good 250 pounds on less than 6 feet. I also had the instant feeling he was *missing* something, and recently so. A mustache, a tumor—something he was still getting used to living without. The slick cosmopolite from the telephone seemed to have quite a few layers, and as I ordered my regulation expense account omelet, I hoped I wouldn't have to go beyond the most superficial one to get to Neil Kinsey.

"Yes, I think of those days with Ali and the others often," he said, sipping some mineral water. "An absolutely ludicrous situation when you think about it. But we were young, so we didn't have to think about it too much. It was . . . esoteric, yes?"

"I know I'm asking the obvious, but why the hell would the Indians trust the French to come up with scripts instead of doing it themselves?"

Servais raised his left wrist to look at his watch with elaborate pause. "You have asked the $64,000 question within four minutes," he pronounced dramatically, "and I will now give you the $64,000 answer. *Because the Italians were doing it for the Pakistanis!*"

He laughed until I had to go along with him. "I adore that question because I adore the answer and the faces people make when I give it to them. But it's true. The studio where I worked signed up with the Indians a year *after* the Italians had been working with the Pakistanis. DeLaurentis, Ponti, one of those producers, they convinced the Pakistanis it would be more profitable for everybody if they could generate scripts in Rome, send them to Karachi for production, then have them dubbed in English, French, and Spanish back in Rome. The key, of course, was finding the kind of expatriate talent in Italy that wouldn't inflate budgets out of proportion. When the Indians saw this was working, they went to the Italians to ask for equal treatment. But the Italians became nervous too many customers would lead to no customers, so they said no to the Indians. That was a mistake. The Indian studios offered ten times as much work as the Pakistanis."

"So the Indians ended up taking their idea to you."

"Not to me personally. At the time, I was merely an associate for a gentleman named Peyrot at Reynaud-Grevin Studios. Peyrot was the one who signed all the contracts and ended up enlarging his bank account. But I did all the supervising of the scripts and dubbing. For mysterious reasons of his own, Peyrot preferred to concentrate on making millions from Deneuve and Delon . . . That's an attempt at humor, Mr. Finley."

I gave him his smile, but I was suddenly back in my apartment. I was watching Phil Caporale follow the ambulance down Fourth Avenue. Like then, I sensed a few holes. "So the real saving in all this was in how much you could get people like Caporale in Paris for as opposed to, say, some struggling actor in Mumbai."

He looked pleased. "You're insinuating something else?"

"I wasn't there. Another continent and another century."

He went for his second seeded roll, had second thoughts, then returned it to the basket. "What other advantage would you see in such an arrangement, Mr. Finley?"

I should have asked for more particulars about his job at the UN before diving in, but it was too late for that. "Well, the way you describe it, there was a lot of back and forth across borders. Scripts there, films here, dubbed films there, god knows what back here. That makes for a lot of paperwork. A lot of invoices. A lot of bank accounts."

"Money laundering?"

"I think that's what they called it even back then, yes."

He was even more delighted with me. "Between whom?"

"I haven't got the slightest idea."

"Peyrot always denied it," he said placidly. "It was the first thing that came to my mind, too. Well, perhaps not the first thing. The first thing was how much money and recognition could I gain at Reynaud-Grevin from this project. The second was how many of the voice-over actresses could I go to bed with. The third thing—yes, sorry to say, only the third—was who was laundering money for whom and for what. I made the mistake of bringing up the subject with Peyrot twice. After the second time, he made it clear he didn't want to hear the question a third time."

"You couldn't have been the only one to have those doubts. When you were at one of these dubbing sessions with Caporale and the other actors, didn't it ever come up as small talk?"

"All the time."

"And?"

"And what, Mr. Finley? Gossip and speculation. They were even further away from it than I was. But don't you think it's time you told me why you were so eager to see me? What is this mysterious project you and Ali are collaborating on? Is he writing his memoirs? Using your skills as an investigator to help him with his research?"

"One more question and I'll answer yours. When I mentioned Caporale to you on the phone, you were surprised, but not *that* surprised. And this after 25 years. Am I the only one to mention him to you recently?"

He consulted the slit of sun that was creeping across the table; he saw something inevitable, and I had the feeling it was my question more than the movement of the planets. "About three weeks ago, I received another call, from somebody saying he represented your Federal Bureau of Investigation," he said. "He asked if I knew Ali and several other people who worked on our Indian projects. When I asked why he wanted to know, he invited me around to his office to discuss it. I told him his interest was not mine. He then became more arrogant, said it was a question that affected me personally. At that point I reminded him that, as a cultural attaché with the French mission, I have diplomatic status and he would have to use the appropriate channels if he wanted to continue our conversation. I haven't heard from them since."

"Caporale came to see me after the same people visited him. He doesn't have your immunity, so they just knocked on his door and upset him with their questions. He would like to know why."

Again, he seemed to process new, but not all *that* new, information. "Mireille," he said after a moment. "It must be about Mireille."

"Mireille Pouchol?"

"One of our dubbers. Ali told you about her?"

"She's a name on a list. Tell me what?"

He believed me, but didn't want to. "Is it possible he doesn't know? Mireille Pouchol was here in New York about a month ago. She was murdered in her hotel room. The Milford Plaza on Eighth Avenue."

I suppose there were any number of coherent reactions I could have had, but I went straight for the incoherent one: I blamed the Professor for having intimidated me into reading the *Times* instead of the *News* in the morning. The *Times* was great for keeping up on world affairs, okay for following movies, and not so bad for ballgames, but a disaster when it came to sensational front-page local news. There just weren't enough gaudy corpses or perp walk photos in the *Times,* and by the time I passed Roger's neighborhood newsstand to catch up on them, it was usually afternoon, by which time my full attention was mired elsewhere. Even staring stupidly across the table at Servais, I could only barely glimpse a headline along the lines of FRENCH TOURIST SLAYING BAFFLES COPS. Or had that been from 10 years ago?

"It's been on television a lot. How could you have missed it?"

That was a different answer. Through sheer dedication. Through a refusal ever to watch again those nattering weathermen and facelifted anchors who smiled cheerily as they warned you that sitting, standing, or sleeping could kill you. Through an iron commitment to forget those morose evenings after Jenny and Susan when I had indeed sat in front of those automatons, despising myself as their equal and wishing every one of us could be trucked out to some landfill and left for the seagulls. But I didn't tell Servais any of that. I just looked impatient he could think I had time for every French tourist who got murdered in her hotel room.

"Forgive me," he relented, "but I wasn't the swiftest about it, either. When I first heard about it, I thought to myself, 'Well, unless she's a dancer or a musician who once performed for the United Nations, that's the affair of our legation in Washington.' I didn't even know who she was right away because she was identified as Mireille Jobert, her husband's name. It was only when the Washington consulate passed on her information that I realized it was dear Mireille. She was 52 years old, Mr. Finley! *My* Mireille Pouchol was not 52 years old! *My* Mireille was a thin blonde with bangs in her middle 20s!"

He had bad feelings about somebody he hadn't seen in 25 years and I had them because I hadn't been watching eyewitless news regularly, and all of that was puny next to another, bigger bad feeling that seemed to start in my kidneys—somewhere around my doubt that Phil Caporale had built up the same aversion to TV news I had. "How was she killed?" I heard myself ask.

"What is the word? When you are hit by a heavy object?"

"Bludgeoned?"

"Yes. Apparently, somebody attacked her in her hotel room. No money was taken, no sexual assault."

"And no arrest?"

He shook his head with a more scrutinous look. "I have not heard of any. But what would any of this have to do with the FBI? Wouldn't it be a local police matter?"

The most irritating questions were the ones I asked myself at the same time others asked them of me. Then I remembered why I was sitting where I was in the first place. "Phil thinks it may have something to do with this Neil Kinsey."

"Ah!"

"That doesn't surprise you, either?"

"I don't know if it should or not. I do know Kinsey and Mireille were lovers. But I'm sure Ali has told you that."

He didn't have time to read from my face how much our good friend Ali had told me. Just then, my omelet and his fish arrived. The waiter's arms also gave me enough cover to zip open my bag on the chair next to me and to reach inside to my tape recorder buttons. I hadn't decided whether I would have shown Klaus's tenants in Sunset Park I was recording them, but Servais's diplomatic status seemed to settle the question where he was concerned: What he didn't know, he didn't have to be diplomatic about.

"Anything you can tell me about Kinsey would be helpful. Have you seen him recently?"

If he'd had a handkerchief, he would have waved it at me and sniffled to go along with his scoff. "Kinsey? I haven't seen him since the day I fired him."

The waiter finally went away.

CHAPTER 4

"**Ali and Inge brought Kinsey** over to the studio one day. They had met him at the hotel where they were living. My first impression was of a little brute. He was not very tall or heavy, but he had a big head and big nose. His eyes were strange, too. He always seemed to be searching around him, like he was on guard against some blow. I don't know why Ali and Inge became his patrons. I would see somebody like Kinsey on the street and walk faster. Maybe they were so infatuated with one another they thought the whole world was theirs to save."

"Caporale and Inge were a couple?"

"You look disappointed."

"Just a bad instinct on my part. I thought he was involved with some other woman over there."

"Who was that?"

"Nobody. It's not important. My mistake."

"No, it was always Ali and Inge. I must confess, her fascination with him always surprised me. It must be the grayness of the Scandinavian mind. What do you think, Mr. Finley?"

"I really couldn't say. We were talking about Kinsey."

"Yes. The gist of it is I had room for another voice, and Kinsey didn't sound like Donald Duck. So, he joined our little troupe. Nobody was happier about this than Mireille. Or, is the word *happy* inappropriate where Mireille was concerned? No one confused gloom and elation more than she did. She seemed to go out of her way to find lovers who would make her miserable. Before Kinsey, there was this waiter . . ."

"So she and Kinsey paired off."

"Correct. They were an inseparable quartet for some time— Kinsey and Mireille, Ali and Inge. They ate meals together, took weekend trips to the countryside together, developed that language between the lines that made a fifth person such as myself feel very much like an outsider. I tried not to care as long as they functioned in the studio, but I must confess I found it irritating at times. If there was any discussion over something as minor as a line reading, all four of them inevitably ended up on the same side of the argument. My engineers used to joke they had become components of some extraterrestrial entity where they had all yielded their individual identities to the entity as a whole."

"But you didn't see it that way."

"No. Ali and Inge were all right, but Kinsey was a drunk and it was soon clear Mireille was receiving full value for her masochism. The worst episode concerned his aspirations to write a film of his own."

"About Indians and Pakistanis?"

"No, and that was what was so droll. About *your* Indians in the West. It was supposed to be a cowboy version of the tales of King Arthur and his knights. Kinsey had apparently been working on it for years. This was to be his entry to Hollywood. Like that other western from the samurai . . ."

"The Magnificent Seven."

"Yes. One day, Mireille brought me a copy of the script. She was all but trembling when she gave it to me because she hadn't told Kinsey what she was doing. Nobody was to know about this grand idea of his. But she was weary of his tantrums, had lost all sense of how much their problems were her fault and how much his, and wanted an outside opinion on at least one facet of their relationship. Was he the genius he claimed to be or simply a lunatic?"

"Which was it?"

"Actually, I found the script amusing. Ranchers rather than kings, hired killers instead of knights, and so on. Nothing wrong with the amusing, but this lark would have cost many millions to produce. I tried to be cautious telling Mireille what I thought, but she interpreted it as a total endorsement and went to Kinsey to admit what she had done. She was hoping my reaction to the script would encourage him, bring him out of this murky co-destructiveness they were living."

"But he beat her up, instead?"

"You're obviously familiar with the breed. There was this evening when we all had dinner with our main Indian contact. Peyrot was in the hospital, so that left the hosting up to me. Sayyid, the Indian, insisted on meeting some of the voices he had only heard, to thank them personally. I probably should have kept Kinsey away, but Sayyid was particularly keen to meet Mireille—she always dubbed the chief woman's roles—so there was no diplomatic way of telling Kinsey he couldn't come. Needless to say, he arrived in a state of inebriation . . . You really want nothing more than that omelet?"

"I'm fine."

"I have always regarded lunch as the most important meal of the day."

"I never have."

"In any case, at this dinner with Sayyid, Mireille couldn't help bringing up the infamous script. I don't know what she was thinking. Maybe that Sayyid would like it enough to persuade his company to finance it. A ludicrous idea, but that was a barometer of Mireille's state of anxiety with Kinsey. Well, as soon as Sayyid made the mistake of asking Kinsey what the script was about, alcoholism took over. What the hell did he care what it was about? Did he think a great artist like Neil Kinsey would entrust such an important project to somebody whose idea of art was *Killers for Allah*? Mireille was a fool even to have mentioned it. It became quite ugly. Sayyid tried to remain calm, but one didn't need to be a clairvoyant to see in his eyes that Neil Kinsey would never work on another film for him. Ali finally dragged Kinsey off to the lavatory. When Ali came back, he came back alone."

"And Mireille?"

"She stayed for the rest of the evening. It was a breaking point even for her. I am certain she and Sayyid . . . well, that would be speculation, hardly more founded today than it was 25 years ago. In any case, two days later, I received a call from Inge saying Kinsey had beaten up Mireille and Mireille would be unable to come to work. Naturally, I informed Kinsey his services would no longer be required. I took it as a modest point of honor I did so about an hour before receiving a call from Peyrot at the hospital demanding the same thing."

"What about all this informer stuff?"

"Ali told you about that? Yes, he would have. He was the most incensed when he heard about it. Myself, Mireille, the others— perhaps we were accustomed to it. We didn't take it too seriously. It was a period when a lot of opportunists found it profitable to treat naive American officials to wonderful political tales about terrorists and anarchists and what-have-you. You could not survive on such extra money, but it made possible the extra bottle of wine or extra package of cigarettes. Kinsey had no scruples about such things. We would be discussing Libya or Nicaragua or something else, he would be making mental notes of it all, and then he would go running off to his CIA man or FBI man or whatever contact he had. I'm sure he helped them build a wonderful dossier on all of us. Then again, the only one in France who didn't have a dossier at the time was the Mona Lisa."

"How did you find out what Kinsey had been doing?"

"From him! He admitted it to Ali! It was the end of their friendship. I can't recall too many details after so long. As I said, Ali took the business far more gravely than the rest of us did. I like to think it's because he felt closer to Kinsey and suffered a deeper sense of betrayal."

"But . . .?"

"Well, considering what you say he has been doing all these years, perhaps he was already planning back then on an impeccable bourgeois life. He certainly wouldn't have found Kinsey's reports, inane as they had to be, much of a help for this teaching career of his."

"Probably not."

"In any case, it was right around the same time that our contract with Sayyid's company expired and Ali decided to return to America."

"That was the end of the whole project?"

"It was bound to have ended sometime, no? Doesn't everything?"

"The timing seems interesting."

"If you think so."

"And you haven't seen Kinsey since?"

"I have no idea if the man is alive or dead. I can't imagine you spoiling my lunch if you told me either way. I also can't imagine why Ali would care one way or another."

"That's another story."

CHAPTER 5

So, I seemed to have been wrong about Caporale and Roberta Weiss, and Caporale seemed to have been wrong in including Mireille Pouchol on the list of the still-living. Did that make us even? I didn't think so unless Caporale was a closet Amish and didn't have a TV set at home. Leaving Servais and heading for the nearest phone booth, I thought it made us so uneven I was ready to return his check. Fortunately, cooler heads prevailed. He already owed me for my ride on the R train and my lunch with the Frenchman. I saw no reason not to throw in a phone call.

I had two possible sources in the NYPD for asking about Mireille Pouchol. The first and more logical one was a Homicide detective named Masterson. But over the last year, I'd already bothered him twice on things I might have found out just as easily by going to the local library—something Masterson had pointed out the second time. But during that second contact, he had also let drop the whereabouts of the source I wanted to speak with after leaving Servais—Dana McGill.

I hadn't talked to McGill in more than two years. The last time I'd seen her had been in the waiting room of the federal prosecutor's office, where both of us had been summoned to give our accounts of a shooting. The shooting had cost her the life of a superior and me the life of the only NYPD detective who hadn't given me the hives. Some days were heavy because nobody seemed to be saying anything to anybody, others were excruciating because you were expected to do nothing *except* talk. By the time I'd finished crossing all the Ts and dotting all the Is for the Justice Department's files that afternoon, McGill was long gone from the waiting room, and I'd known she was as talked out for the next century or two as I was. I wouldn't have waited for her any more than she hadn't waited for me.

I was tempted to hang up as soon as the operator at the 107 told me to wait a second instead of telling me what I wanted to hear ("I'm sorry, but Lieutenant McGill won't be in today.") Instead, I cursed Jean-Claude Servais, Caporale, and Mireille Pouchol. "Hello, Paul. How you been?"

I didn't recognize the tone at all. I'd kept her at such an arm's distance for so long, having only Masterson's information she'd been transferred to the 107 in Queens, that only a metallic, alien bray belonged to my memory. Instead, there was warmth.

Or, might have been. What did five words tell you? Aside from how much I wanted to believe my impression?

"Sorry for dropping down out of the blue on you like this . . ."

She laughed. "How were you *not* going to unless we never talked to each other ever again?"

A sense of humor? A sense of humor in Dana McGill? Could this be the same Homicide sergeant who had usually looked at me as though police hiring standards in Nassau County must have been even lower in my day than they had become in hers? "Got me there," I blurted. "I guess this is a bad time for calling . . ."

"No, no. What's up?"

"I want to buy you a coffee. And pick your brain about a homicide."

"Which?"

"A French tourist named Pouchol or Jobert. First name Mireille."

"The one at the Milford Plaza?"

"Right."

"That's in Manhattan, Paul. I'm in Fresh Meadows."

"I know. I just wondered whether there was any scuttlebutt even out there in Queens. For a client. By doing him this favor, I get to keep up my reputation as Mr. Insider. Good for word-of-mouth and business. Any dollar that comes down the pike . . ." I

suppose I might have gone on in that vein until Verizon's robots
cut me off. But then I had a better idea: the truth. "Anyway, that
was the original idea of calling you. But now that I've got you on
the line, I'd really like to see you."

Why stop at reading great significance into five words when I
could read even greater significance into a two-second pause? I
wanted to believe getting together must have occurred to her at
some point, too.

"Okay, but it'll have to be tomorrow and catch-as-catch-can.
I've got a manpower problem out here plus a killer flu going
through the command. I can't be away from the desk too long."

I took down her driving directions for the 107. We agreed I'd
drop by the precinct around five the following evening. If she
wasn't there, I would just have to wait until she came back.

I hung up and headed down into the pit of the R train for
the trip back to Brooklyn. I told myself I had about four hours
of stops to decide whether to get off at Sunset Park to check out
Klaus's slum. That felt like the least of my remoteness anxieties
after talking with McGill. Who was she but a cop who had once
worked for a cop I had gotten to like but whom I had also known
for all about three weeks and who was now dead? When I had
thought of her over the last two years, it had almost always begun
with a picture of her holding Allen Bernstein as he had slipped
away from two bullets in the chest. It had been a maddening ending to a plot to kill a diplomat. Too many of the wrong people had
died and too many of the wrong ones had gone on living. Because
we had stopped the killing, I had, for once, received more handshakes than threats from officialdom. But Bernstein and a couple
of other bodies had been the cost of the handshakes.

Maybe that was why I'd willy-nilly invented an extra connection to McGill. You should never underrate your strengths, and
I've always counted self-pity as one of mine. Sometimes you can
follow that sucker right into other people's worlds and, for a little
variety, entertain the illusion that you're not the only person
walking around on the planet with a sack of grief, frustration, and
angst over your shoulder. When I had met McGill and Bernstein,
they had been dancing around each other as ridiculously as any

two people too old for puppy love could have been. Separated by a good 20 years, by rank, and by NYPD relationship regulations, they had both taken to ignoring one another personally the way you ignore the gorilla sitting on the living room couch watching Archie Bunker reruns. Two people couldn't have had more lust and affection for one another—or more determination to hide it within the daily swamp of a Homicide division. They were cute, they were pathetic, they seemed to have been born at least a half-century too late with all their concern for the social proprieties. Did I envy them? Damn right I did. The two of them then—and McGill alone now—seemed to have had the direct opposite of my experience: They had worked at passing off closeness as remoteness. That afternoon on the subway, I still found that trick more intriguing than Americans, Swedes, and Frenchmen dubbing anti-Pakistani Indian movies in Paris.

CHAPTER 6

Thanks to Frank Martinez, I did my duty on Fourth Avenue. The address for Klaus's building in Sunset Park turned out to be for a corner bodega with several apartments upstairs. Since the bodega owner Martinez had nothing to do with the apartments or the undeclared number of people living in them, he had no worries about Immigration in showing me the crumbling walls and cockroach packs that had come to endanger his business. "I got nothin' to hide," he said, leading me to the back of his single-aisle store and waving me into my picture taking. "What I don't tell you, the Health Department can. They're always in here sayin' this and that. I tell them it's from the apartments upstairs, it's the whole buildin'. Klaus don't give a shit what's goin' on. But Health are deaf people. They just write their summons. You go upstairs, Mister. Go see how they're livin' up there."

I passed. I had eight Polaroids pretty much in focus. One of them—of a water line extending from the ceiling of the storeroom down to the floor—seemed fit for one of the galleries the *Times* had called "trendsetting." There was no reason to stretch my luck by going upstairs and running into people less cooperative than Martinez. So, I just left him my card and got back into the subway for the last two miles to 86th Street. I might have spent the ride having a few reveries about my future as an art photographer if not for my favorite broker. He was sitting as nonchalantly in my car as he had been on the way over to Manhattan.

A mocking wave wouldn't have covered it a second time. I tried to think of something that would annoy Brian Seldes, that they hadn't already fed into their Paul Finley program. There was robbing or killing the son of a bitch, of course, but that would have led to other complications. In the end, I decided the best tack was a show of Weary Wisdom—standing up as the train pulled into 86th Street, shaking my head all-knowingly, and even managing a jaded chuckle as I glanced down at the broker. And for the tiniest fraction of a second, I thought, he did indeed look irritated with my condescension. What other victories can you expect on the R train?

CHAPTER 7

Mrs. Chalian came out into the hall as I was opening my door. She was a round little woman with Little Lulu curls and eyes that were never quite part of her smiles. "You have a package from Federal Express, Mr. Finley. But I can't lift it."

I wished I couldn't, either. As soon as I saw Caporale's name as the sender, I knew the huge carton against the woman's vestibule wall held the collected film works of Neil Kinsey. "I couldn't have the poor man lug it back to his truck," Mrs. Chalian said. "I hope you don't mind I took it."

"Not at all. Thanks a lot."

She lingered in the hallway until I had to thank her again and close my door. As I went into the kitchen for the box-cutter, I didn't know if I was more annoyed by Caporale sending me the stuff without telling me or Mrs. Chalian looking at me as though I had just received assorted body parts. And beneath these candidates was the third one: that having Kinsey's movies in the apartment represented more of a commitment to Ali and the Great Indian Dubbers than $500 bought.

There was no note inside, just five reels numbered one to five with a grease pencil. To judge by the yellow Reynaud-Grevin stickers on the cans, Kinsey hadn't been too squeamish about ferreting around in studio closets during breaks from his voiceovers. The same stickers were on a couple of the reels inside the tins. None of them looked like they would squeeze inside my VCR, meaning they were going to make for clutter in my living room before I either found Kinsey or returned them to Caporale. And when a client didn't bother pointing out that one of the people he'd included in his wild goose chase had been murdered a few weeks before, returning them seemed the stronger bet. On that assumption, I tore off the return address in Garden City and stuck it in my top desk drawer.

I turned on the daily Calvary known as my message machine. First, there was the Professor wanting to know if Caporale had been in touch. I was sure he'd already gotten that answer from Caporale, probably right before calling me. Joe Carroll was never satisfied playing matchmaker, he also liked reviewing the honeymoon with all parties. Then there was Gerald Harrah announcing he was back from Colorado Springs and was "curious" if I'd found out anything about Mrs. Harrah. The sexual association was so stark I couldn't help laughing—thinking immediately of my conversation with McGill and suddenly feeling fewer compunctions about throwing Sarah Harrah over the side to her husband's lawyer sharks. Bay Ridge Don Juans could be so whimsical in their affections!

Number three was Cynthia to report that Miles Harkleroad was in the hospital with a stroke and that the Green Fox regulars were putting together a little money for a couple of months' rent he owed where he lived. Did I want to contribute? No, not really. When old Harkleroad wasn't going on about how overrated Jackie Robinson had been or how underrated Hitler had been, he had been restricting ideal UN membership to countries clustered around the British Isles and the Statue of Liberty. I'd always thought it a tribute to Johnny Yeager's oppressiveness that I'd never been quite able to rank Harkleroad as the Green Fox skel I most wanted to avoid. I supposed that failing alone was eventually going to cost me a twenty-dollar donation to Cynthia's fund.

Number four was Caporale, and he disarmed me right away with the tone of the little boy with a Marlboro in his mouth who wanted to confess he'd been smoking. "One of the names on that list . . . well, actually she's dead. If you haven't found out already, it's Mireille Pouchol. The papers say she was killed in a New York hotel last month. You probably heard about it. Just didn't connect it to the list I gave you . . ."

"Wrong, Phil babe."

He broke off as though he'd heard my voice. There was some movie-like music in the background from where he was calling. Then he was back, trying to sound as defiant as he was confused. "The fact of the matter is, Finley, she called me when she got to the city, said she wanted to see me. But I was taking off for a conference down in Philadelphia and I told her I'd call her when I got back. I would have, I really would have. I didn't want to, but how could I have gotten out of it? She had my number, she could've just called again. She said it had something to do with Reynaud-Grevin, the company we worked for. What the hell did that mean! She wanted to know if I'd seen Kinsey??!! Swell! All these years and that's what she's calling about! Like I'm supposed to be his keeper for the rest of my life! . . . Anyway, it didn't sound all that urgent, and she said a few days wouldn't matter. When I got back, though, she was all over the papers and the television . . . I guess I must seem like a clinical case to you, putting her name down on that list . . . Well, okay, maybe I had an ulterior purpose. Maybe I've also been hoping you'd find out why she wanted to talk to me . . . No, not even that so much. Let's put it this way: I wouldn't mind you hearing I didn't endanger her in any special way by not seeing her before I went to Philadelphia. I'm not saying to focus on that. Hardly. I need you to find Kinsey so I can rid of the movies. But if in the process . . . well, why repeat myself?"

I listened to the shrill whistle of the machine longer than was good for my ears before thumping it quiet. What had I said—he needed a lawyer more than an investigator? In fact, he needed a shrink more than either. But then, I reminded myself, it wasn't only about Phil Caporale anymore. In the middle of everything, there was a real body—Mareille Pouchol's—having nothing to do with his complexes.

I stretched out on the couch under my soothing ocean storm in *Calm.* I surveyed the terrain as masterfully as Ahab once had. Clear on the horizon was what earnest people had recently taken to calling a "disconnect." On the one hand, there was this tale of expatriates in Paris that traced back a leisurely 25 years. On the other hand, there were the killing of Mireille Pouchol-Jobert, the zeal of Seldes about wanting me and others to drop by to see him, and the haywire voice I'd just heard on my machine. On one side, take a stroll through history; on the other side, move your ass. Yes, definitely a disconnect. Maybe even a full-blown disconnection.

All of this put me in the mood to nod off thinking about movie heroes disconnecting train cars. Burt Lancaster in *The Train*. Charles Bronson in *Breakheart Pass*. Ernest Borgnine in *The Wild Bunch*. I knew there had to have been some movie where the hero got his hand cut off by a train that rolled back on him after he had separated the cars, but I couldn't think of any. What I thought instead, as I dropped down, was that there was such a scene in the reels sitting on my floor and that I was the one losing the hand.

CHAPTER 8

I woke up to the telephone. It was that loveliest of all wake-ups: rotten pears in the mouth, twilight outside the window, and the Chalians next door clicking plates and cutlery as they went at their supper. Even if I'd turned a light on before dozing off, the room would have been lightless. Everything I had missed I should have waited to miss a little longer.

As penance for having nodded off, I picked up the phone before it clicked over to the machine. "Mr. Finley? Brian Seldes."

He was peppy, peppy, peppy. Without his card on my desk, I could have mistaken him for an insurance salesman. "So what?"

"So I think we should talk, Mr. Finley."

"About what?"

"C'mon, fella. We know who you are. Why play games?"

I tried to picture Seldes coming on to Caporale, Cynthia, and Servais in the same tone. Only Caporale scanned as taking him seriously for more than a second. "Tell me something fascinating, Seldes, or the next sound you hear will piss you off."

If we had been in the same room, he would have slapped me on the back. "That's good. Okay, try this. You might be involved with people jeopardizing the security of the United States."

"I'm a Mets fan. I'm used to it."

"The world doesn't have much room for that kind of glibness anymore, fella."

"This isn't fascinating. Bye, bye . . ."

"Wait! Wait a second! . . . All right. You online?"

"What of it?"

"Go to Google. Call up J-A-B-P-U-N. Punjab reversed. One word. I know you have my card. Call me after you see what's there."

My choice was to stand there for the rest of my life with a dead phone in my hand resenting his presumption about his business card or to do what he said. It helped to think that turning on my computer and going to JABPUN worked off more of Caporale's retainer.

JABPUN started out as a black screen with two red boxing gloves tapping against each other. I got it: They were *jabbing* one another. Then the monitor opened out into some kind of gold and rust and green screen with small emblems of white elephants. I thought I got that, too: all things Indian. The letters for JABPUN then began doing their own dancing in and out of one another so that PUNJAB came out a couple of times. My third get was that I was dealing with someone who had an inflated opinion of his own sense of humor: Not just puns, but puns on top of puns. The name Neil Kinsey came to mind as the Indian colors dissolved, making room for the first screed.

The lettering was supposed to make me think of Sanskrit, the *Kama Sutra*, and Bollywood ads, so I thought of all those things. But Kinsey had also obviously had a limited budget for his fancy design ideas, so once the texts started coming on, the white elephants, temple dancers, and pictures of Gandhi were few and far between. Why run the risk of being distracted by such profundity, anyway? The first rant was about how the Pakistanis were bent on destroying India and Hinduism. It cited the sort of "intelligence sources" usually mentioned in "The X-Files" for the information that Pakistani terrorists had already installed nuclear devices in New Delhi and Agra and were only waiting for a "signal" to detonate them. The second and third rants, two months old, were more of the same. The next one wasn't. It started out: "Once upon a time, a group of terrorist foreigners working for the French film company Reynaud-Grevin . . ."

I was disoriented by more than the halfwit tone of what I was scrolling. Caporale and Servais had both said their movies had been anti-Pakistan. So how had that made Caporale and the others "terrorist foreigners" bent on India's ruin? The answer came in the second paragraph:

Ostensibly, these people were employed to propagandize on behalf of India. In reality, they were embarked on so ridiculing genuine Indian concerns about Islamabad that warnings of the Pakistani threat would lose all credibility in the long run. Moreover, members of the company became so arrogant about their mission that they openly addressed each other in their adopted Muslim names. One American, for instance, became known to everyone as Ali. The slut who shared his bed, a Swedish woman of no talent whatsoever became referred to jokingly as Fatima because that was the role she was usually called upon to play . . .

I cackled loud enough to freeze the chatter around the Chalian kitchen table next door. That seemed right: Mrs. Chalian saw me as a nut who talked to himself when he wasn't ordering up from the cemetery and I saw Neil Kinsey as a wacko prowling the streets of the Bowery. His *shtick* might have been Hinduism instead of Christianity, but it was the same rotgut. What had set off Seldes and the forces of the Republic was the kind of meatball who'd once pestered pedestrians but who now went after people with computers. Welcome to high-tech progress.

My second reaction was to think of $15-million-a-year shortstops who batted .235. So much expense for so much banality. Why would a Phil Caporale want to save *anything* belonging to this guy? Even Gerald Harrah looked good by comparison: At least his wife *was* screwing around behind his back.

I scrolled down the last editorial. In this rant, Kinsey identified "Ali" explicitly as Phil Caporale, which meant the FBI at least hadn't had to waste taxpayer money getting their agents in Paris to dig up Reynaud-Grevin's old employment rolls. And that wasn't all. Somebody else specifically located was my *femme fatale*, Roberta Weiss. Except she wasn't Roberta Weiss anymore, she was "Roberta Klein."

I sat staring at my monitor. The trouble was, I had taken to watching too many movies on TV lately, so there could have been any number of characters named Roberta Klein who had killed, been killed, loved, or been loved in my life. But somewhere in the garbage bag of my memory, and near the top of it, I could have sworn there was someone by the name of Roberta Klein. I even had a picture of her: stocky, white blouse and black skirt, short black bangs, moonish face.

Of course, Kinsey also had a picture of the Muslim threat to India. I snapped off JABPUN before I started my own website called ROBERTA.

CHAPTER 9

I disobeyed orders by not calling back Seldes. Instead, I phoned a few fashion magazines to track down the third woman on the list, Inge Matson. I figured Caporale's *mea culpa* deserved that much effort from me. Besides, whatever else she was supposed to tell me, I wanted Matson to explain how she could have so blithely upset my fantasy by stealing the dashing history professor away from Roberta Weiss/Klein and her ninja killer children. I got nowhere until I came across a secretary at *Maxim* who insisted I call her Wiggy. "Inge Matson doesn't work for magazines, sweetheart," Wiggy told me. "She has her own modeling agency. I worked there last year."

"You're a godsend, Wiggy."

"Money wasn't so great. She was nice, though. Except she always wore these big bows. You're a guy. You like women in bows? I always think it's like, 'Okay, here I am, the wrapping around the box of chocolates. Start unraveling me.' Isn't that what men think when they see bows?"

"You wouldn't know the name of her agency, would you?"

"You sound pretty helpless, sweetheart. How about getting a directory and looking it up under Inge Matson? Gotta go. Nice chatting."

Wiggy was right. INGE MATSON INTERNATIONAL was in bold letters on the White Pages. On lower Fifth Avenue in Greenwich Village. I jotted down the phone number and address but had no intention of calling or visiting before having another heart-to-heart with Caporale. The more I thought about it, the movies littering my floor and all the quivering and quailing on my message machine seemed a lot more complicated than what could be covered by a $500 check and a merry be-on-your-way-with-my-list-of-the-living-and-the-dead. I took it as a happy omen that it was Wednesday, the evening of the Professor's weekly soiree, and that it was 50-50 Caporale would be there. Well, maybe not 50-50, more like 90-10 against, but it seemed like enough of a chance to take a ride out to Garden City. Whatever I had to put up with in gab about the Third Punic War could be paid back with some stirring truths about Mireille Pouchol.

I spent another half-hour finishing off a malpractice interview transcription with a chiropractor named Bogan, then hit the road. I was blinky enough on the drive to look into my rearview mirror a couple of times for a better look at who was behind the wheel of the tan Mercedes hugging me. If Seldes or the agent of some other planetary power had thought it important to have my broker friend on the R train, why not on the highways and byways, too? But then I saw a kid pop up in the back seat of the Mercedes and decided nobody was recruiting *that* young.

The Professor's block of one-family houses was as quiet as ever. The idiot Pattersons still had their plastic ducks on the lawn, the Ruizes still had a basket over the garage door even though both kids had long since moved on—one to the Army, the other to a Wyoming agricultural school. The Professor's heap of a Chevy still protruded out of his driveway with its rear end over the sidewalk. I assumed the Rothmans next door had long since given up asking him to make the effort to nudge the car a few feet closer to the garage and out of the way of people who had the crazy idea sidewalks were for pedestrians.

In the best of cases, Joe Carroll looked like an old fish with two tufts of gray hair where his gill openings should have been. Tonight, he looked like he had grown Brillo pads. "I just called you," he said. "Why don't you get a cellphone like normal people? Didn't know you were coming out."

"Just decided."

He grunted as though that was typical unreasonable behavior, left the door for me to close, and gimped inside. I followed him into the kitchen, but he kept going, down to the basement, the first headquarters of Finley Investigations, Inc. "What're you doing?"

There was no answer. Only when I got downstairs in the bleary light of the basement and smelled the varnish did I see I'd interrupted a Mr. Fix-It Moment. Atop the worktable in the far corner was a cheesy wooden music box I'd never dared touch on its living room shelf. The thing hadn't made music in decades and its catch was rusted over, but it was apparently the first thing he'd ever bought for his wife Ruth and had willy-nilly become a symbol of their 34-year marriage for him. For some reason, he had finally decided the catch and hinges needed polishing. "If you're making work for yourself, you can come clean my apartment."

"Phil Caporale's dead." With his broad square back turned to me, my first thought was he was addressing the wall behind the worktable. "Committed suicide early this afternoon."

"That's not possible." He turned around with the music box. He could have been frowning at either one of us, but I could have told him the box catch was going to gleam again before I did. "I just heard from him! Well, not directly . . ."

He let the idiocy of my objection sink in, then went back to rubbing at the hinges. "I was trying him all afternoon. Wanted to know if you two had connected. An hour ago, Florence answered. She found him in the tub. He'd slit his wrists. Cop took the phone after a minute. She was hysterical. Never heard her like that. Sounded almost human."

I didn't know Florence and didn't know why her natural reaction to finding a husband dead merited something sounding close to contempt. But Florence seemed like just a baton twirler in a whole parade of things I didn't know. "Suicide note?"

"Didn't get the chance to ask. But she didn't sound like she had any doubts. Said he'd been acting odd lately. Ever since those FBI guys he told me about visited him. You know all about that, yeah?"

"Yeah."

"What kind of trouble was he in?"

"To hear him, none. He wanted to return something to an old friend."

"What was that?"

I sat down in the captain's chair with the broken rungs. The desk I'd once used had been pushed against the wall and buried under boxes, but the chair was still waiting to jab into my spine like old times. "Home movies."

"What the hell for?"

"I don't know, Joe!"

He considered that an unsatisfactory answer, but liked what I looked like even less. He drew out putting the box back on the table. "You look at the movies?"

"No, I didn't look at the movies." And something else I didn't want to look at was what that confused phone message had been about. Had it been code for a confession? "I only got them today."

He crossed over from the worktable to sag down on one of the basement steps; it was where he had sat at night when he had been hungry for more company than the TV or one of his history books. "So tell me."

I didn't need him to ask twice. It was a comforting feeling telling him everything that had happened since Caporale had rung my bell. As always, he followed me from his staircase perch like an examiner at one of his orals finals: He didn't *want* to drive a truck through what I was saying, but he had the engines revving on a whole fleet of them just in case. I'd missed those sessions since moving to Brooklyn; phones weren't the same thing. And maybe I'd also missed Joe Carroll the accomplice—the father who had allowed his daughter and granddaughter to take off from his house while I'd been sleeping off my Christmas drunk. However else I painted it, I'd never lived with the Professor for two years after the car accident; what I had done was share a cell with him on Remorse Row. Now, telling him about Caporale and Servais and Kinsey, I had that accomplice back, for sure as hell, nothing from JABPUN to Neil Kinsey's movies to Caporale's suicide would have been part of our world if he hadn't sent me his History Department protégé in the first place.

When I finally shut up, he shook his head. "You make the poor bastard sound more interesting than I ever thought he was."

"You know what this looks like, I hope." His glare warned me against saying it. "Why not, Joe? He kills Pouchol, then he can't stand living with himself anymore."

"And why would he do that?"

"How the hell do I know? Maybe they had the secret hots for each other in Paris. Maybe he didn't want her reminding him of the old days. Forget the why. You've got two big whats right in front of you. Murder, suicide. It's a bridge. Any cop at all could walk across it."

"You're full of shit, Finley."

"You say so."

He had so many fingers on his hand he looked fatigued even to have to start ticking them off. "One, I knew Phil Caporale."

"That makes one of us."

"He couldn't kill anybody."

"Including himself?"

He dropped his hands sheepishly. "So I didn't know him perfectly."

"That supposed to be funny?"

"No, it's an invitation to get your head out of your ass!"

"Right. He's your protégé, so he couldn't have killed anybody."

"For starters. Then there's Amritsar."

"There's what?"

"Amritsar. Where the British massacred the Indians, right after World War I. You must've at least seen *Gandhi*, for Christ sake!" I knew what he was talking about—sort of. "A few years ago, just before I retired, I audited Caporale's class. I guess I wanted to hear all my best and brightest one last time. His lecture for the day was on Amritsar. April 13, 1919. General Reginald Dyer." He looked over to his worktable and the music box; his married years weren't the only thing very far away. "It was fucking bloodless! I sat there seething the whole hour. 1,500 people shot down and he's telling these kids about it like it's just more old water dripping from the faucet! Here, boys and girls, you have the Indians massing in protest these *habeas corpus* restrictions. And over here you have Dyer determined to break up the protest.

The order is given to fire, and people start dying. That was April 13, 1919, boys and girls. Write all that down."

"And that's why he couldn't kill Mireille Pouchol?"

He nodded without hesitation. "That's right."

"Because he had a headache that morning and couldn't work up the kind of righteous indignation you would have?"

"Then he should've called in sick."

I had rammed into the Wall. As Jenny had once said, they might have gotten rid of the one in Berlin, but the one in Joe Carroll's house would outlast anything the Chinese had. "Phil Caporale couldn't *see* other people, let alone kill them. A man like that, nothing matters to him but settling his books at the end of every day so the assets equal the debts and he can go to bed knowing he hasn't helped tilt the planet off its axis. The Indians had their reasons for doing things, the British had theirs, and Phil Caporale had the task of making sure nobody got too bothered about anything. He called it objectivity. I should've never hired the guy, but I was stuck and . . ."

He fell so silent the stairs under him seemed to improvise creaks to cover his embarrassment. I looked away so he wouldn't feel me staring at him. I tried to imagine why, after so long, he had suddenly decided to fix the music box. Something sparked by the news about Caporale? Fix up the fixable before it was too late?

"These movies," he said finally, "I'll bet you he never looked at them in the 25 years he had them. His curriculum was getting back at this Kinsey guy who betrayed him, and that was it. Book closed."

"Servais said something like that."

"The French aren't always wrong. But there's another reason he didn't kill Pouchol, Paul. *You.* Why go through all this hiring you, making that call you got?"

"Maybe he just couldn't get it out. He wanted to tell me, but . . ."

"Screw the buts! Here's a guy a few minutes away from his last bath and he's going to get tongue-tied with you about confessing what's about to drive him to the tub? To a machine, yet? Bullshit! Right to the end, what was he talking about? Squaring things with you! Adjusting more ledgers! Keeping the accounts right! More dripping faucets!"

"Well, *something* sure as hell got to him, Joe!"

He nodded. "Yeah, and you better find out what."

"What're you talking about? No more Caporale, no more client."

"How much you charging these days?" He didn't dare look at me. "I'd like to know for my own sake. Who knows? We might even find out something that'll help Florence."

"You don't sound like you even like her!"

"When did I say that?"

"'Almost human.' I don't get a picture of Mrs. Warmth."

"That's not the point here, Finley. If you're jumping to the conclusion you are about this French woman, you're probably not going to be the only one. I've known the Caporales a long time. If I can help Florence avoid some asshole Sunday feature story in *Newsday*, I'd like to do it."

"And suppose it turns out to be true?"

"It won't," he said evenly. "Phil Caporale didn't kill Pouchol. And that's not why he killed himself. As a favor, kid. Just a few days. Okay? And any expenses you have, I'll take care of them."

I knew he'd put it that way deliberately, as an outlet for both of us, and I had no intention of ignoring the escape hatch. "First you're talking about my fee, now we're already down to expenses."

He smiled. "I'd really appreciate it, Paul."

"Tell me why at some point?"

"Maybe."

I didn't know why I thought it was worth mentioning, but I did. "Ever hear of a Roberta Klein?"

"Who's she?"

"One of this merry band of Paris dubbers. Her name rings a bell, but I don't know where from. She wouldn't be one of your Wednesday night people, by any chance?"

"Jesus, I almost forgot! I got wine in the freezer!" He was up so fast I wondered how Caporale could have been so thoughtless to do what he had done on a Wednesday. "Word gets around the campus about Phil, there'll be a mob scene here tonight looking for details."

"You're reminding me why I was glad to get out of here."

"I didn't invite you back tonight, either."

He took the stairs so heavily I thought he was going to go right through them. I sat listening to him upstairs thumping the freezer door and swearing. There was still another one of those disconnects, of course: Caporale and Pouchol, fine, but what about the Where's Waldo game Seldes was playing? How did that relate to everything?

"Roberta Klein?" the old man yelled down from the top of the stairs.

"Yeah! Is it possible I met her here one night?"

"Never heard of her! Sounds like a classical pianist!"

Some doors were easy to open. Instead of trying to force the key through the mail slot or the hinges of the dog flap, all you needed was someone like Joe Carroll pointing toward the keyhole. Not a pianist, I finally remembered from the *Times* listings on the R train, but a painter with a show that had opened a few days ago. There had even been a picture of her. White blouse, black skirt, chunky.

CHAPTER 10

I waited around until the first few people filtered in for the soiree. As much as they'd come for some inside information on Caporale, I'd held out a thin hope one of them could tell me something I didn't know. But after the arrival of a campus librarian, a married graduate student couple, and a neighbor from around the block, the old man was still doing most of the talking—about Phil Caporale's classroom eloquence. For one night, anyway, Joe Carroll had nothing invested in the Amritsar massacre.

I loaded up on enough of the French bread and taleggio the graduate students had brought to take care of supper, then headed home. "Don't forget to mail me that bill," the host called out after me.

On the way home, I tried to think positive things. Most of all, there had been the Professor's help in tracing Roberta Klein. I reassured myself I still had my copy of the *Times* with the gallery listings, that it had been only the Business section I'd left on the subway. And why worry if I still didn't have it? There was always the *Times* online, some candy store in Bay Ridge open until midnight . . . the goddamn public library!

I caught my swerve ahead of a blue Honda just in time. A rush of anger seemed to come out of my every pore. Somebody was playing with me, and I didn't want it to be only Phil Caporale. Brian Seldes was a much more satisfying target. At least he was still alive. Cracking that prick's head into his Outbox was just the *start* of what he had coming! For what? For sending Caporale over the edge? Who cared about that? I hadn't liked Caporale anyway. For being indirectly responsible for the *pro bono* work the Professor expected me to do? Closer, because who the hell had ever accused me or Joe Carroll of being *bono* about anything? Who the fuck had made Brian Seldes God??!!

Maybe it was this religious frame of mind that left me distracted while I parked half a block down from my building and then stalked back up the quiet night street. Lights were everywhere—in the windows, in the lampposts, in the stars. The one place they weren't, I realized too late, was under the archway separating the sidewalk from the gate to the courtyard of my apartment building. What was there instead were two weightlifters who looked like they had barely had time to slap on their T-shirts and jeans in rushing over from the gym to see me.

"You Finley?" the one with furry eyebrows asked.

My first thought was of the .38 sitting atop my socks in the bureau drawer upstairs. My second thought was it was too late to have thoughts.

"It's him," the second one, three inches shorter than his brother, said.

I figured this was an opening to whatever threats the morons had in mind. But instead, Brows just came up with his left hand and caught me flush under the left eye. I have just begun to fight, I told myself, as I crashed back into the doorbell grid and warned my face not to say a word.

"Keep the fuck away from places you don't belong! You got it?"

I couldn't get any part of me to pay attention. My legs hadn't been hit, but they insisted on falling. The fury I'd been working up in my chest against Seldes went down in the same heap on the archway stone in front of the bells as the rest of me. My shoulder blades hadn't banged up against any of the bells hard enough to raise help. My left cheekbone acted as though it had been attacked by a swarm of wasps.

"He got it," Little Brother said. "Let's go."

They were reasonable morons, I had to give them that. A single-stamp message and they were swaggering away toward deliveries elsewhere. Not only that, but they'd found a parking space right in front of the house! It was all I could do in overcoming my admiration for them to get up to my knees in time to read their plate as MG4313, not so sure of the last two digits.

My face didn't look half as bad in the bathroom mirror as it felt; I was sure a few hours' sleep would cure that. I was also sure the Brows brothers hadn't been sent by Seldes. *Keep the fuck away from places you don't belong* didn't sound like his kind of message. Why had I so quickly thought of the slugs as brothers?

Because I had a file on my desk saying the final phase of Klaus the scumlord's intimidation tactics had been to send his "sons" around to shut up protesting tenants.

Because I'd made still another mistake in leaving my card at Frank Martinez's bodega.

Because Siegfried and Roy, or whatever the hell they were called, had been a natural nightcap for Finley's thrilling adventures on the day.

CHAPTER 11

The *Times* said next to nothing about Caporale the next day, so I went around to Roger's candy store to pick up a *Newsday*. Long Island paper or not, it wasn't much better—statements of shock from university colleagues and neighbors and a list of organizations to which Caporale had belonged. Wife Florence was nowhere except for having found the body. The case officer, a Lieutenant John Romano whom I didn't know, ruled out anything except suicide. Bureaucratically, that seemed quick. The handful of times I'd been in his spot, if there had been the slightest trace of another possibility, my boilerplate phrase had been "our investigation is not yet officially complete." Apparently, Phil Caporale was as officially complete as any corpse could be.

CHAPTER 12

The 107 precinct was on a leafy residential street off Union Turnpike. Between all the private houses and the web of highways surrounding them, it looked like a neighborhood ripe for burglaries and car thefts but not bothered by too much of anything else. I wondered how the command suited McGill. After Bernstein had been killed, she had been promoted, but to a desk at Police Plaza. Was Fresh Meadows a decompression chamber for easing her back out to the streets? Had she been disappointed the assignment meant mostly hot wiremen who could be on the Grand Central, Van Wyck, or Long Island Expressway speeding toward other boroughs before Mr. and Mrs. Smith realized their new Nissan was gone?

She saw me before I killed the engine. She was standing next to a car in front of the house with two other detectives and doing all the talking. Without missing a beat in her instructions, she gestured for me to stay where I was. I recognized her tight movements, but not much else. She had let her raven hair grow down to her shoulders, and there was no more recently lost baby fat in her face. Between the black bag hanging off her shoulder and the glasses and ID badge on cords around her neck, she looked entwined in strings, but with total self-confidence about which one jiggled what. I'd never seen her in anything like her tan suit before, or for that matter in low pumps. Two years ago, she had gone around in clunky brogans, knowing she would be expected to do most of the footwork for the overweight Bernstein. The shoes alone seemed to say she had moved on.

She got rid of her ID as she came over. I hadn't completely imagined her warmth on the phone: Her smile didn't seem to have any hidden agendas. "Know what I'd really like right now?" she said, walking around the front of my car to the passenger seat. "A lurid ice cream to ruin the supper I'm not going to get to eat anyway."

"I passed a Carvel's a couple of blocks down."

"Exactly what I had in mind."

And with that, the awkwardness was over. No handshakes or kissy-kissies or anything else exaggerated as she climbed in next to me and I went back up to the Turnpike. She smelled of lilac and sun and grass and anything else outdoors that came to mind. "A John Doe in the park," she said, as though I'd been sniffing her like a hound. "Must've been laying in his cardboard box a couple of days."

That was it until we parked in the Carvel's lot, ordered two chocolate cones, and sat down at a picnic table at the side of the place to eat them. She wondered about the nice purple weal I'd grown under my left eye, I wondered about the new craze for doors that could be pushed as abruptly as pulled when you approached them. She thought I'd gained a couple of pounds, I thought she'd lost a couple. She thought maybe it was the bad-fitting shirt I was wearing, I thought maybe it was because she had always been wearing chunky clothes two years ago. We both thought the buses and cars tearing up and down Union Turnpike were convenient for not blaming ourselves for having to strain for the next gambit. I'd never noticed before how green her eyes were.

"Okay," she said finally. "You first."

I told her everything I knew. Her interest couldn't have been less like the Professor's. While he had doted on the Indian movies and the JABPUN website, she made her cone an afterthought only when it came to Pouchol-Jobert and Seldes. It was a totally professional attention: Paris dubbers and the Internet didn't pose jurisdiction questions, but Manhattan murders and the FBI did. As for Caporale's suicide, that had already been filed away by Nassau County, hadn't it?

"You really ought to stick to the USA, Finley," she said when I had finished. "You seem to get into trouble when there are other parts of the world involved."

I was supposed to admire her reference to our chase through South American politics with Bernstein, and I did. I was supposed to get over any idea she was still as fragile as she had been at our last meeting, so I got over it. "The Pouchol woman," she said, not wanting to see *too* much approval. "Milford Plaza. 12th-floor room. Unidentified intruder bashed her over the skull three times. Weapon a metal table candleholder with assault marks but no fingerprints. Wiped clean. Remember the place we're talking about here. The Milford isn't a desk with a bell and a detective watching the elevators. Escalators from the street make it more like a mall than a hotel. Anyone at all could have gone directly from the escalators over to the elevators and up to Pouchol's room without attracting attention."

"If this anyone knew where the room was."

"One theory. Another is a prowler going floor to floor. Maybe she just picked the wrong moment to open her door."

"Prints elsewhere than on the candleholder?"

"Thousands of them. Aren't we both glad it's not our problem?"

"So there were valuables taken. Tens of thousands of dollars' worth. Necklaces that traced back to before the French Revolution."

She bit into her cone with a smile. "That's good, Paul."

"No robbery?"

"No robbery. About three thousand in traveler's checks. A couple of rings that would've kept her on her feet even if she'd lost the checks. Some euros and an expensive tape recorder in her attaché case, too. All the tapes were blank or new and unused.

"Even the one in the machine?"

"There was none in the machine."

"Maybe she just bought the recorder."

"French make. You ask the damndest questions. For somebody just trying to win brownie points, I mean."

"You seem to have asked the same ones. For somebody in Queens asking about a Manhattan homicide, I mean."

"So we should both change our habits."

"No sexual assault, I presume."

"Right."

"So the working hypothesis is . . .?"

A motorcycle went ripping down the Turnpike loud enough to earn her frown—and the few seconds of thought she needed. "You know how this works," she said. "I reach out to somebody in Midtown South and ask a lot of questions. Then they get curious about my curiosity."

"What did you promise them, Mac?"

"Your details. Things like what you just told me—maybe on a piece of paper? I mean, Caporale and Pouchol within such a short time after all these years? Wouldn't *you* want that on paper in their place?"

"Why the hell didn't you just tape me?"

"Because that would be my tape and this has nothing to do with me."

I was the one who suddenly needed a motorcycle. It wasn't the idea of typing up everything I had told her; even with my picking and pecking, that would have been an hour's work at most. But there was no way I could ever sign my name to something like that without having some bored Manhattan detectives summoning me down to a fart-smelling office so I could show I told the same story with my mouth as I did with my word processor.

"You're about to whine."

"I'm thinking about it. Tell me something that would make all this helpfulness worth it."

She considered that reasonable. "Alex Olmos, the guy working the case, has no idea if it means anything, but the lady might not have been here just to record the sounds of the lions in the Bronx Zoo with her tape recorder. She was an accountant by profession. Apparently worked for some company that's been on the front pages of the French papers for months. Some kind of takeover scandal, unfriendly raiders, all that Michael Douglas *Wall Street* movie stuff that's always bored the hell out of me. What exactly she was doing here Alex doesn't know and the French cops don't seem to have gotten any clear answers from her employer. At which point . . ."

"Olmos's eyes glazed over and he said that's a French problem."

"I never *got* the popularity of Michael Douglas. Do you? I mean, now he's even married to that beautiful Zeta woman half his age . . ."

Thanks to the Professor, I'd once picked up a few hundred bucks at Adelphi teaching a course called Investigative Techniques. It had been the usual Learning Annex entertainment for the bored and the drifting, except it had come with the formal backing of a university department and the bored and the drifting had been credit-hungry students instead of soccer Moms in the mood for more than pottery lessons. As McGill went on about her tastes in Hollywood leading men, I suddenly remembered the conviction I'd felt one day in that classroom pontificating that during every case, the average investigator had three happy intuitions; not one, two, or sixty-three-and-a-half, but three. I'd had no idea that day where that number had come from, and I still didn't. But thinking about Roberta Klein seemed to leave two more healthy stabs in my satchel. "This French company in the middle of all this to-do," I tried. "It wouldn't be a movie company, would it?"

She had to play it back to herself before admitting I was serious. "The one that did all these Indian things?"

"Right."

"I didn't ask. Are you sure we're talking about the same Mireille Pouchol? You said yours was some kind of actress."

"It's the same one. Servais confirmed it. Besides, this dubbing thing was 25 years ago. What were you 25 years ago?"

"The most rambunctious kid in Mrs. Schwartz's kindergarten class."

She held it for about three seconds. Then she laughed—full teeth, crinkles under her eyes, the barest wisp of chocolate on her upper lip. I was very glad I had decided to ruin my supper, too.

CHAPTER 13

"Think we did okay?" she asked as soon as I pulled in back across the street from her precinct house.

"When I called, I really wanted to hang up. I didn't want you hearing my name and then thinking of Bernie."

Her laugh was a hollow whoop, but not as false as it should have been. "And what the hell else do you think would pop into my mind when I hear Paul Finley's calling? You've had a couple of aliases in my life, you know. For a while, you were Finley the Shit who got Bernie too involved in that mess. Those politicos might have killed him, but you were the one who put him in the line of fire. Then you were just Finley the guy I wanted to forget about because I felt cheaper trying to cheapen you. Then, when you called yesterday, I realized you'd become somebody else altogether. You were Finley Who Had Been There, somebody who could reassure me at my new awareness level that we weren't the ones who fucked up and got him killed. Want to do that for me, Finley?"

With no more ice cream cones between us, I went immediately for the seat belt over her tan shoulder. Anything was more comfortable than the bad-old-days glare she had finally worked up for me. "If I started thinking about all the people I've . . ."

"I don't give a crap about other people. I'm asking about Lieutenant Allen Bernstein. Killed in the line of duty on August 27, 2001. The one who earned the gratitude of two countries and a police department for dying when he did."

At times, orders had their merits. "No, Lieutenant, we didn't fuck up."

She waited for a second, two seconds, then relaxed her green eyes and unclasped her seat belt. "That's what I decided last year, too. Sometimes you get the bear and sometimes the bear gets you, and that's all there is to it. But it's good hearing you say it."

I watched her retrace the same steps around the car she had taken to climb in the first time. I hadn't said anything about the reading glasses that flapped off her chest, I realized: That would have been another time-killer back at Carvel's. But then I didn't need any more particulars about what had improved or what had deteriorated in the two years since I'd last seen her in the federal prosecutor's office. She had improved, I would have regarded even slow deterioration as progress. End of story.

It was in that buoyant mood that I headed home. Since Jenny's death, my worst bouts of loneliness had come right after seeing somebody whose world hadn't spun out of orbit by noticing how lonely I was. I'd decided this was some reverse Svengali itch: *I* wasn't the one who wanted to do the possessing, I wanted all my Trilbys to think of nothing being more urgent than *their possessing me.* By now I'd also accepted there was more than one hypocrisy in this. As I'd already proven a few times, nobody was easier to justify breaking up with than a possessive Trilby. They could never live up to their ambitions.

CHAPTER 14

I skipped the tail end of Happy Hour at the Green Fox. I wasn't up for donating $20 to the Miles Harkleroad Fund and even less for shagging after passing thoughts I was a Miles Harkleroad in-waiting. What I was in the mood for least of all was either of Cynthia's guises as little sister or mother and the repartee we'd gotten into the habit of exchanging for apologizing we couldn't feel more for each other. Being in bed with her seemed as long ago as some family Thanksgiving.

The first message waiting for me on my machine was from Gerald Harrah. I was feeling envious enough of Mr. Westbeth and spiteful enough toward Harrah to return it right away. By the time his secretary believed that I wasn't selling real estate and put me through, I was ready to do what I was good at—I compromised. I still had a business to run, and who knew how many cuckolds Harrah ran into every day? So, while he tried to sound level and disinterested, I told him about Sarah staying inside Westbeth for more than three hours, but omitted the details about the cab and the uptown restaurant after that. It was up to him to decide if she had gone to see some dashiki designer. He thanked me without much conviction. I told myself I was out the Bass Ale from Mr. Westbeth's restaurant.

Before going off to see McGill, I'd put in several calls without too much to show for it. Apparently, everyone had been waiting for me to get out of the house so they could phone back without any danger of having to talk to me. Jimmy Heyer at Motor Vehicles told me license plate MG4313 belonged to a Walter Klaus, a real estate broker with an address in the Park Slope section of Brooklyn. The Pandora Galleries woman had to confirm she had spoken with her boss and that, unfortunately, it was indeed policy not to give out the home addresses of exhibiting artists. Blanche Walsh wondered if I had heard the terrible news about Harkleroad.

I was disappointed Seldes hadn't run out of patience waiting for me to call back after seeing JABPUN. It was a waste of anguish. The first message on my e-mail said: CONDOLENCES ON DOCTOR CAPORALE'S PASSING. WE REALLY SHOULD TALK. So, he wasn't only on top of the news, he was on top of the e-mail directory. He was Power and I wasn't. And so? What else was new?

I heated some Chunky soup for supper, reminding myself with every stirring of the pot that, the Professor's good intentions or not, I had nowhere to go with Phil Caporale and his old soulmates. The trouble was, my guests kept clearing their throats to suggest otherwise. The film cans didn't move from the floor in front of the bookcase, but they knew as well as I did what I'd decided in throwing out the Federal Express box with the garbage before going off to see McGill.

Then the name Boardman came to mind, and I ran out of the excuse that I had nowhere to project the movies.

CHAPTER 15

The Pandora Galleries was a Soho walkup of bare spaces sectioned off by plywood walls and smelling of violets. The woman sitting at the reception desk at the top of the stairs, a student with a taste for Marcel Marceau makeup, looked grateful to be able to look up from her business management textbook and flash her smile at anyone at all. The only other browser was an elderly man in a Yankee windbreaker and Panama hat. I took a brochure to kill a few minutes for establishing my presence. It seemed Roberta Klein was sharing the exhibition with a Carol Golina. The area with the receptionist was all Golina—watercolors that might have been seascapes or might have been the code lines on cans of soup. I tried the next cubbyhole. A clumsily printed sign said I'd found Roberta Klein.

What had I expected? More Indian colors from JABPUN? Portraits of Phil Caporale? What I found were geometrical shapes resembling sidewalk asphalt patterns. The first was a green triangle between two cream squares. In the second one, the triangle was at the bottom of the canvas, colored orange, looking overwhelmed by the cream squares and by a blue trapezoid. In the third one, the green triangle was back, but this time standing on its head and overlapping one of the cream squares. A couple of other canvasses had changed the squares to green and had them surrounding the trapezoid, with the triangle off to the side like some objective observer. The longer I stared, the creepier the feeling I was looking at people, not geometry.

"What do you think the triangle means to her?" The old guy in the Yankee jacket looked enthralled by all the shapes.

"To her, probably just a shape and a color. But I see people."

"Who's that?"

"Nobody in particular. Just people. What do you see?"

His chest rumbled with catarrh, but he didn't take his eyes off the green triangle with the cream squares. "The world, the flesh, and the devil; isn't that what they say?"

My mistake, I told myself; the leaflet would be next. "I guess."

"The world and the flesh are great," he grinned. "It's that god-damn devil, always making us think the worst of one another. That's your triangle, son. Letting that fucker interfere with the world and the flesh." He patted me on the shoulder. "Nice talking to you."

An epiphany! What else could it have been as I watched him trudge back out of the space and into the cubbyhole behind us? The old guy with the bad taste in baseball teams was actually the angel Gabriel come down to point me in the right direction in so many things—tough investigations, my love life, finances, enlightened political stances.

If only he hadn't chosen that moment to clear his lungs with as gross a gargle of phlegm as I had ever heard!

And if only Marcel Marceau's disciple hadn't looked at me with so much sadness when I returned to her to ask for more information on Roberta Klein. "I'm sorry," she said in her tiny squeaky voice. "We just received word this morning that she's died."

CHAPTER 16

I'd had enough. I'd had enough of Phil Caporale and the suburban fortress he had defended to the death. I'd had enough of some gutter bum spinning out his hallucinations on the Internet. I'd had enough of the other gutter bums toying with lives with telephone calls and business cards because they had the power to do it. And I'd had enough of my brilliant intuitions and made-for-cable mind. Sitting behind the wheel in front of the Pandora Galleries, I could have squeezed out enough bile to make an ocean. Roberta Klein had been the key to everything? Certainly, and for that she had died. But not at the hands of some masked intruder swinging a candleholder or under the wheels of a city bus secretly owned by the North Atlantic Treaty Organization. No, none of that. As the receptionist had told me in her bleak wonder, Roberta Klein had died of breast cancer!

And even that flash hadn't ended it! What else could a Finley imagine immediately than a breast cancer *caused* by the same conspiratorial forces that had killed Mireille Pouchol-Jobert and Phil Caporale? I had mocked the little girl because she had bought her white makeup from a tomb? I could have given her lessons in how to trespass on the dead.

For the first time in a long time, I sank back into the sore haze that had descended as soon as State Trooper Donald Wolf had knocked on the Professor's door to report what had happened to Jenny and Susan. The deeply philosophical days, weeks, and months of Paul Finley. My favorite insight from that time was that death idealized life. You went to a wake or funeral to say nice things about the departed. You went into miserable dark rooms where you couldn't forgive yourself for not having been as perfect as the departed had been. Any hint the departed *hadn't been* perfect made you a creep. And then the last twist: The departed had created standards. If they had been perfect and you still weren't, why the hell continue to clutter up the planet? Just to make bartenders and shrinks and priests feel appreciated? Life was too glorious for that, and if you didn't understand that, life was as much beyond your understanding as death was. You didn't belong in either place. You belonged in the limbo where you were.

A mother approached the car with her brood. She was pushing a baby carriage with an infant girl and wearing the same fatigue pants as the six- or seven-year-old boy walking alongside her. She had her head buried in a comic book, and the way she was scrutinizing some panel like a jeweler searching for a flaw, it didn't look like the boy's. The kid peered in at me. He looked curious, then just unimpressed, as he tottered along. I wondered if that was the kind of look store window mannequins received every hour of every day. I saw the kid's point.

I also had the perfect appointment for my bright outlook.

The address left on my e-mail by Seldes was for a pocket office building on 21st Street in Chelsea. It wasn't Federal Plaza and it didn't have the look of anything else being subsidized by me and the U.S. Congress. The street door was unlocked and the lobby desk hadn't been used in years. The wall directory listed personal names and companies like VIEWER MEDIA CONSULTANTS and FARO DYES. With one exception, the letters were more gray than white, and a few had fallen into the gutter behind the glass. The exception was Room 403, where everyone from SELDES, BRIAN to CICUT, JOHN to BELLINI, MARY seemed to have gathered; the letters spelling out their names looked fresh from the factory. No mention of the FBI. I'd never heard of an agency that wanted to be anonymous at the same time it went barging into Garden City homes and Brooklyn bars trumpeting what it was. Whatever was going on up in Room 403 was clearly of a piece with a business card that gave a name and number but no affiliation. I had a bad feeling I'd been taking something far too much for granted.

The peeling elevator car deposited me on the fourth floor with only a single unnerving creak from its cables. Room 403 was a recently installed wooden door with no name on it and an intercom phone on the wall next to it. I reminded myself I hadn't come as far as I had to beat a retreat and ponder strategic alternatives. Whether they were shipping twine or anthrax to North Korea inside, the day (the week, the month) would have been a bust without getting through the door to Seldes.

The buzzer led to a big, fluorescent-lighted room divided into at least a dozen workspaces. I saw heads and computers in the cubbyholes and calendars and Rand-McNally maps on the walls. The only sounds were of keyboards being clacked and someone at a back desk sneezing.

"Mr. Finley!"

Seldes was standing in the doorway to a private office flush with the entrance. Sitting at the desk right outside the office was my broker from the R train; his nameplate said JOHN CICUT. He was too busy on a telephone headset even to look up at me.

"Please come in!"

I gave Seldes a point for not trying to shake hands and followed him inside. The office was a modest square with two advantages over the bullpen outside: the window over Seventh Avenue that took up almost the entirety of one wall and an old-fashioned metal desk lamp instead of the keep-their-eyes-open fluorescence from the ceiling. There were a couple of framed photos on the desk, but they were turned away from the single chair for visitors. As I sat down, I decided the pictures were of mating aardvarks.

Brian Seldes was in his 40s, and didn't look so much like the Hoover G-Man Caporale had described as some kind of factory floor boss. He also didn't know when to leave well enough alone. He was tall, but with an exaggerated stiffness to his spine, as though he'd never heard the Marine sergeant's At Ease order. A cowlick called attention to his thinning hair. A maroon turtle-necked shirt accented his paunch. I had the feeling he liked his anonymous little building. It didn't encourage social interaction.

"Should we cut right to the chase?"

"What would that be? Phil Caporale?"

He became grave—at least I was supposed to think so. "We were sorry to hear about that. Man was apparently under a great deal of stress."

"You didn't notice you were giving him more?"

Gravity hour over. "Whatever was bothering your client—I assume he was? —was bothering him long before we ever interviewed him. What interests me is if that something was Neil Kinsey."

"Ask your friend Cicut outside. He should know."

No apology. "You seemed worth a one-day surveillance. And where did that lead us? Most immediately, to a foreign national."

"He's French, I think."

"But not an old friend of yours. A new one."

"We do lunch every once in a while. That okay with you?"

"Look, Mr. Finley, I just follow the dotted lines. We interview Doctor Caporale to ask if he's seen Kinsey. He says no, but suddenly he's visiting you and you in turn are chatting up foreign diplomats. What possibilities does that leave? Doctor Caporale wants you to find Kinsey because we've unwittingly reminded him Kinsey owes him money? Or, he knows where Kinsey is, but doesn't want to be followed there, so he sends you to contact people who might. To warn him, perhaps?"

"Warn him about what?"

He stretched his legs out over the edge of the desk. I hadn't seen his tasseled moccasins outside a shoe store window in years. "C'mon, fella. A little professional courtesy across the desk here. To warn Kinsey we're looking for him . . . You think that's funny?"

"I think you live in a narrow little world, Seldes, but I haven't figured out the universe yet. This sure as hell isn't Federal Plaza."

"No, it isn't." He made it sound like some vital defiance. "Did you have the opportunity to watch JABPUN?"

"So?"

"What did you think?"

"I'm sure the man believes in what he says."

"Man?"

"We were cutting to the chase, remember? Kinsey."

He glanced up over my shoulder, seemed to consider closing the door, then went back to studying his knees. "Maybe I should

explain we're not in Federal Plaza because we're seconded to another agency altogether."

Only then did I notice the walls had none of the usual plaques
or pictures of Seldes shaking hands on the White House lawn.
There wasn't even a flag in the room. Just a lot of recently painted
green wall and two glum wheaty prints of farmland that would
have fit nicely next to my seascape *Calm.* "Homeland Security."

He nodded readily. "They don't just sit around playing with
color alarm charts. But even with all the reintegration of investigative bureaus, they occasionally have special inquiry needs. We
assist in those cases."

"That's nice. And who cares?"

"Only the bad guys, we hope. You a bad guy, Mr. Finley? No, I
don't think you're a bad guy. And that's why I thought you could
help us. For starters, JABPUN wasn't Kinsey's creation. It was
mine."

Under my plan on the way over, I should have already been
storming out of the office. Instead, I was groping toward the feat
of crossing my leg and remembering the Professor's crack of how
"Homeland Security" sounded like some police outfit from apart-
heid South Africa. "That's nice."

"It seemed like a good idea at the time. Smoke out what there
was to smoke out. People can be so single-minded about their
manias sometimes they're grateful to find kindred spirits. Their
failure *is* communication."

He thought that was funny. I had a buggy feeling he knew
Cool Hand Luke was one of my favorite movies. "Lovely."

"Yes, the idea was," he said, the humor interlude over. "But
then somebody higher on the food chain decided to reorganize
priorities after 9/11. They thought we already had too much to
do here to take on JABPUN too, so they assigned it to somebody
else. Guess who?"

I wanted to be back with the old-timer in the Yankee jacket
and Panama hat. At least with him, I had *thought* I understood
something.

"The short of it is Kinsey impressed someone as an ideal webmaster. He had the computer background, knew the right people

after years of free-lance work for them, he was off the books, etcetera, etcetera. What nobody saw coming was he'd use the website to settle old personal scores."

"So take away this marvelous toy the government's given him."

He smiled benevolently. "That's when it started getting complicated. One day he was working from a little studio he had in Minneapolis, the next day he'd disappeared. The building manager, his landlord, a woman he was seeing—nobody had a clue where he went. We don't, either."

"So much for JABPUN. We're all going to miss it."

"We'd love to think that was all. But four days after he disappeared, we had a possible sighting. At the Milford Plaza, here."

I thought of the last scene in *Land of the Pharaohs*. All the high priests and the evil Joan Collins wife were inside the pyramid, the murdered pharaoh's resting place. Then the high priest nodded to one of his minions, who immediately took a hammer to a cup on the wall. The cup splintered, sand began flowing out, leading to a chain reaction of other cups splintering, more sand falling out, wooden supports collapsing, and rock by rock, the pyramid closing down internally. The evil wife screamed when she realized she was going to be trapped inside with the loyal priests and husband she had murdered. I didn't want to be inside, either.

"You're saying Kinsey killed Pouchol?"

Suddenly, he wasn't saying much of anything. He liked the tassel lagging left on his right shoe or maybe he didn't like it. A low telephone buzz from the bullpen outside could have been me calling and getting the wrong number. Or maybe I was the impatient driver honking at somebody downstairs on Seventh Avenue. I agreed with Seldes: I just wasn't there.

"A definite possibility," he said finally. "Pouchol's room records say she called him right before he disappeared. Someone answering his general description struck a bell with a deskman at the hotel. Nothing conclusive, but he sure wasn't behaving all that rationally before he vanished."

I liked it; I liked it a lot. It did away with Phil Caporale the killer a lot more convincingly than the Professor's intuitions about Indian massacres. "Caporale didn't mention any of this."

"We didn't say anything about it to him. There was no reason to. But my point is, Kinsey and Pouchol the old lovers from Paris getting together again after all this time . . . Well, we don't need a Neil Kinsey telling Diane Sawyer how their reunion got fucked up at the Milford Plaza and oh, incidentally, this is how I've been making my living lately."

It took me a second to accept he was serious. But then I remembered federal prosecutor Murphy after Bernstein's death and the Feds I'd worked with as a cop. "Embarrassment??!! This is all about embarrassment??!!"

"Doctor Caporale was evidently under severe pressures, and that ended tragically," he tramped on. "You yourself have been in contact with a foreign national known to have had an association with Kinsey at one time. What it's about, Mr. Finley, is whether Caporale or Servais told you the whereabouts of Neil Kinsey."

I'd been unfair to Caporale twice over. Not only hadn't he taken his last bath in remorse for having killed Pouchol, but he hadn't been the only cat licking its fur in shame after being thrown off the kitchen table! "That's all? I tell you yes or no and that's it?"

"I understand about client privilege even after the client . . ."

Actually, it had nothing to do with that. If it meant making life much simpler with one word, I wouldn't have hesitated to say *no*, stood up, tried to see whose pictures had been framed, taken a longer look around outside, then pressed for the elevator to return to the street and eternal happiness. But ever since Caporale had walked into my living room, clear talk, keeping one's word, and all those golden things had been a little elusive. Did I trust Brian Seldes to correct that trend? No, I didn't. No matter how unimportant I might have been to him in his grand scheme of things, he had still sent two clowns into Cynthia's to raise a lot of dust. "Good, I'm glad you do," I said. "Especially if you're so convinced Kinsey killed Pouchol. Because that'd make Caporale, deceased or not, an accomplice after the fact, wouldn't it?"

"You're being silly, Finley . . ."

"Must be those old cop tics of mine."

"I'd love nothing more than to hear the police have another suspect in custody. But they don't."

"They don't have Kinsey, either. How come? You're not sharing with the cops working the case? I thought Homeland Security
lived for cooperating with law enforcement agencies around the
country. The President himself told me that."

"I'm not going to get into a pissing contest with you, Finley."

"Good. Then tell me what you really want or I'll be shoving off."

I gave myself a count of five before standing up. He smiled at
three. "I'd be particularly interested in what Servais told you."

"Ask him yourself."

"I'm pretty sure he's told you he cited his diplomatic immunity
as a reason not to cooperate. That can be corrected, but would be
a tedious process. I'd prefer to settle it here and now."

"Great. And maybe there's something I want to know, too."

"What?"

My *quid pro quo* knee-jerk hadn't thought that one through.
Some particulars on what the people outside were working on
might have been instructive, but for what—party chat at the Professor's next salon? Fast as it crept up on me, there seemed to
be only one answer. "Tell me about Kinsey. How he ingratiated
himself to your friends in Washington."

He didn't know what to be suspicious of, only that he should
have been. "I've just got paper. I've never met him."

"So tell me what's on paper. And then I'll see if I can help you."

I could usually tell when people didn't like me: They aimed
their eyes at some spot in front of my chin they didn't really see. I
was on the far side of their one-way mirror: No matter how much
I waved or jumped up and down, I'd been sentenced to invis-
ibility. Much harder to figure out was when people didn't like me
but wondered how useful I could be. I rarely got a sense of how
optimistic they were feeling. "We could be talking about a grave
security issue here, Finley."

"Yeah, you keep saying."

He thought about it an extra second, then collapsed his legs
to the floor, and went over to close the door.

CHAPTER 17

"**After Paris, Kinsey bummed around** Europe a couple of years. He came back to the States, went to Chicago. Did TV commercial work, then hooked up with a ghetto demagogue who was running in the primaries for mayor. The candidate never got past first base, but the campaign got Kinsey a lot of exposure. Political spots, prominent TV commercials—he capitalized on it pretty good for awhile there. Then he got in on the ground floor of some on-line media outfit. Apparently, they were a little too early on the scene. There was more talk about what they were doing than income from doing it. Kinsey didn't have the patience to wait for the flower to blossom, so went out to California. I'm not sure what he was doing out there. Trying to break into the movies, I guess."

"Sell a script. A cowboy version of King Arthur and the Knights of the Round Table."

"Why not? He stayed out there for a couple of years. Odd jobs, from what we understand. Next we have him back in St. Paul. He worked for a frozen food company there, shooting some commercials, then helping them computerize their operation. The owner of the company also happened to be the biggest financial backer of . . . an important American. Kinsey's circle widened. He became everybody's special technical advisor. One Administration followed another, the frozen food man and his creature faded from the scene, but Kinsey kept being useful. He made enough to set up offices in Minneapolis. Didn't seem to belong to anything but a local video club."

"So where did all this Indian expertise kick in? There must've been something in particular to recommend him for it."

"Not all that much. He did websites for ethnic groups up there. One of them was Indian. I guess Person A led to Person B to Person C and Person C remembered he was connected through Person D. There're people out there right now you never heard of who could give you a reference, Finley."

"And that was enough? 'Here, Kinsey, we have this new operation and we want you to manage it. Get back to us if some lunatic e-mails you?' Nobody ever saw what he sent out ahead of time?"

"Of course it was vetted. I saw some of it myself."

"And it was all wonderful until he started dishing the dirt on his old acquaintances in Paris?"

"I think he was told once he was going overboard, wasn't following his directive. His mental state wasn't as appreciated as it might have been."

"I guess not."

"Make of it what you will. I'm hardly going to deny we've had some organizational glitches here and there. But we had no reason to raise an alarm until he didn't answer repeated queries. Our people on the scene said he just didn't show up at his studio one morning."

"And this would be around the time Pouchol called him?"

"The diatribes about Caporale and the others came the very next day. Then phfftt! No warning to the people who worked there with him or to the building landlord. The woman he was seeing was very upset, but she couldn't think of any foul play reasons for his disappearance. His neighbors didn't think of him as Santa Claus, but he wasn't an ogre, either."

"And so you began bothering Caporale because . . .?"

"Why 'because?' Because Kinsey attacks the guy out of the blue. It didn't seem like much of a reach they'd had recent contact."

"But he named them all on that website. Not just Caporale."

"And we contacted them, too. Like I said, the Frenchman got huffy. Roberta Klein wasn't in great shape. The Matson woman's on another planet. Kinsey was somebody she knew ages ago when she was living down here on earth, and who wants to take that long trip back through space just for accommodating us?"

"I like her already."

"Now you know as much as we know about Kinsey's whereabouts. The question is, is that as much as Jean-Claude Servais knows about them?"

"He hasn't seen Kinsey in 25 years."

"That's what he told you? You believe him?"

"I can't think of a reason why I shouldn't."

"He's well known in Hinduphile circles, did you know that?"

"*Hinduphile?*"

Nothing. "He didn't tell you that, I bet. Or did he tell you that one of the other numbers on Pouchol's hotel records was the French mission to the United Nations? Did he mention that?"

"So what? Pouchol probably called Klein and Matson, too. From what I hear, they all used to be pretty tight."

"My point. Maybe they were all planning a reunion, but for some reason that bothered Kinsey."

It was the kind of conversation you had with Miles Harkleroad at the Green Fox: the more demented the arguments, the wearier the feeling that the main issue was the steadfastness of the person making them. "I don't think I can help you any further, Seldes."

He barely raised his eyes as I stood up, just folded his hands over his budding belly and nodded. "Tell me why I should believe that."

"You have no choice?"

He consulted with his photo of the mating aadvarks for a moment, then smiled. "Thanks for coming by, Finley."

"You don't want talent like Kinsey getting away from you. You sound made for each other. Hope you find him."

"That's a given."

CHAPTER 18

I took the Manhattan Bridge instead of the tunnel back to Brooklyn. I didn't want cavernous thoughts, I wanted luminous horizons. The road back to the Neil Kinsey movies sitting on my living room floor was paved with crystal, shimmering intentions. I would get home, call Florence Caporale, and tell her I'd drop the reels by her house whenever she felt like it after the funeral. Then I'd call the Professor and tell him there was no reason to look any deeper into Phil Caporale, that even the Federal Government knew for sure he hadn't had anything to do with Mireille Pouchol's death. I didn't know how, but I'd try to get along without either Neil Kinsey or Brian Seldes in my life.

Then I made the mistake of getting off the bridge. The skylines were lower, the traffic slower. Once off the Flatbush Avenue extension, I was back into the street grids that had inspired Roberta Klein's last exhibition and I was still five miles from home. The only good thought I had traveling them was Killer Kinsey. Just because Seldes was another dangerous Federal clerk didn't mean he couldn't have been right occasionally. For some reason, Kinsey killing Pouchol made it seem almost as though I'd done something concrete for my late client Phil Caporale.

For once, I opened my apartment door into a telephone call I wanted. Dana McGill's voice made me think I had a genie living in my jar of Maxwell House Instant. "The answer to your question is yes," she said. "This big business fracas in Europe is over the Reynaud-Grevin studios. Am I saying it right?"

"You're asking the wrong guy."

"The married name, Jobert? He's an executive at the studio. In fact, he looks like the top dog. The name you mentioned—Peyrot—is chairman of the board. Looks like Pouchol married the right producer."

"Who's the other party in this business spat?"

"Visiv Telecom. Another whale trying to swallow the ocean."

I looked over my desk to what passed for my furniture. It didn't look better informed. "Thanks, Dana." My coolness sounded unnecessary even to me, and I understood her silence. "I mean, if I was trying to tie Pouchol to an international conspiracy, I'd feel enlightened."

"*You* would. But not Alex Olmos."

"Oh, Christ, you've been making promises in my name again."

"You made me curious, and now he is, too. He's an okay guy, Paul. A little temperamental sometimes, but okay. How about a drink tomorrow night? Nothing official. Just three people talking about the state of law and order in the Midtown South command."

I couldn't refuse and I didn't want to refuse. And the nice thing was that I could use one feeling to alibi the other.

CHAPTER 19

I hadn't seen the Cameo manager Boardman in four years, and he had made sure he had a shot at another four. When I'd called him and told him what I wanted, he had resisted until I told him I needed only a projectionist, not him. Somebody named Glynn was to be the solution: I could drive out to the Island to see Kinsey's movies under Glynn's eye before the Cameo was due to open and Boardman wouldn't owe me any more favors.

I pulled in across the street from the movie house. Nothing much had changed in four years: a dusty block sloping down from the main strip, a sports memorabilia place, a couple of abandoned storefronts, and some woods at the foot of the street. The biggest changes had been in the sooty marquee. Instead of specific titles, it now just advertised ADULT FILMS. And the lettering announcing that weekends were devoted exclusively to martial arts pictures also seemed bigger. That was part of Boardman's arrangement with the town fathers who allowed him to stay in business. It was as hypocritical as everything else about the operation. If the local priests and rabbis ever found the energy to go to court against the Cameo, Boardman could always claim he had observed all the Sabbaths with kung-fu, not pubic hair.

The gate was still closed, but Glynn, a tall black guy in a jeans shirt, was sweeping the lobby behind it. He acknowledged me with a sigh and a grimace that had probably come from a conversation with Boardman, then made a production of putting aside his broom and walking over to unlock the gate. "Man says you got an hour, no more," he said. "You're on the clock as of now."

"Just don't use it up threading the film, okay?"

Glynn thought that was funny, closed the gate again, then took the film cans and led the way inside and up to the projection booth. The drearily lit orchestra had already been drowned in some putrid cherry deodorant. Even the old cigar smoke of the projection booth was a relief.

"I'll tell you right now you got too much here for an hour," he said, mounting the first reel. "Sure this is the one you want to start with?"

"I'm sure." The only thing I was sure of was that the five reels had been numbered. Beyond that, there was only another Finley Instinct to count on: that if there was anything interesting anywhere, it was more likely in the later pieces. Of course, the Finley Instinct had no guarantee the numbering reflected a chronological order, but why expect everything?

Caporale had been right about the *pissoirs* and Metro commuters. Ten minutes into the first reel, I had seen every Parisian who had taken a leak in Montmartre and Montparnasse 25 years ago. I was also ready to attest that people who got off the subway came up stairs and those who wanted to catch a subway went down them. Some of the Citroens still looked like the cars Nazi commandants had used in World War II movies, waiters were thankful when they retrieved their plates with money, the newsstands sold *France-Soir*, the women wore maxis or midis, and the men wore those striped colored shirts with white tab collars TV announcers had condemned to a merciful death.

"What is this shit, man?"

"King Arthur and the Round Table."

"Yeah? Somebody forgot the swords."

It went on like that for 25 minutes. The *cinema verite* was anything that had crossed in front of Kinsey's wobbly camera. Then he was inside—with bad lighting and blinding flashes and an even shakier hand, but inside. A thin blonde with bangs was irked to have the camera intruding on her as she sat in a window seat knitting what looked like a bed comforter. I knew it was Mireille Pouchol (the still-alive Mireille Pouchol of 25 years ago) even before she flashed him (flashed Kinsey and Finley and Glynn) with a yank at her blue halter. She had very small breasts and a bird-like chest.

"Hey, maybe we're warmin' up here!"

But that was all for Mireille Pouchol's breasts. There was some leader, and then a glaring pan of hideous red wallpaper shifted everything to a different indoor scene. Suddenly, there they all were—minus Kinsey the cameraman, anyway. It was some kind of get-together. Caporale sat on a big leather chair smoking; he was still short and paunchy, but his eyes didn't look as heavy and he had almost a full head of hair. The spindly redhead on the arm of the chair and waving at the lens must have been Inge Matson; she too was smoking and chugalugged whatever she had in a mug. Servais was on a couch between Mireille and the stocky elf I knew was Roberta Weiss. Roberta was working on a joint, both Servais and Mireille had wine glasses. This time, Mireille didn't flash Kinsey, she just gave him the finger, jerking it upward awkwardly as if showing him she had perfected the gesture after his teaching. Servais laughed and gave Mireille a peck on the cheek, but then turned to Roberta and didn't come up for air. She didn't mind, either, except for having to raise herself to pass her joint over to Inge before diving back into his face. Apparently, Servais had left out one of the other people at the infamous dinner with the Indian Sayyid: He had been paired off with Weiss as much as Kinsey-Mireille and Caporale-Inge had been couples.

"Fuckin' home movies, man!" Glynn turned from his peephole with distaste and walked a couple of feet away to light a cigarette. "Happy folks," he muttered. "Always love to see happy folks."

How many times would I have made a similar crack? But then and there, it sounded just mean—a futility from *our* world, the world of Finley and Glynn, a planet removed from a night in Paris 25 years ago when Phil Caporale had still had hair and three more people had still been alive.

My lungs missed an exhale. I didn't like it when they did that. Even though I hadn't had a cigarette in years, I was never quite sure when the gang already on board was going to start the Bon Voyage party.

Matson passed the joint to Caporale, who gave only a fake pass at inhaling before standing up and passing it back to Pouchol. Pouchol took it with a long glance at Caporale. She had seen the fake, I thought. And sure enough, there was Caporale poking his finger into his Adam's apple the way he'd done in my apartment. It had been his tell for all phony and awkward things Caporale.

The camera went back outside, to the concrete walkway along the Seine at night. There was a glimpse of a bridge in the background, but the camera couldn't wait to herky-jerk down to a body. It was a man in a suit on his stomach. The camera stayed square in the middle of his back, as if his jacket had some special significance. Nobody had mentioned Kinsey's necrophilia tendencies. Or was that just more *cinema verite*—you saw Mireille Pouchol flashing her tits, you saw rush hour commuters going down to the Metro, and you saw the corpse of a businessman after he'd been mugged or had dropped dead of a heart attack? It was all grist for the mill.

Except this time there was also a hand reaching down in front of the lens. The cameraman wanted a better shot of the corpse, and he had hired his hand to grasp the left shoulder and turn the body around. The hand was really bad at it. First it was tentative, then it managed only to leave the head drooping away from the camera as the shoulder came up. The head didn't turn more than an inch or two before the hand finally gave up. All that was visible was an ear with slick-fine black hair above it.

Then the angle changed. This time the camera was in front of the head, above it. The distance was too great for the hand to reach down again, but there was slightly more body to be seen. The hair might have been from a crow. The forehead was bumpy and dark. A few feet off to the right side, there was what looked to be a pair of frameless glasses.

"Maybe you want one of the other reels," Glynn said behind me, pacing the box of a room. "Before you blow all your time on this one."

What did an Indian businessman's left ear look like? What did an Indian businessman's forehead look like? What did an Indian businessman's skin look like? Were they different from, say, a Norwegian businessman's left ear, forehead, and skin? I really didn't know. There was no reason I couldn't have been looking at a dark Norwegian, not to mention an Italian or a Spaniard or a Filipino.

No reason except I was positive I was looking at the corpse of the Indian film guy Sayyid.

CHAPTER 20

Glynn gave me an extra half-hour on the cuff and a half-hour beyond that for a twenty-dollar bill. There was nothing else on bodies along the Seine. I wouldn't have been up for it if there had been. I already had four corpses—Pouchol, Caporale, Weiss/Klein, and Sayyid. Twenty-five years apart and dead from the most widely different causes possible, but all connected to the Indian movies. Was that the office average? If I'd studied the records of, say, a single department of Met Life Insurance employees over 25 years, would I have discovered one had been murdered, one had committed suicide, one had died of cancer, and one . . . well, might have been murdered, might have had a heart attack, or might not have been dead to begin with?

I didn't care about Met Life employees.

The breathing fit came on the second I told Glynn I didn't want to see any more, to rewind the reel that was mounted so I could collect it and get out of his hair. I hadn't had a serious spasm in years, but it came back as the most familiar of old friends: a wall coming down in my windpipe even as I told myself it was nothing, just breathe through it without thinking of anything but waves hitting the shore or palm trees or cute fawns and raccoons and lion cubs. And then my chest got into it—not as the spare room under my throat it should have been, but as another boulder.

"Hey, man!"

Glynn was on me before I could tell him contact—all kind of contact—was suffocating. I did what I'd done with the police psychiatrist right after the funeral for Jenny and Susan: I made a frantic sign for pouring water from a glass. I didn't need water, I just needed Glynn, as I'd needed the shrink, off doing something away from me.

"Gotcha! Hold on!"

He was out the door of the booth and clambering downstairs to the fountain before I had to repeat the gestures. I thought about waves and idyllic valleys and stars—places where there was no danger of running into people. Then I thought about Jenny and Susan and Lieutenant Alan Bernstein—people I had no chance of running into. In fact, add to that list Mireille Pouchol, Phil Caporale, Roberta Weiss/Klein, and an Indian named Sayyid. There were medical examiners who weren't as surrounded by as much death as I was. When had *that* become my trade? Or maybe I just wasn't counting accurately. On the other side of the ledger, the living ledger, there were all the Sarah Harrahs and Klauses and the friendly dentists who yanked molars on the right when they had meant molars on the left.

They were the living???

I gave it one big intake, and finally, my lungs broke. Catarrh meant life. It wasn't pain, but who had everything? By the time Glynn hurried back with a Dixie cup, I could drink the water out of politeness.

"What the fuck was that, man?"

"Too many corpses lately."

He knew it wasn't what I'd meant, and didn't want to know what I did, but at least he had an opening for a crack. "You should see the shit I see up here every week! This is amateur night!"

CHAPTER 21

The bar in the Village Dana had suggested turned out not to be a bar at all, but a teeming Italian restaurant. My good vibe entering Da Francesco was it wasn't in midtown, so the famous Alex Olmos couldn't just drag me around a corner to meet his favorite typist in his favorite interrogation box. The bad vibe was we might be stuck with him for a three-course meal.

They were already there, drinking red wine at the bar. Olmos was a muscular wedge with a brush cut, pock-marked face, and open smile; unlike Mrs. Chalian, his eyes went with the smile. But I also had the feeling he'd gotten A's in all the class courses warning about hostile body language. He was smooth enough to get it in right away that he could only sit in the back with us for a half-hour tops because he had a birthday party for his 10-year-old son waiting for him at home. As the headwaiter led us to a back booth, Dana threw me a I-told-you-he-was-okay look. I didn't know what to throw back at her. There was the assumption she and I would be left alone for dinner. There was the warm, sexy way she was dressed—aqua shirt, black skirt, and tiny pearl earrings. Not a single table in the restaurant was occupied by cops on a break, lonely singles, or widows reluctant to break old habits. Everybody in the brownish lights of the place seemed to be there because they had wanted to come, and most of the everybodies were couples. Despite Olmos's presence, I thought, I would have to refer to the evening at Da Francesco in my memoirs as an actual, living *date*.

"So Dana says you have interesting tales to tell."

And I told them, right through my afternoon at the Cameo (minus how the movie had choked me up). Olmos didn't take notes. He didn't take his brown eyes off me at all except to sip at the wine he had carried from the bar. He interrupted only once—to remind me he wasn't *that* incompetent, that he too had come across both Kinsey's Minneapolis studio and Roberta Klein's numbers on Pouchol's hotel telephone records. He had even visited Klein in her Hoboken home in the hope of learning something, but the woman had been too ill to be of any help. Otherwise, he listened curiously, patiently, and skeptically. Dana sat next to him silently with her arms folded across her chest, throwing regular looks at the diners entering so I wouldn't feel double-teamed. She even flagged down the waiter for a refill of her wine without asking either of us if we wanted to go with her. She was still the friendly but disinterested party from Fresh Meadows, and wanted both of us to keep it in mind.

When I finally shut up, Olmos raised his arms in mock exasperation. "What about JFK's assassination? You left that out."

Dana came back to us with a laugh; the worst part of the examination was over. But Olmos wasn't quite ready to run home and eat birthday cake. "So what you're saying is that whatever's bothering all these people goes back 25 years, probably to this Indian guy."

"Simplest scenario? Kinsey learns about Pouchol making time with Sayyid. He doesn't sound like somebody who'd have a real tight grip on something like jealousy. Or maybe he just obsesses about the guy after their little restaurant scene over his screenplay. One way or another, he ends up with Sayyid down near the river. He does the deed, then he films the scene. Maybe he already knows in his head that's the closest he'll ever get to doing his King Arthur and the Round Table."

Dana grimaced. "Yuck!"

"Right. But all these people were close. Servais was clear about that. There's no way the others didn't at least suspect what happened to the Indian. And that's not figuring in Kinsey's apparent habit of blabbing about his good works when he drank too much."

"So we got four people who wouldn't be surprised by what you think you've seen in this movie."

"I'd say at least seven."

"Finley!"

"Count them yourself. Kinsey, Pouchol, Caporale, and Matson. Then Servais and his girlfriend Weiss. You got to figure Servais's boss, this Peyrot. And on from there. Somebody like Sayyid doesn't just turn up dead without a lot of questions being asked. The worst Homicide detective in the world asks if Sayyid's had any bad scenes before joining the deceased."

Olmos drained his wine glass. "So half of Paris knew about this and nobody did a goddamn thing?"

"Sure they did! Servais lied about it to me, just like he didn't spell out his relationship with Weiss, but it can't be pure coincidence that that's when they broke up their dubbing operation. Suddenly, Reynaud-Grevin goes back to the tried and true ways of making billions of francs. Caporale, he comes home, takes up the academic life he was meant to take up. The others scatter. Except for Pouchol, anyway. She sticks around and ends up marrying into the company."

"All to protect this loose cannon Kinsey? I don't think so."

"I don't, either. There was more than Kinsey and Sayyid involved. There was all this hocus-pocus of the dubbing operation itself. Somebody in Calcutta hiding this bundle of money, somebody in Paris washing that bundle. Too many questions about Sayyid, and who knows where the French cops end up? So better for all concerned to pass it off for whatever they passed it off as, shut down, and tell all the foreigners they're free to go home. Ten to one, the French records of the case will say something like a mugging gone wrong."

Olmos had seen aliens before; he just hadn't identified my particular planet. "Sure, the French records. I'll be studying them real soon."

"Your computer to their computer. How hard can it be?"

He didn't dignify the question with an answer. "And all these years, Caporale and the others have known Kinsey killed the Indian and never said anything? You're asking a lot."

"Some knew, some might've just suspected. Their version of don't-ask-don't-tell." I remembered what the Professor had told me in the basement. "I only met the guy a couple of times, but

it wouldn't surprise me if Caporale had this movie in his basement all these years and never looked at it . . . I mean it, Alex.
People get used to living with shadows. They only turn around to
see them when they're sure they'll be gone." She stared at me so
inquisitively, I grinned. It didn't work; she knew I was squirm-
ing. "Besides, he had another excuse altogether for holding on to
the movies. How Kinsey was some two-bit informer on political
things. That might've been true, but so what? Caporale wasn't
some radical who planted bombs. No way Kinsey's tidbits could've
threatened him seriously, and no way he keeps up all this vindic-
tiveness for so long if that's all there was involved."

"People change. Maybe Caporale was Fidel Castro in another
life."

"Not the one I saw in those movies."

"Yeah, well, that's what it keeps coming back to, isn't it? What
you saw in those movies." He glanced at Dana to say something,
but she was busy searching for new patterns in the rose table-
cloth. "I mean, you could've seen a drunk. The guy on that film
might not even be dead."

"To me he was dead."

She finally raised her eyes from the table. "Okay, Paul, let's
accept all that," she said. "That's Sayyid on the film and that's
Neil Kinsey posing the corpse for his sick mind. Servais and the
others cover it up. But even if all that's true, what's that got to do
with Alex's problem? What's it got to do with Pouchol being dead?"

I was afraid somebody was going to ask that. "I'm just guess-
ing . . ."

Olmos couldn't resist. "As opposed to what?"

"She told Caporale she wanted to talk to him about something
to do with Reynaud-Grevin. She and her husband have a stake
in keeping the place out of the clutches of this Visiv octopus . . ."

"Yeah?"

"What she came over for was to line up the other people who
knew about Sayyid's death."

"Because?"

"Because in some way that nasty little secret got into the
middle of all these negotiations for taking over the studio." I was
losing both with every word. "She was setting up the defenses for

her husband with her old pals because somehow Visiv found out what forced the end of their little dubbing enterprise, found out about Kinsey."

"Which is also a guess," he reminded me.

"Which is also a guess."

"Anything else?"

"There's this whole thing between the Feds and Servais because of who he is. I don't know how it factors in exactly, but the guy is certainly a liar. He didn't tell me about Weiss? Okay, I didn't ask. But the story of why they broke up the dubbing thing was bullshit, and so was his not knowing right away who Mireille Jobert was. The head of a studio? A cultural attaché who used to work at the place?" Olmos's frown said he wanted to talk to Servais about as much as he wanted to talk to me again. "Just a thought."

He took that as his cue to push back from the table. "How about you lay these flicks on me so I can get home to my birthday party? Maybe I can get one of our techs to look at them before next spring."

As soon as we hit the street to go to my car, Olmos pulled a cigarette and lighter from his jacket pocket. "I really hate drinking without smoking."

"You get used to it. Kind of like doing police work without a badge."

He gave me my smile and I cursed not having found a parking space closer than three blocks away. I felt as I once had as a kid on Christmas—being sent out for a carton of milk while my brothers and sisters had been opening more packages under the tree. Dana's asking for the menu as we'd walked out didn't seem like enough of a guarantee I wouldn't miss important time.

"You're famous, you know," Olmos said, savoring his first drag. "The way I heard it, you were the only PI Bernie ever met he didn't want to turn into a bank guard."

"You knew Bernstein?"

"Yeah. But that's a long time ago. Maybe we should move on."

The urge to hit him came on so fast I was as dismayed as he clearly wasn't. He even thought I was funny. "*All* of you should. She doesn't want you to be a bank guard, either."

"And you're saying this because . . ."

"Because I'm Dear Abby. You know what McGill has, Finley? She has tall eyes. Even when she's sitting on the same level with you, across the table like tonight, her eyes have to lean down to make you feel comfortable. You didn't notice that tonight?"

"No."

"Look closer next time."

We got to the car and I pulled the reels out of the back. He had been expecting cassettes. "Jesus Christ! I didn't know they had these anymore!"

"The reel that's numbered five. I've only looked at four and five. I'm pretty sure the other stuff is earlier, but I'm not a hundred percent positive. And when you see the sequence with the dead guy, you'll notice some glasses near the body. That might help you with the French cops."

"I can't go on the subway with this shit. Flag a cab. I've got to drop them off at the station house before I go home."

I went out into the street looking for a taxi. The seconds thudded around my watch when I thought of Dana looking expectantly at the door. Had I been clear I'd be back?

"What about Seldes?" Olmos asked, juggling the cans against his chest.

"What about him?"

"Should I tell him you've done this favor for him?"

"Like you said, you already had Kinsey's studio number from the hotel phone charges. What about the others, by the way? She called Matson and Servais, too."

He shrugged as the cab I caught pulled up. "If she just got to a switchboard . . . well, we didn't have you there to tell us what last name to punch out in the company directory."

"See? You missed me and you didn't even know it."

"*Buon appetito.*"

"Happy Birthday to your son."

The cans started falling out of his grasp as soon as he ducked into the back seat. I could hear the temper Dana had mentioned as I hurried away.

CHAPTER 22

Naturally, there were ways of chipping away at the idea I was out on a date. I got to work as soon as I sat back down in the booth. Was Da Francesco a place she had come to with Bernstein? (No.) Somebody from the local precinct recommend it? (No.) Did she ID the John Doe she'd found in the park carton the last time we'd met? (No.) I didn't care all that much about the baseball playoffs with the Mets once again out of them. (Oh, how fascinating to know.) By the time we were both ordering veal piccata, I didn't know why she wasn't running screaming out of the place to a lasagna in her freezer at home.

And she thought I was hilarious!

As soon as the waiter left with our orders, she burst out laughing—the same, full-faced laugh she had surrendered at Carvel's after talking about being in kindergarten. Only this time she wasn't the five-year-old she had in mind. "You took a special crash course, right? In how to put your foot wrong? You called up Pace or NYU and told them you were going out to dinner with me and you needed to cram in some lessons on how to be awkward real fast. And they accommodated you!"

For about three seconds, I heard every note, hammer, and pedal of the piano jangle as it fell off my back and crashed onto the floor. For the next couple, I just gaped at her until the Dana McGill sitting across from me was no longer the Dana McGill who had tramped around Bernstein's office like somebody in training against whatever floor was under her.

"What're you looking for?" she asked, puzzled.

"Olmos says you have tall eyes. They always look down on people."

"It's his inferiority complex. He's short."

"I don't think he meant that."

"Well, I'm glad you boys got it off your hairy chests outside. How about you? All this shadow stuff you were talking about before? You talking about Caporale or yourself?"

"I thought I was talking about him."

"And you got that from him because he was using you as a filter for dealing with his untidy world."

"That's what my clients usually do, yeah."

"And that's okay with you."

"It's a pact between me and my creditors."

"Just with them?"

"What're you saying?"

She tilted her head so curiously she seemed on the verge of picking up the candle from the table and putting it in front of my face for a closer inspection. "You represent this Caporale to his former world," she said. "You're going to get rid of these old movies for him, you're even going to say hello to his old Swedish lover for him. While he could still believe in it, he thought of it as hiring a PI to do what a PI's supposed to do. Now you, on the other hand, you think of working for your client as . . . Oh, isn't that funny! It's the same thing! Doing what a PI's supposed to do."

"Your point being?"

"Who's needed his little buffer more—you or Caporale?"

"You're saying I disliked him because he reminded me of me?"

"What I'm saying," she said evenly, "is we've all got occupational hazards that sometimes don't seem all that hazardous. They help us through the rough patches. I'm sure in some way your job helped you a lot after what happened to your wife and daughter. Anyone who hired you—that was who gave you a reason for getting up in the morning and for hitting the gas when the light turned green. Caporale was just the latest."

"I would've called you anyway."

She smiled. "And I would've answered your call. When do you think that might have been, Paul? Before the Tricentennial, do you think?"

"Am I that transparent?"

"It's not just now. Even back with Bernie. What's this—the ninth, maybe tenth time we've shared a little space together? I've never heard you mention, not once, some friend besides your father-in-law."

"Like who?"

"That's what I mean! Never go to ballgames with somebody? Play poker? Go to a bar? Do all those male bonding things? And okay, we've hardly had the relationship where you'd talk about women you've seen or are seeing. But body language, vibes, aura—they all tell me there hasn't been anything that serious for you lately."

If I had planned, I could have defended my life by mentioning Cynthia and the regulars at the Green Fox, the occasional calls I got from old Rotisserie league pals on the Island, and the people who showed up for the Professor's soirees. Want to talk about sex? I could have staggered her with an Argentinian researcher, a professional closet organizer, and a secretary from the New York Islanders front office. Yes, I thought, I could have wasted all that preparation since none of it would have prevented her from staring across the table at me with the same self-assurance about what she had said.

"Work takes up a lot."

"Sure, it does. You never saw a more dedicated paper pusher at Police Plaza. I got the traffic moving between borough commands like nobody had in 10 years. Result? The whole building shook with cheers when I got moved out to the 107. I'd go home, and my world was Igor, my cat. He's 12, going on 100. He doesn't beg for food, that would mean he'd have to get up and wander into the kitchen for it. I must bring it to him. I can't remember the last time he even bothered to swat at a fly in his face. But one time, just before I got transferred, he made my day. He did something he hadn't done since he was a kitten—got up on the window sill and jumped up to the top of this old secretary I got from my mother. I was *thrilled*! Igor wasn't dead yet! There was still *life* in my apartment! That was the most exhilarating thing that'd happened to me since Bernie died—a goddamn cat jumping up on a piece of furniture! And that's the state I was in for—what? —a year or more. How many years you working on it now?"

"There've been . . ."

"I'm not just talking about getting laid. Although that wasn't New Year's Eve, either. I'm talking about the big world. How long has it been since you've been out here with us in it?"

"I just heard this from Olmos!"

"I don't care about him. I'm the one asking. How long?"

The first answer was since I'd been out with somebody who had talked to me the way she was doing. "Saying it's okay out there?"

She tilted her head for another look and wasn't discouraged. "It can be rough," she said. "But I don't think it has to be fatal."

"I've heard that from Oprah."

"Good. You've heard it from Oprah and from Olmos. But now it's official because you've heard it from me. Let's have another wine."

She looked away for the waiter just in time. I would have taken her hand if she had left it on the table.

CHAPTER 23

We laughed enough and drank enough Chianti with our veal to excuse whatever we wanted to do after leaving the restaurant. The option was still there in front of her brownstone when we were telling one another we didn't want to have to appeal to excuses for the rest of the year that began the following morning. She had already done that—no tragedies, fun in one case. But didn't we already have enough furniture between us without adding a what-the-hell bureau? Not everybody was as spry as 12-year-old Igor. Why not get the tiniest bit more insurance that we wouldn't fall on our asses? Starting when? How about within the first week of the year that began the following morning?

"Good Night, Paul."

I smelled her kiss all the way back to the car—orange something from lipstick she must have put on when she had gone to the Ladies Room. Getting behind the wheel, I felt like I'd just completed my first high school date. I had touched all the right places on reconnaissance, had recovered from all my idiocies from the first few minutes, could think of the adventure of it all only as extra. It took me a second to accept that the mobs jamming the sidewalks on both sides of the street so close to midnight were because of the weekend, not because a parade had been organized to celebrate Finley's rise. I was sorry to have to drive away from them toward strictly car places like highways and bridges. I wanted to celebrate it, too.

CHAPTER 24

I was all set to waste Sunday plowing through the *Times,* catching up on bills and billings, and watching the last Mets game of the year. Then I came across the Obituary page. There was the usual scientist from the Manhattan Project, the usual off-Broadway actor, and the usual newspaperman from Columbus, Ohio. What was not so usual was a two-paragraph item on Roberta Klein of Hoboken, New Jersey, who had obviously had more of a following than me and the guy in the Yankees windbreaker. The line that caught my attention was "*survived by husband Jacob and daughters Rachel (17) and Mireille (16).*"

Of course, there was always the possibility Roberta Weiss/Klein had just liked the name Mireille in general. It didn't necessarily mean some special enduring friendship with Mireille Pouchol or make it 100 percent certain Mireille Pouchol had crossed the Hudson to tell her sick friend things Olmos had felt too awkward to pry out of a dying woman. But on the other hand, there was Kinsey's movie with the two of them sandwiching Servais. Had they done the same thing without Servais in the middle?

I didn't have the willpower to sit around the apartment all day with that fantasy. Besides, if Roberta Weiss/Klein hadn't been especially close to Pouchol, why would she have chosen to live so close to a drive from Bay Ridge? The pros and cons? There seemed to be three cons: bothering the family in the middle of mourning, not learning anything if I did bother them, and the fact that Olmos had already visited without learning anything. The pros? Only one: the chance of finding out for sure why Mireille Pouchol had come to New York. Wasn't just that possibility worth more than sitting around and watching the Mets play a pointless game? Oddly enough, I agreed with me.

I was on Washington Street in Hoboken shortly after noon. Seventy degrees and a peek-a-boo sun had filled the sidewalk places with brunchers, and there seemed to be twice as many more in the restaurants. Everybody seemed to be hauling a Sunday *Times* or Newark *Star-Ledger.* I went for the first pay phone I found to get an address for Jacob Klein, then pulled out my city map for the happy discovery that Bloomfield Street ran parallel to Washington and that my target was only a 10-minute walk from the telephone booth. The address was for a two-family house on a block of them. The gods of delicacy and tact hardly owed me anything for my mission, but they gave me a freebie anyway by having the widower instead of one of his daughters open the door.

Jacob Klein was a balding mid-50ish, with a big moon face and a waistline spread undermining his 6' or 6'1". The eyes that peered out through his rimless glasses looked ready to jump back into his brain before they had to see anything else grim. He seemed to take it as the lesser of two evils when I told him I was a one-time dubber who had worked with Roberta in Paris and had come by to extend my condolences. As he was ushering me inside to a living room with more chairs and couches than a furniture store, I realized I'd just spent the first of the lies Caporale had put into my account the day he had come to see me. Old movies, old friends, new lies—I'd never had a client leave me such a rich legacy before.

I recognized Klein's edginess only too well. He wanted me to sit, he couldn't find enough space between all the chairs for his own feet. Would I like a coffee? Or maybe that was stupid, maybe I wanted something stronger? Then again, who drank so early on a Sunday? He didn't mean anything by that. The main thing was, did I want anything? And when I said no the last time, it was as if he'd caught a glimpse of the awkward host in a mirror, looked embarrassing to himself, and finally surrendered to the larger of the two couches. "As you can imagine," he smiled, "it hasn't been a great few days."

"Was Roberta sick long?"

He nodded with a glance at a bowl of candies on the coffee table. "Good days, bad days. In and out of the hospital. I think the worst part was she began feeling guilty about what it was doing to *us*. That's stupid, isn't it? But that's what was bothering her. The girls got mad at her for that. But that's how you deal with it, right? You get angry."

There was another green triangle above the fireplace. But this one had no cream squares around it. "I went to the show at the Pandora Galleries."

"Oh, yeah?"

"There was this old-timer there and we got to talking about the green triangles. They obviously meant a lot to your wife. Did they have some particular meaning for her?"

He had to shift gears to talk about something so abstract and wasn't at all sure he wanted to. "The Green Triangle series? I don't know. I suppose on some level. She was always doing some variation on them. That one there, she had that in her loft before we ever bought this house."

"From Paris?"

"I'm not sure that long . . . Well, now that you mention it, maybe so. You never saw it over there?"

The question sneaked up on me; *both* did. And he didn't look the least apologetic. "No, we didn't know each other that way."

The smile was freer, of a surviving husband. "Just wondering. Maybe I just want to account for more than I'll ever be able to account for."

"You'll never catch up."

"Sound like you're speaking from experience."

"As a matter of fact."

He took it in with a nod, then looked back up at the painting from a calmer distance. "Robby was really good. It took me awhile to realize that. I thought any opinion I'd have . . . well, I just didn't trust it. It was *me*, for Christ sake!"

I laughed with him and listened to the resume he suddenly wanted me to have. Corporate finance background with degrees from Wharton and NYU, had first known Robby in Europe, then had met her again years later in New York, had gotten tired of the international business world and now taught economics at the Stevens Institute a few blocks away. Both the girls were in high school and bent on college, meaning he would soon be learning more about higher economics than he had ever wanted to know. But he didn't foresee a crisis. Between loans and what Robby had been selling regularly . . . I kept nodding, thinking his every syllable was getting me in deeper. The old form, the one I'd been trained in, was to let people unbend, feel secure, so I could gain their confidence. But that suddenly churned in my chest as a goal beyond crassness. I didn't want to know anything more about Jake Klein, his dreams, or his feelings.

"Did Mireille get to visit before . . .?"

"Mireille Jobert? Oh, Jesus! You knew her, too? . . . Of course, you would. We were shocked when we heard what happened. She'd visited Robby in the hospital just the day before."

"I take it your daughter was named after her."

For the briefest of seconds, his grin came from somewhere before the memories demanded by death. "You should've heard those conversations! I had nothing against Mireille's name. I liked her a lot. She visited us here a few times, we saw her in Paris. But *Mireille Klein*!!?? And the damn spelling! I'd say to Robby, 'Even spell it M-I-R-A-Y if it means that much to you. But why torture the girl through all her school years with that French spelling? It's bad enough she's going to have to go through life explaining how she isn't French, she was just named after a friend of her mother's!' As you can see, I lost that one. When Robby made up her mind about something, that was it. And Mireille, she's always acted proud of her name. Mireille—big Mireille—became her special aunt. Her exotic aunt. Know what I mean? The kid was even more devastated than Robby when we heard what happened . . . Paul is it? . . . I guess they'll never catch the bastard that did it now."

I reached for another of the lies Caporale had banked for me. "The weird thing is, just before Mireille was killed, she called and left a message saying it was important we talk. I never found out what it was about."

For a second, I thought I'd gone too far. The look he gave me was for some fatal mistake. (Mireille Pouchol had made it one of her life's missions never to leave messages for anybody?) Then he nodded to himself, took one of the candies, and nudged the bowl over to me. "You get screwed by Reynaud, too?"

Walking up a mountain of sludge is not the worst of experiences; far worse is trudging up a hill of sludge and suddenly realizing your feet have lost traction, you are sinking, and you will never have the consolation even of knowing what garbage you were trying to surmount. "Oh, that!"

"Yeah, 'Oh, that!' All these years later and Mireille hasn't let go. She's married to some big shot in the company now and she says she's . . . she *said* she was determined to get back some salary you all were owed. I don't know how much you were counting on that money, but I find it ridiculous. I mean, I've got money owed to me from a restaurant where I waited tables in 1981! So what? Ancient history. Let's move on."

"She talked to Roberta about this?"

"I walked in on them at the hospital! Robby had her good days and her bad days, and this wasn't a good day. But there's Mireille with her tape recorder and Robby looking like she's doing everything she can to remember. Like Robby could have given a damn how many francs she had coming through the last five devaluations. I threw her out."

"Mireille?"

"I swear to god; I threw her out. I thought of her as family. She was Robby's oldest friend from Europe. But there she was with her tape recorder like *60 Minutes.* I got a real uneasy feeling. Like maybe she and her husband Jobert were having a bad time, and she was going to make him pay literally with this old debt. There was a grabbiness about it all, and I didn't like it. Robby was in no condition for that kind of thing."

I shook my head with him at the inexplicableness of it all. And knew Mireille Pouchol and Roberta Klein had not been talking about some unpaid salary. "You actually heard her asking about this back pay?"

He took another candy. "Not right there, no. They cut it off when I walked in. Robby told me what the questions were about later. You can imagine who got it for throwing Mireille out! *I* was the one who'd upset Robby, not Mireille. Even the nurse accused me of making all the scenes. I'm sorry to say that was the last time I saw Mireille . . . Whose voice did you do in these Indian things?"

"Ali. I was usually Ali the terrorist."

He smiled. "What else, right?

I took a red candy, mainly to gain a moment. I thought it was cherry, it turned out to be strawberry. "I didn't mention any of that to the cops."

"Cops?"

"Yeah, they came in two shifts. But you don't want to hear all this. The last few days I just yammer on when I don't know what to say. To be honest, Robby never mentioned you. I thought I'd heard all the names. There was a Phil Caporale. Neil Kinsey. Nobody seemed to like that guy."

"That was the consensus, yeah."

He glanced back up at the painting. His eyes saw one thing, his glasses another. Then he came back down to me with his new objectivity. "Why don't you just tell me what you want to know, Paul? If I can help you, I will. But I really don't feel up to more bullshit."

It was another order, as with Dana back in the car in front of her precinct house; and once again, it pushed the humiliation I had coming back to a later time. "Two shifts, you said?"

He dropped his head back on the couch with a sigh and gazed up at the high ceiling; whoever I was, I wasn't going to help his life. "A sergeant named Olmos, from Manhattan," he said. "He wanted to know how Robby knew Mireille when they had last seen each other. Robby had just come home from the hospital that morning, so she wasn't all that energetic. Olmos looked uncomfortable the whole time he was here, couldn't wait to leave. Then, a few days later, I came home from the Institute and Rachel, my older one, said the cops had been by again. Different ones. They didn't look so uncomfortable, asked Robby a lot of questions about Mireille and the old Paris crowd. Finally, Rachel threw them out." He came back down from the ceiling. "That do it for you?"

"I'm not a cop, Jake."

"You're not here for Robby, though."

"No."

"I knew that when you called her Roberta," he said, trying to grin over his anger. "The only one who ever did that was her mother. And you're not Ali the terrorist. That was Caporale. I heard enough stories about that to know the guy's lines of dialogue."

There was no more reason not to dive for home plate, head first into shin guards. "The second cops who were here," I said, picturing Seldes and Cicut, "what did they ask?"

"I don't know. I wasn't here."

I waited. He waited. Then he rewarded me for not knowing what else I could say but thank you and goodbye. "This has to do with Mireille, right?"

"Right. I'd just like a reason for what happened to her."

I hadn't planned on it to sound as though I were some old boy-friend or Pouchol blood relation, but his face softened so quickly, I knew that was how he had interpreted it. Then, without a word, he was up off the couch and going out to the hall staircase and bouncing up to the second floor. I couldn't remember having that much spring in my legs after Jenny and Susan had been killed.

I got up and worked my way around the chairs for a closer look at the triangle. The frame glass seemed especially thick, the green limier than from a distance. I imagined the elfish-looking girl from Kinsey's movie working in front of an easel in a Paris garret. Then I remembered the stocky middle-aged woman in the white blouse and black skirt I'd seen in the *Times*. Then I thought of Mr. Maggio's geometry class and all the different kinds of tri-angles he had drawn on the blackboard. This one was definitely a scalene job, all the angles different. Nothing equaled anything inside, but it still all came out to something that fit the waiting name of triangle. Where was the old man in the hat and wind-breaker when I needed him? What had Robby and Mireille been talking about before being interrupted by Klein?

Klein came back down with two gray-green stubs in his hand. "Robby was a packrat. She saved everything. These were the last two pay stubs she got from Reynaud. This was the kind of thing I guess Mireille was looking for. Maybe they can help you."

I took them. The stubs were so old the typed date of January 1991, a payment amount of 3,700 francs, and Roberta Weiss's name were close to fading into the paper. "Doesn't really say much, does it?"

Klein shrugged and went over to the coffee table for another candy. "Not to somebody who wasn't there, I guess not."

That *touché* seemed to earn him one last question. "Any of the others contacted you? Maybe for the funeral service?"

"Kinsey I never met, and Robby didn't know if he was dead or alive. I think she said Caporale was a teacher, but I never met him, either. Inge, I called. She came. The Frenchman? The one show of Robby's he came to, I didn't see any of that continental charm that's always advertised."

"Servais?"

"Yeah. The guy had a leer frozen to his face, wouldn't take his hands off Robby all night. She finally had to take him over to a corner and tell him I knew all about them, Good Night, and have a pleasant life. I certainly wasn't going to call him for the service. Maybe that's why I was trying to account for you before. I got a little defensive after meeting Servais."

I moved to the door with the old pay stubs in my hand. It occurred to me he'd given them to me just to have them out of the house—getting rid of his wife's last lie to him.

"Maybe you can make sense out of what happened to Mireille," he said, shaking hands. "At least that would account for one of them."

I walked away from the house as fast as I could. I didn't hear him close the door, but I couldn't imagine why he wouldn't have. In his place, I would have also been more careful about opening it the next time.

CHAPTER 25

I stopped off at the Green Fox when I got back. Cynthia wasn't there, and as soon as the bartender Gregory told me she wasn't, I didn't know what I was doing there, either. I stayed for a couple of drinks, anyway. What that got me were the latest medical reports on Miles Harkleroad from Gregory and Blanche Walsh ("doing well for his condition, God bless him") and the cigar box for contributing a twenty to the Harkleroad Fund.

By the second scotch, it was easier to laugh at myself. What exactly had I been hoping—finding Cynthia so we could slip back into the kitchen for a quickie? It had never happened that way, and there was no way in hell it would have happened that afternoon, but just the thought of it seemed healthier than all the deaths going on in my parallel universe. Jake Klein, noble widower, had been the last straw with his I'm-okay-but-not-really and his useless pay stubs. How could anybody who claimed to teach economics have been that naive? No wonder stock markets crashed!

I tried to be interested in the Mets-Pirates on the TV, but couldn't manage it. The game was meaningless to both teams, so the players weren't just going through the motions, they were going through them at flash-forward speed to get out of Citi Field, fly home, and be with their families for the winter. As a plan, that seemed like me wanting to get to the Green Fox to pull down Cynthia's pants in the kitchen: *Somebody was getting cheated.*

I said no to Gregory's buyback, thanked Blanche for her "God bless you," and went back to the apartment. It was my worst move since I'd left it. The place had been hit by a very selective tornado. The living room bookshelves with my files hadn't been touched, but every coat and pair of pants from my hall and bedroom closets had been tossed on the floor. The cabinets under the kitchen sink had been left gaping open, but not the food closets above the table. The oven had been searched, but not the dishwasher; not my desk drawers, but the couch cushions were up against the coffee table.

I didn't hear anything from the Chalian apartment. They usually ate out on Sunday afternoons. I sat down at the desk. I kept the obvious thought suspended as long as I could. I saw the desk hadn't been totally neglected, after all. The pens, staples and paperclips in the middle drawer made funny new designs; Robby Klein might have appreciated them, but I didn't. The cancelled checks in the top side drawer were still in a rubber band, but they were sliding out from it. My splurge on Finley Investigations stationery was now minus a few top sheets where the paws of my intruder seemed to have contemplated making spitballs. Caporale's return address from the Federal Express package was on the floor under the side drawers. My friend had apparently looked at it, decided it hadn't told him enough or only what he had already known, then tossed it aside. What he had known, of course, and what had made him do his burrowing only in spacious places, was that I had the Kinsey collection. Reel cans might have been stashed in a hamper or an oven, but not behind my files, so why bother looking there?

I wouldn't have minded Gregory's buyback for the survey of my disordered realm. Would Seldes or Cicut have been so transparent in their tossing of the place? I wanted to think so, but preferred the idea of the master filmmaker himself, come to retrieve his wares. What better news for both Seldes and Olmos than that Kinsey was in town? I felt good for them.

For about a fraction of a second. Because to believe it'd been Kinsey meant also believing he'd talked to Caporale before the suicide. There was no other way he would have known about me or my having the movies. And that idea was far too twisty. Caporale had been lying to me about Kinsey, had been in contact with him all along? Kinsey had been in Garden City the day Caporale had gotten into his tub? No, I didn't want thoughts like that. I wanted simple, simpler, simplest. I'd finished with the heavy lifting the second I'd seen Olmos off in his cab with the film cans.

It took a few bends while I rehung my clothes in the closet for simple, simpler, simplest to strike. The canceled checks reminded me of Caporale's signature on his $500 retainer: The signature of someone right-handed who had never forgotten Sister Rosemary's penmanship classes. But the writing on the return address on the Federal Express package, I checked again, was that of a lefty. Some History department secretary? Or Florence Caporale?

I wanted to know that answer more than if the Mets beat the Pirates. It felt right that the only place I'd get it was at a funeral.

CHAPTER 26

The requiem Mass for Caporale was a mob scene. There must have been 200 people jamming the little church. More than half of them seemed to have some university connection—groups of threes and fours with serious but tentative faces, like study groups waiting for somebody to say something offhand to break all the gravity. The family, including a lot of overdressed nieces and nephews who hadn't started school yet, filled the first dozen pews or so. I was surprised to see the Professor sitting alone in the very front pew with Florence Caporale: He'd never told me he was *that* close to the family. My favorite feeling stirred: *I was missing something.*

One face I wasn't surprised to see was Cicut's. Even if I hadn't had my house ransacked, I would have figured the funeral for a possible Neil Kinsey sighting. He didn't look surprised to see me in the last pew, either. "I thought they didn't have Mass for suicides," he muttered, sliding in next to me. "They change that, too? Jeez, anybody can be a Catholic these days!"

I left him to his Kinsey search. Since the Professor was evidently so close to the Widow Caporale, I decided he could relay some of my trickier questions to her. I also wondered if Inge Matson had read about Caporale in the paper. She was the only one left on my list.

"Seldes said to give him a call when you get the chance."

"That won't happen." There were two women midway down on the other side of the aisle with the kind of red hair Matson had had in the Kinsey movie. The one nearer the aisle was too young, hardly in her thirties. I had my *Maxim* friend Wiggy to thank for being sure the second one, three pews closer to the front, was the Swede: The lady had topped off her black suit with a stupid looking silver bow on the throat of her blouse.

"Then he said I should tell you we're pretty sure Kinsey's in town."

I kept my eyes on the priest, probably more intently than at any time since I'd been an altar boy. What Cicut was supposed to see was fervor, not calculation. Let us pray.

"Seldes just thought you should know."

"I don't know why. But tell him I appreciate it anyway."

He liked me; I knew admiration when I saw it. If I'd been able to pay him a salary and give him health insurance benefits, he would have quit Seldes for me right then and there. As it was, though, he could only shuffle out of the pew and wander around behind me and over to the side aisle. He might as well have put on a blue uniform and called himself Clancy as he strolled down to the front scanning the faces of the mourners. With my new dedication to simple, simpler, simplest, I shook off the idea he was more interested in warning Kinsey than grabbing him.

There was a parade to the pulpit to say nice things about Caporale. A niece remembered how he'd chaperoned her first grammar school dance because her father had been at sea with the Navy. A teacher of Portuguese confessed how astonished he'd been by Caporale's knowledge before taking a *Roots* trip to the Indian territory of Goa. Some kind of finance guy from the college talked about the grants and scholarships Caporale had attracted to the History department. I wasn't the only one who got itchy with the bloodlessness of it all. Some of the school cliques began whispering among themselves. Florence Caporale allowed herself a long contemplation of a stained-glass window showing some prophet in a long white beard and charcoal black eyes. The priest sitting to the side of the altar seemed to blow his nose more than any snot required. Even crabby Miles Harkleroad, I thought, would have triggered funnier and warmer remembrances. It was as though Phil Caporale had lived his entire life—or at least the last 25 years of it—in the middle of a frozen pond.

I was the first one outside when everything was finally over. Cicut was second, and he went straight to his blue Odyssey with a nod and drove away. I thought that was kind of lax of him if Kinsey decided to skip the Mass and go directly to the cemetery. But then again, I was beginning to think he'd come as much to deliver his message to me as for any other reason. The Professor came out gripping Florence Caporale's elbow. She was a lanky, graying woman a bit curved at the shoulders. There was nothing bending in her eyes, though: She had traveled to Hell and the details of the trip were nobody's business but her own. For a second, I couldn't remember where I'd seen her expression before, then it occurred to me: on the prophet on the stained-glass window. Caporale had made her sound like Flo the wife with the rolling pin. He had exaggerated: She hadn't needed any trivial weapon like a rolling pin.

I hung back as she stood on the top step of the church and blankly accepted the condolences of the people who wouldn't be going to the cemetery with her. The Professor saw me and shook his head. I didn't know what he'd thought I was planning, but the gesture was irritating. He had been the one to insist I keep digging and he had been the one who had clearly been evasive about his ties to the Caporales, but I was the one who was being warned off from doing something goofy.

He had been looking in the wrong direction. As soon as Inge Matson stood in front of Florence Caporale, I felt a lurch from my chest. Maybe it was some old-school attitudes about lovers meeting over the coffin of their honey, but I felt a sudden tension even 20 yards away. What I hadn't seen coming was Matson saying something and then Florence Caporale suddenly swinging up her hand to catch the Swede full in the right cheek.

The Professor's fish eyes popped. Conversations seemed to stop in a dozen places. Then, as quickly as she had raised her hand, Florence Caporale put it back on the shiny black bag she was carrying, imparted one final glare, and started down the steps toward the waiting limo. She wasn't quite as steady as she wanted everybody to see, but the Professor caught her elbow again just as she seemed about to totter. He kept his eyes down, door handle level, as he walked her briskly to the limo, then got in with her.

For some reason, I thought of Mr. Westbeth putting Sarah Harrah into her cab.

Inge Matson might have been a black plague victim in one of those old movies where the town square emptied in a panic when a body collapsed to the ground. She seemed triply numb as she cradled her cheek: once for the slap, once for the outrageousness of it, and once for the way everybody else was scattering away from her. For a second, she thought she had found a place for appeal when the priest stepped out into the morning sun. But he had arrived too late to see anything and merely smiled kindly at her as one of the many mourning the tragic end of Phil Caporale. Somebody waved to him from the curb and he hurried down the steps to get into the car that would take him out to the cemetery.

Aside from some kids, fascinated by the odd behavior of adults, only a couple of the parish pros risked looking at Matson directly. She had little choice but to use me to try to recover. "That was different."

There was a lot of cleft in her enunciation. I smiled back at her, probably just as falsely. "People aren't at their best on days like this."

She bit off an answer, then dismissed me from her thoughts and came stalking down the steps so awkwardly on her thin legs and heels I thought I was going to have to give a bigger assist than the Professor had given Florence Caporale. But on the sidewalk, she was still walking as though her feet were on stilts. "Get out of the way, get out of the way," she ordered impatiently, waving to the limo and the other cemetery cars, but audible only to the two of us. "I need a taxi."

The limo and the family cars finally cleared the curb to go off in their motorcade; only then did she seem to realize she wasn't on Broadway. "They must have taxis out here, yes? Where are they?"

Like Caporale's other friends, she had turned the bend of 50 by a year or two. Her cheeks had ganged up on her since her slinky days in Kinsey's home movies and she wore too much makeup, but there was still something of an imp in her blue eyes. She didn't sound like she had wasted too many hours using them to look at anything outside Paris, New York, and other metropolises.

"I suppose there's a stand down on the main street. Won't be cheap, though, if you want to go back to Manhattan."

"Well, I'm not going to take that damn train again! Once in a lifetime should be enough!"

"You took the LIRR all by yourself! You must've really liked Phil!"

I didn't consider it a make-or-break gambit, exactly; I still had my car and the promise of a ride back to New York as an ace. But if the head of Inge Matson International took herself too seriously, it was just as well I found out right away how long that ride might be. She narrowed her eyes with a wonderful takeoff on suspicion, and I knew who she was. She didn't take herself seriously *all* the time because that gave her room not to have to take other people seriously at all. "Who are you?"

"Paul Finley."

"A teacher?"

"No."

"His lawyer or something?"

"No. I'm going to the city. Want a ride?"

She took a Parliament out of her bag to think. She knew she would accept; she just needed a moment to make sure she hadn't overlooked some deeply hidden reason she shouldn't. "How do I know you even knew him?"

"I know all of you. Kinsey, Robby, Servais. You're Inge."

"Oh."

"My car's across the street."

She lighted her cigarette and, mainly for show, took another look up the street to see if I was her only possibility. "Lead on, gallant gentleman," she finally conceded.

I might as well have been the one getting into a cab and she might as well have been the driver. She had all kinds of fares: She didn't like wearing a seatbelt and would have been perfectly happy sitting in the back if that bothered me; she really needed a cigarette and hoped I wouldn't mind; she didn't know where I was going in the city, but she had to be back in her office down near Greenwich Village, so if that was too much of a problem for me, she was willing to accept some cab stand ("but where there is a taxi, not where I have to stand around to see if they still use it as a stand"). I did a lot of nodding until we got onto the expressway.

"I screwed her husband a hundred years ago, so she slaps me! Maybe she needs passion where she can find it. What do you think?"

"Would you be listening if I answered?"

"You want to annoy me, yes?"

"I don't think she slapped you for being Phil's old flame. I think she slapped you because she blames you and the rest of the gang for driving him to suicide."

The idea horrified her, but it had also been swimming around too long in her own head to merit a *good grief, man!* "Why do you say that?"

"Tell me about the movies."

"What movies? *The Terror of Allah*? That dreck?"

"Kinsey's movies."

She closed the hand without the cigarette on her black-skirt-ed thigh. A weaving green Mazda ahead of me didn't let me see any more. "Those things he and Phil were always shooting? Who knows where they are!"

"I do. They're with the cops investigating Mireille's murder."

Nothing. Even the fist came unclenched so she could roll down her window to get rid of the butt. "I didn't even know Kinsey kept them."

"He didn't. Your boyfriend did."

"That I can believe. Neil didn't know where his clothes were unless he was wearing them. But Phil, he saved everything."

"You're not curious why the cops should be interested in them?"

"They look at everything when you kill yourself, don't they?"

"New York cops, I said. Mireille Pouchol?"

She couldn't get back into her bag fast enough for another Parliament. I could scratch her from being the one in my apartment, I thought: The living room would have looked like an ashtray. "That is an ugly story. I don't like thinking about that."

"I assume she contacted you like everybody else? All this business about Visiv trying to take over Reynaud?"

"Who are you, Finley?"

There were so many plausible lies beckoning that the truth felt almost cleansing. "A private investigator Phil hired. He wanted me to give the films back to Kinsey."

"So you gave them to the police, instead?"

"One thing led to another."

She stared ahead, blowing smoke at the windshield. I could make out what looked like a cut across her right instep. Then again it could have been the kind of rash Jenny had once had on her insteps and elbows. I wondered how long it was going to go on: Would I ever be able to look at a towel without thinking about how Jenny had once used a towel?

"Yes, she did call me," Inge said, in less of a trance than she wanted to sound. "For some reason, she thought I'd be interested in all this Visiv business. I understand it was important for *her*. She was married to some executive at Reynaud-Grevin. Just like Mireille. She always acted so frail, the victim of men and gods and circumstances. But she always seemed to end up with what she wanted."

"You sound envious."

"Hardly. I don't have the energy for the front she was always putting up. Coquetry is overrated. In her case, it also left her with a few black eyes."

"You mean Kinsey?"

"Kinsey. Pierre le Fou. Whoever. You seem to have a great deal of useless information. You should sell it to a newspaper."

"So she told you all about this Visiv business."

"She told me nothing because I didn't see her. When she telephoned, I said I'd be glad to see her for a drink or lunch if she wanted to be social, but I wasn't the least interested in hearing about all this financial boorishness. I hire accountants for that kind of thing in my company and hire lawyers to keep an eye on the accountants."

"Why don't I believe that?"

"Because you're dense?"

"Okay, you didn't want to talk about Visiv and Reynaud-Grevin with her. But couldn't you have gotten together, anyway? I mean, the two of you do go back."

"I told you, Mireille concentrated on what Mireille wanted. I was immediately moved to the bottom of her Must-See list. She'd try to call me the next day to set up something, she said. I didn't stand guard on the telephone, and two days later she was dead."

"That says something about you, too."

"What are you talking about?"

"Well, if I crossed the Atlantic to talk to people about something and one of them said it'd be great to see me but no talk about that one thing, I'd make an appointment anyway and try to slide my agenda in. You must've been pretty convincing on the phone no meant no."

Sometimes blowing air meant annoyance and sometimes it meant embarrassment. I thought I heard both. "What do you care about any of this? Phil hired you and Phil is gone."

"Somebody else has asked me to tie up the loose ends."

"There are always loose ends. Even in Phil Caporale's life."

"Now that *doesn't* sound like envy."

"It's his day. Let's be pleasant."

It seemed time to withdraw another lie from the account Caporale had opened for me. "He spoke well of you. I think he always missed you."

I was glad I didn't have to return her stare—or couldn't see the expression she was seeing. "You're quite the bullshitter, aren't you?"

"It's not true?"

She went back to spitting smoke at the windshield. "Phil was a nice little boy when I met him. Very uncomplicated because his idea of what was complicated—whether he should be a teacher or not, whether he should miss his first Christmas with his parents—was endearing. Then, like everybody else, he met some real complications and stopped being a nice little boy. Nothing original about any of that."

"Probably not."

"So I don't think you should be making money from such things."

"I'll keep that in mind."

"Do."

She was serious, titanically serious. Whatever my phone friend Wiggy had said, I couldn't see working for Inge Matson as a dream job. I was also getting a picture of the three women from Reynaud-Grevin as an iron triptych. Matson dispensed advice like a hanging judge, Pouchol had no time for small talk when takeovers were being threatened, and Robby Klein, per her husband, hadn't brooked much argument about things like a daughter's name. From what I knew of them, the Paris men in their lives seemed like wusses by comparison.

I dropped her off at Fifth and Tenth without any more enlightenment for my hack service. All that was missing when she got out was the tip. "Thank you," she said over the slam of the door, and off she went toward an office building next to one of those big empty-space boutiques that seemed to sell glittery paper cubes. I had never figured out what stores with those huge tinsel blocks in the window were trying to tell me. That anything you bought inside was as much a gamble as what you could earn from a pair of dice? That even the most solid-looking purchase was made of paper? For once, my mental ravings paid off. Because I sat there for 30 seconds puzzling over the mysteries of commercial window designs, I was late for the light at the corner. And because I was late for the light at the corner, Inge Matson was too hasty about coming right back out of her building and, shutting off the cellphone in her hand, looking for the cab she hadn't been able to find in front of the church on Long Island.

It cost me a couple of honks from a Ryder truck, but I ignored the light until she had found her cab and streaked out ahead of me. Two turns later, we were headed for the Upper West Side. All the way up, I beat off the sirens whispering I was going to make Finley Investigations proud. What I was about to discover, I insisted, was the address of the shrink where Inge Matson rushed to blurt out such tragedies as being slapped in the face by a widow and being driven back to the city by an obnoxious stranger. I recited that mantra loud enough that my radio started giving me odd looks.

The cab stopped before an apartment building at West End and 78th. A guy looking like a baseball catcher gone to seed stood under the awning, an overnight bag on the pavement next to him. As soon as the back door opened, he grabbed the bag and hurried into the cab. Who had described Neil Kinsey to me? Servais, that day at lunch. He had made him sound like Peter Lorre, somebody you didn't leave alone with the kids. As the Professor had said, the French weren't always wrong.

My radio still didn't think it was time for High Fives. The immediate problem was keeping after the cab to find out where Matson was taking the JABPUN webmaster. East, said the taxi driver, through Central Park. And then what? The trees in the park were already warning me: They looked too skanky for early fall. It was *too* perfect. Another *Land of the Pharaohs* moment. All the sand running out of the cups and all the chambers were sealed off one after another. I had made one-and-a-half promises to Caporale. The whole promise was to try to find Kinsey, and that I had done. The half-promise was to give Kinsey back his movies. That too I could do, but only with the help of Olmos, who could simultaneously bag the killer of Sayyid and Pouchol! And before Seldes knew what had hit him! Throw in the head of a successful modeling agency as an accomplice—her long legs all over the front pages of the tabloids—and that didn't make for just a golden day, that was a day from a precious element the Atomic Table had never heard of!

And who could believe it for a second?

The next stop on the Inge Matson Tour was 48th off Second— another apartment building with an awning. Here there was also a doorman quick to get to the cab and open the back door. Kinsey stepped out with his bag, didn't think for a second about waiting to help Matson out, just made a beeline for the front door. The doorman didn't like that, was as concerned about Kinsey barging through to the elevators as giving Matson a hand out of the taxi. He could hardly wait to slam the cab door and to scamper inside.

Matson pinched down the skirt of her suit, gave her fate a big sigh, then stalked in after the doorman.

I went around the block wondering what I was going to do next. The doorman's behavior with her told me Matson wasn't a tenant with Christmas tip powers. Did I just go down the alphabet with the doorman until my name matched one in his apartment directory?

But then the United Nations reminded me what neighborhood I was in. Why not start with S as in Servais?

CHAPTER 27

Olmos arrived with confirmations—that Caporale had indeed been in Philadelphia when Pouchol had been killed and that Servais lived in the building across the street from where we were standing. He still didn't look grateful for my call; what he mainly looked in his corduroy jacket and silk shirt was cold. "What do you want, Finley?" he asked, raising the collar of the jacket against a nasty wind from the river. "I have no warrant for going in there and if I ask for one, I can write off the rest of the week."

"You've just eliminated Caporale! Doesn't that make Kinsey even more of a lead with Pouchol? At least a material witness?"

"And we'll jump him when he comes out to buy a lotto ticket. Thanks for the heads-up. Anything else?"

The bliss from his son's birthday had clearly worn off. "We still have the movies. I could go up and tell him I have the reels in my car for his house guest and I'd appreciate it if his house guest could come down and take them off my hands. My last obligation to Phil Caporale, thank you very much. How can Kinsey say no? He broke into my place to get them, didn't he?"

"I didn't know you'd wrapped up that burglary."

"Okay, he *might* have broken in. But that's where my money is. He wants that Sayyid film back."

He thought about it more reasonably than he wanted to. "And while you're up there, I'm freezing my nuts off down here."

"C'mon, you know it's worth a shot. You get Kinsey and you have him all to yourself to ask about Pouchol. No French diplomats are involved and you beat Seldes at whatever he's playing."

There was something like a grunt, then: "The guy in the movie, the dead one—Sayyid did wear glasses. And yeah, the French did file it away as a mugging."

"You talked to them?"

"No, I'm making it up so you can feel good about yourself. We talked to the Indians. I figured they were more likely to have Sayyid on a top box in their warehouse. Plus, they speak English. We don't wait for you to come up with *all* the good ideas."

"Anything else on those reels?"

"How the hell should I know? I looked at the one you said. I've got two guys looking at the rest. They liked *Lord of the Rings* better."

The feeling from the car came back: Things were falling into line too neatly. Finley Investigations hadn't been on this kind of roll since I'd named the actors who'd played the four gunslingers in *High Noon* for a free round at the Green Fox. "Okay, go ahead," he finally said. "But keep it to the movies. Nada about Pouchol. The French haven't been bothering us with the usual calls to the State Department on her, and I want to keep it that way. If Servais wants to come down, tell him Caporale wanted you to give them only to Kinsey. Just don't take forever up there."

I almost used up the forever in the lobby. Beefy Joe the doorman was happy to call upstairs for me, but then became unhappy when Servais told him he wasn't receiving. He became *very* unhappy when I insisted he call again and let me talk to Servais. Beefy Joe handed me the intercom receiver as if parting with his last dollar.

"I'm sorry, Mr. Finley, but I really cannot see you right now . . ."

"Inge left something in my car."

"Excuse me?"

"Inge Matson? You know, from Paris? She left something in my car, and I'd like to return it to her."

On the way up in the elevator to the 14th floor, I wondered whether Swedish peasants—Inge Matson's ancestors—had once shouldered their way through life laying off one bluff against another. When Sven showed up in a new village, did he tell Lars in the first hut he had been sent by Gunnar from the neighboring village and did he then tell Max in the second hut Lars had told him to drop by? I doubted it had worked that way back then. How many doormen could you find in an old Swedish village, anyway?

Servais stood in his doorway at the end of the hall. His tie was down from his collar and his sleeves rolled up to his hammy forearms. I thought of a fire hydrant with a false smile. "I have a very short lunch hour today and I have a guest, Mr. Finley. So, I can take whatever it is."

"You already have. Neil Kinsey. Or do we want to talk about that out in the hall here?" He shot his eyes over my shoulder down the corridor to the elevator. They were working toward sulking, anger, and a lot of other good defensive things. "Just me. The guy you told you hadn't seen Kinsey since the day you fired him."

Give him his experience: He was used to dealing with representatives from the Tonga Republic. "A surprise for me, too," he smiled edgily. "Maybe we can clarify some things together. Come in."

Seldes would have been at a red alert level if he had walked in with me. The door opened into an enormous square of a sunken living room not so much lit as glistening from a show window; outside were the East River and Long Island City in IMAX. The furniture was some Ivory Soap fantasy of white on white. But what would have sent Seldes into paranoid overdrive was what he would have called the Hinduphilia. Every wall hanging and knick-knack had an Indian theme: monkey gods, gilded shields, ebony elephants, small grillwork sculptures in the rusts and greens Kinsey had used on JABPUN. Could there be any doubt the ceiling-high shelves in the far corner were books on how to blow up Pakistanis in Cleveland?

"You're very intolerable, aren't you, Mr. Finley?"

Matson sat smoking and wagging one thin leg over another on one of the two white couches; her bow seemed part of the furniture. "I've never been asked that before."

"It wasn't a question."

Servais went down the two rugged steps ahead of me. He had become so hospitable so fast I wondered what side door Kinsey was using to get out of the building. But then I saw the overnight bag on the floor behind a chair. "I've got something in my car for Kinsey. If he doesn't want to come down for it, I'll just throw it away."

"These famous movies?" She still sounded indifferent.

"I promised Caporale. This is Kinsey's last chance to get them."

Servais sat down and, hands folded across his stomach, studied me as some kind of floor act. "And you take this obligation so seriously, you followed Inge here?"

"Not just here," she snapped. "He first had to follow me up to my apartment. He's been following me since the funeral."

"And for what, might I ask? Neil is hardly some criminal fugitive, Mr. Finley. Aren't old acquaintances allowed to see each other?"

As long as the question had been asked, I didn't think I was breaking Olmos's instructions in answering. "I'm sure he's told you he didn't cut off his newspaper delivery before leaving Minneapolis and that some of his employers are anxious about his whereabouts. Remember them? The same guys who invited you around for a talk?"

"If it's an interesting story, I'm sure he'll tell us about it. Or does that make *us* suspicious characters, too?"

Servais still seemed to be missing something—a mustache recently shaved, a mole just lanced. The odd thing about that feeling, of course, was that I hadn't known him when he'd had the extra thing. "Is it worth it for somebody in your position? Here's somebody official people want to talk to and you're the genial host after all these years. You didn't pocket his severance pay in Paris, did you?"

He seemed on the verge of glancing at Matson, then caught himself. "And that would be your business how exactly?"

"It's not. Just call him out from whatever door he's hiding behind, I'll give him his movies, and we'll all get on with our lives."

"You told me you gave these films to the police."

Whoops, one piece of truth too much. "I did, and they gave them back to me. They thought they were boring."

It should have ended right then and there. Goodbye, Finley. Goodbye, brilliant gambit for getting Kinsey out of the apartment.

With anybody else, it would have. But Inge Matson hadn't spent so many narcissistic years dismissing the importance of other people to worry now about their little contradictions. "Well, go get your damn movies and bring them up," she said, grinding out her cigarette in an ashtray on her lap.

"I don't like all this traffic in and out downstairs," the Frenchman said, suddenly looking fussier. "Can't this wait for another day?"

It was the right moment for reminding him he had been putting up a lot of unnecessary obstacles, starting with his failure to mention knowing who Pouchol's husband was. But he saved me that idiocy by reading my hesitation as determination. "All right. Just leave them with the doorman."

"I think I've done all the lifting I'm going to do with those reels. He wants them, he comes down for them."

She didn't give Servais the chance to argue. "Neil! Come in here!" she barked without turning.

Hungry eyes and sandwich-board trim aside, Neil Kinsey wasn't any craven Peter Lorre in close-up. As he opened the door in the corner next to the bookshelves and stepped out into the living room, he didn't apologize for the space he was taking up. Just the opposite, I smelled the bravado of the hustler. He worked to outside fantasies, not inside perversions. He was sure he was going to win at something, he just didn't know what it was yet.

"This is Mr. Finley, Neil," she said. "He has something he says belongs to you."

"Wonder what that could be."

I guess there was a supermarket list of reasons for what I did next. Right in front of me, there was the dwarf rhino beauty of Neil Kinsey. He hadn't shaved in a couple of days, the dye was wearing off his hair, and his Hawaiian shirt was probably only the top layer of his affectations in Minnesota. He thought we were all comical and strolled around the couch as though he supposed he had three-and-a-half seconds to toss me a few peanuts. Later, I also factored in the nervous neatness of Servais's living room, with everything gleaming too much in its place. And that was without counting Florence Caporale for immediate inspiration, the trashing of my apartment, a 25-year-old murder the creep seemed to have dodged, and his milking of the public teat for people like Seldes. Throw in the shiner from Klaus's two goony sons and Darlene Anderson, who got sick the night of our junior year hop. There were so many reasons a list was superfluous: Just buy the whole supermarket. It just suddenly felt *necessary* to answer his whiff of Lifebuoy by giving him until two feet away and then smashing him across the mouth with the back of my hand.

The yelping was almost as nice as watching Kinsey go over the arm of the couch and reach too late for where he had been hit. Matson jumped up in so much alarm she didn't notice the ashes jumping up with her out of the ashtray and over the back of her hand. Servais was protesting to the General Assembly. It was my first Finley Thug Moment in years and felt overdue. I had forgotten how calming it could be. As long as everybody was being enraged and panicked, I could concentrate on the control centers, the front door and the intercom next to it, to make sure nobody ran for either. I liked thinking the three people in the room had never heard of me back in the nineties when they had been plotting in a Paris studio to blow up the Taj Mahal. Without realizing it, they had already been on track to our meeting on East 46th Street. Kismet!

"Tell them why you had that coming, Kinsey. Or do they know why?"

Matson said something indignant, Servais said something even more indignant. Kinsey, though, said nothing, as though he *did* believe he'd had it coming. Mainly, he looked disappointed there was no blood on the hand he ran across his mouth. Maybe it was only because of how Servais had described him at our lunch, but I didn't think killer, propagandist, or burglar, I thought *drunk*. The kind who looked for bar fights so he could be knocked around and could make that a deposit down on his next drunk. I had a feeling the squirrels in his head were already ordering a round on me.

Which somehow didn't quite come out as Mireille Pouchol. Sayyid in a drunken rage a century ago, yes; Pouchol, no.

"What makes you think I want those shitty movies?"

"You were interested enough to break into my place after them."

He thought that was hilarious, and I liked seeing some blood on his front teeth. But I would have been happier if he had lifted himself out of his ball over the couch arm. He was *really* beginning to remind me of a drunk: somebody who just stayed where he fell. "I'd say you called Florence Caporale and she told you where I lived."

"You don't have to answer him, Neil. He has no authority."

He had tuned out Matson more than I had. "Yeah, I called her. Tried to. Too many numbers to punch out."

"What's that supposed to mean?"

He finally got off his shoulder blades and sat up. "Inge said Ali killed himself. I had this idea his wife wanted a condolences call. I got through the area code before I realized what I was doing. I never even met the woman! And if Ali was still Ali, he never mentioned me to her. So, I hung up. Good thing. If she slammed Inge, she might've sent a contract killer after me!"

Mr. Ling on Fourth Avenue did my shirts. He always used an abacus. Except for one day when he knocked the abacus off the counter, smashing it up enough for some of the beads to go rolling across the floor. I wished I hadn't thought of Mr. Ling. "You saying you didn't break into my apartment to get those reels?"

"I think Neil is saying he doesn't even know where you live," Servais said emphatically.

"Till Inge mentioned you, Finley, you were just an anonymous Nielsen viewer. Sorry. But they who labor in the shadows also serve."

Believing him wasn't going to help, so I didn't. When it came right down to it, breaking into my apartment was a bigger crime than killing Sayyid 25 years ago, killing Pouchol a month ago, or driving Caporale into his bathtub a few days ago. I couldn't mention any of those other things anyway. "You're the only one who had an interest in that stuff."

"What? Frenchmen sitting around sidewalk cafes? Oh, yeah. I want to relive those good old days. Made me the artist I am today."

My head was brimming with cracks. About Sayyid. About King Arthur as a cowboy. About JABPUN. But they had all been taken already for Kinsey's leer of self-loathing. "See?" Matson's smirk said. "*This* is what you've been wasting your gas on all day!"

I might have stood there in suspended animation for the rest of the afternoon if Servais hadn't opened his mouth. "Go get the damn things, Neil. Then Mr. Finley can go his way."

"I don't want them."

"Well, I do! I don't want to be bothered by this nonsense anymore!"

"Just get them, *cheri*," she seconded, calming herself by lighting another Parliament.

I latched on to the scow moving up the river before Kinsey could get me to applaud his toying. He didn't need my agreement anyway. Manipulating the others was all part of some profound contempt. Who could respect the bartenders of life who kept filling up your glass?

"Well, it sounds like you're going to have to give me these things," he finally gave in, using the couch arm to raise himself. "Good things just never seem to go away."

I was too busy watching his hand on the couch to see any look he exchanged with the others. I still wasn't sure he wasn't going to go for another fall until we got to the door. I was counting on it. Anything to screen a new certainty I'd be delivering less to Olmos than had seemed the case a few minutes ago.

"It's been lovely, Finley," she said.

Servais was too close to getting me off the premises to ruin it all with cheap sarcasm. "I'm sure all this confusion is because of the tragedies we've all had lately," he said, grabbing for the doorknob. "Mireille, then Robby, then Ali. There is just so much we can take."

Kinsey's heckling laugh as he ambled down the hall to the elevator seemed answer enough to Servais's pompousness. The one thought I could have done without was that Killer Kinsey wasn't such a killer, after all.

CHAPTER 28

"The nice thing about Jean-Claude and Inge," Kinsey said in the elevator, "is you can forget about them as soon as you leave them. They don't burden you with their significance."

"Oh, you mean the slut with no talent?"

A half-second before the mockery there was real surprise. "You're a JABPUNite? Great shit, man! You wouldn't also happen to belong to some terrorist network, would you?"

"They seem to have gone out of their way to put you up. How do you account for that after the way you attacked them?"

The dried blood on his teeth had become a badge of honor. "Let's think . . . They're both foreigners and they can't read English?"

The elevator doors opened before I pictured another bulls-eye on his mouth. Olmos came up as soon as we had cleared the building. Kinsey's dismay lasted only a couple of seconds before he went back to remembering all the worst there was to remember about people, but that was long enough. I needed to see the tiniest soft spot, weakness, or vulnerability, and I thought I'd seen it. People like me could still hurt him. There were Thug Moments and then there were Dynamite Thug Moments.

Kinsey wasn't going to make any trouble Olmos couldn't handle, but I volunteered to tag along to Midtown South. Both looked at me as if I had skipped the punchline to a joke. I watched them walk up to Olmos's double-parked Acura; they were old pals who couldn't wait to get away from strangers so they could rehash the good times.

I drove home with a carful of ferrets. They were jumping up and down in the back, gnawing at the seats, running back and forth on the dashboard. Where was the feeling of accomplishment I should have had? I had earned every penny of Caporale's $500, hadn't I?

First job for the Professor: Ask Florence Caporale whom she had told about sending the films to me. The idea that it had been Seldes or one of his henchmen was infuriating twice, three times over. I should have seen it right away, should have understood Cicut's approach at the church with his bulletin about Kinsey being in the city had been their diversion for divertible minds. Or maybe I shouldn't have seen it. Maybe I was too much the child of pure, innocent modes of thought. Somebody who, yes, had his Thug Moment every few years, but who was still too pure and innocent for all the doublethink people who rented Chelsea offices. Maybe the Professor and his friends were at war with the Brian Seldes of the world for the wrong reasons. Maybe the Seldes of the world were dangerous because they encouraged us to think like them, we simply couldn't, and so we thought of ourselves as being outsmarted and stopped thinking altogether.

I snapped on the radio. Did the Knicks need another guard? Finley sure as hell did. That was the other part of it. Within two minutes of meeting the slice called Neil Kinsey, my defenses had crumbled. He wasn't Harry Lime, more like Harry Lemon. He hadn't cared about the film cans. And me? After all my counting on him as Killer Kinsey, the answer to two murders 25 years apart, I was ready to make the slug Humanitarian of the Year for his instinct to call Florence Caporale with his condolences.

I looked for music. I didn't want Bach or rock or rap or jazz or Sinatra. I wanted something like Rodgers and Hammerstein. "Bali Hai," something trebly and ethereal along those lines. I wanted veils and violins accompanying my Bambi prancings around the stage. I was missing EVERYTHING. Why not score it and collapse in a swoon at the end?

The closest I came was a Meineke commercial.

CHAPTER 29

I tried to let it go for a couple of days. I took nice little Polaroids of the Klaus buildings in Jackson Heights and Greenpoint and got them off to the lawyer before I became mesmerized by my artful framings of soggy plaster. Then there was Walter Ochs, a Cobble Hill vet who seemed to have a problem keeping alive nine-month-old dogs and an even bigger one keeping their corpses around after they had suddenly died on him; just coincidence they were usually German shepherds, pit bulls, and other breeds good for training for dog fights? At least one owner of a dead and vanished animal didn't think so.

In short, there were whole minutes I didn't think about Neil Kinsey, Phil Caporale, or Robby Klein's green triangles. And even when I did think about them, I spent most of my brain candles telling myself not to think about them. Olmos hadn't called to say what he had gotten from Kinsey? Oh, hey, the guy's busy on a hundred other things, too. Seldes hadn't called to renew his invitation for another sit-down? Hey, what did I matter anymore? And hey, even if my instinct about Kinsey was right, that he had only killed Sayyid, wouldn't some cop in some city somewhere along the line come up with evidence proving Pouchol had been snuffed by Monsieur Jobert's wicked first wife or greedy oldest son? None of it was my business anymore. Where *Allah's Henchmen* was concerned, the balcony was closed.

Then the Professor ruined my vacation. His call was on the pretext of asking if I was coming out to his Wednesday gathering and would I bring a little extra wine if I was? No, I wasn't so I couldn't and had my tickets for whatever people wanted to have tickets for to prove it. (What I mainly wanted to avoid was another salon evening dominated by talk of Phil Caporale.) The old man didn't draw out the pretense. "So they'll drink Sprite. How's my case going?"

"Your case is over. What happened to Caporale happened because Caporale wanted it to happen. No Kinsey darting around the Caporale bathroom and rearranging the props."

"Why're you so sure?"

"Kinsey's a lush, Joe. Big attitude, small everything else. Homeland Security was made for him. They told him he was important so he played the part. Anything else has been too ambitious for him for a long time."

He churned that over a moment, then came from another direction. "I talked to Florence. She says she never saw what was on those films."

"What else is new?"

"She said Caporale started obsessing on them about three weeks ago. She didn't get it. Told him just to throw the goddamn things out if they bothered him so much. He said no, he wanted to give them back to Kinsey and told her he'd hired you for the job."

"So she decided to take the bull by the horns."

"Right. If he was going to keep futzing around about the damn things, she'd take care of them for him. When she told him what she'd done, he went bonkers. Made a big scene. Slamming things. She got out of the house, stayed away all day. When she got home, she found him in the tub."

I'd heard that sequence before, on Finley FM. "Whatever."

"You listening?"

"I'm listening. And if you want to get technical, I think it's bullshit."

"It's what the woman told me. As a confidence."

"So she believes it and you believe it."

"And you don't."

"I don't know what I believe. But I'm sure it didn't go down the way you're saying. But who cares? There's not much we can do about it now anyway. Keep her confidence, Joe."

"I'm not the only one she told."

"There was nothing in the paper. Who else?"

"The only person she would've dared tell. You."

"I've never spoken to the woman!"

"But she doesn't know that. She's under the impression you called her to extend your condolences. It was your Chelsea friends in your apartment, Paul. The same ones who're listening to us now, I suppose."

My first thought was to remind myself I'd already worked that out, that there hadn't been any other possibility. But Seldes or Cicut or maybe the guy behind the partition who had been sneezing the day I'd been there, one of them *being me*, that suddenly cleaned out my stomach like a second burglary. "Those fuckers."

"I guess Florence's story made them curious."

I didn't have enough fingers to put around Seldes' throat. "Thanks for ruining my day. Just don't ruin it anymore by mentioning it where those cans are now."

"There's a cause and an effect in there, Paul."

"Absolutely. And I'll work it out one of these years."

"What's the matter with you? What I just said is important."

I wasn't in the mood for Joe Carroll the private investigator any more than I was for Brian Seldes the second-story man. "Would you give it a rest? Caporale was going to give me the movies anyway. Sounds like he just didn't like Florence polishing his bowling ball. Cause and effect? He had a morbid fear of his wife wearing the pants, even for a trip to Federal Express. He was more certifiable than either one of us saw."

"When in doubt, go with crazy."

"It's the only explanation."

"Know what you sound like? The general who keeps rushing the six troops he has left from one wall of the fort to the other and can't understand why the Rebs are coming through the gate."

"Just as long as you're there to tell me where I go wrong."

"The *people*, Finley, the *people*! When Caporale got dressed in the morning, it was right laces first, then left. If he found the left laces already tied, his whole day was ruined."

"On that note . . ."

"No, on this one. Florence said he started being obsessive about the films 'three weeks ago.' Throw in another week when he kept a stiff upper lip even with her. What does that get us back to?"

"I know. Pouchol."

"You know. Good. Then that's where you start."

"Start what? That's the theory you didn't want to believe, remember? Besides, Caporale was in Philadelphia. That's solid."

"I said start with Pouchol, not with Caporale killing her. They're different things."

"It's over, Joe!"

"Because you've run out of stamina?"

"Because we'll never know. Because it could be one thing or a hundred things and you don't always figure out which."

"What a wonderful philosophy!"

"I've been inside the web, Joe. That's what it is—not your Civil War fort, but a fucking web full of bugs. And all you do is get icky dead flies in your brain."

There was too much silence on the other end. "Don't pull this shit on me, old man."

"When Caporale came to me looking for a job," the toneless voice finally came back, "I was his sixth or seventh stop. He'd been turned down everywhere. Not because he didn't have credentials. He had his Masters, top grades, anything you'd want in an assistant for the spot I had for European history. Except he didn't want to hear about European history. His academic qualifications, his travels, Jesus, even his Italian background—he wanted them all behind him. What he was looking for was the second slot I had open, for modern Asian history. I thought he was kidding. I said to myself, 'Oh, Christ, another one.'"

"Another what?"

"Trendy careerist! The Pacific Rim, that was the flavor of the month, the fast track. Tokyo, not Rome. Beijing, not London. Why aim for an international conference in Paris drinking red wine when you could be having mai-tais in Singapore?"

"But you hired him for it."

"I hired him for it. He worked at it. Got two PhDs in his spare time. Wrote two books that sneaked out of academic circles, got into the History Book Club and Readers Subscription. One was about Clive, the . . ."

"Joe."

"Clive committed suicide, too, you know that?"

"You didn't want to, but you hired him."

"I hired him. And he built the life he had. The Amritsar life of the soulless academic. Just running out the ground ball. Twenty-five years of kids listening to him like the day I did."

"That's got nothing to do with why he killed himself, Joe."

"Then fucking find out why he did!"

The phone went down with a bang. It took me a second to realize that he still hadn't explained why he'd hired Caporale in the first place.

CHAPTER 30

Everything the woman had said was a question; that was what kept swimming around in my head as I hit the Manhattan Bridge behind a *News* delivery truck. "Paul Finley?" she had asked. "This is the Emergency Room at St. Clare's Hospital? In Manhattan? Are you acquainted with a Neil Kinsey?" I couldn't work out how that mint julep habit of putting a question mark after everything had ended up in a midtown hospital.

At four in the morning, with only me and the *News* truck to show the advantage of having a bridge connect Bay Ridge in Brooklyn to Columbus Circle in Manhattan, the other questions could wait. The one, for example, about why Neil Kinsey was no longer in the custody of Alex Olmos and why Olmos had neglected to impart that piece of trivia to me. Or the one about how Neil Kinsey had ended up in a "serious accident?" And then there was the one about why Neil Kinsey had asked for me instead of his reunited buddies from Reynaud-Grevin. That kind of thing belonged in my Later On box. The important thing, as I'd told the mint julep nurse on the phone, was that as long as her call had woken me up anyway and as long as Brooklyn and Manhattan were in the same city anyway and as long as I would've had to move my car to the opposite side of the street in a few hours anyway, I couldn't wait to get over to see her and Neil Kinsey.

The City That Never Sleeps was a roaring *fiesta* of invisible tourists and conventioneers at four a.m. They were on every freezing street corner whooping it up in front of the barred and screened stores, garbage cartons, and newspaper mounds of homeless. The traffic lights sounded like drums when they switched from red to green. The fluorescent lights seemed to have been left on in the skyscrapers for future archeologists. I had called Phil Caporale certifiable? The only difference between us seemed to be that he had run the water in his tub first.

I kept up this positive train of whining until I walked into the somber glaze of the hospital emergency room. All the people I hadn't seen on the street seemed to be sitting on chairs against the wall holding on to some part of themselves while medical people flitted around in the baby blue colors the Montreal Expos had once worn. I went right for a black woman at a tiny desk who looked like she had gotten her job after years of bouncing drunks from draft-and-rye joints.

"Kinsey, Kinsey," she said, sizing me up as someone who needed to start dropping better names. "We call it a substance abuse problem. We got enough real problems in here."

"I'm sure you do."

"Caterina! Take him back to Number Six!"

Caterina, a tall, gangly Latina who looked used to the woman's dispatches, waggled a finger at me and led me to Number Six. Inside the curtained-off bed was a cast with Kinsey somewhere in it. His left leg was in traction, bandages started around his head, covered his right eye, and ended under the right side of his chin. His nose looked even bigger and squatter for having been kept outside. "My man Finley!"

For once, a nurse didn't tell me I had only so many minutes. I felt like chasing after Caterina to remind her of her duties. "You look good, Neil."

"Don't try matching boilermakers with poets. First, they out-drink you, then they lead you into the street where cars are still moving."

"You got hit by a car?"

"More like I hit it. What's the matter? You look disappointed. Think some crazed killer got me? The same one that got Mireille?"

"The mind's a great thing to waste. What'd you want me for?"

A spasm of something came through his medication, and he gritted a smile for the dirty hands clutching the sheet over his chest. "You people in New York should get more funding for your hospitals. I got stronger things in my bathroom at home. Guy says I'm going to need an orthopedist for a long time. No, what I need is some Demerol for a short time."

"I can ask . . ."

"Never mind. Sit down, sit down."

"They frown on that in emergency rooms. Why'd you have them call me? And what happened to the cops?"

He seemed grateful for a happier thought. "Right, your pal Olmos. Well, sad to say for him, I had a bus stub in my pocket showing I arrived here the day after Mireille was killed. That kind of took the wind out of his sails. Yours, too, if you'd been there, I guess, huh?"

I reminded myself I'd already written him off on Pouchol. "That's the only thing you talked about?"

"No. But aren't cop-suspect conversations privileged? Wouldn't I be breaking some oath to tell you about them?"

My first thought was that it must have been the way I'd just slapped on some clothes to get out of the house; no shave, no brushing my teeth, barely a comb through my hair. And with Kinsey able to see out of only one eye, maybe I *did* resemble a horse's ass. "This was your idea of a joke—to get me over here like this?"

"We talked about a lot of things," he said. "Why Mireille called me. What I think might've happened to her. Why I left Minneapolis the way I did. Indian-Pakistani politics. And finally, my movies. The prick refuses to give them back to me. Part of that's my fault since I told him most of the reels were Ali's. Including our favorite little scene along the Seine. But on top of that, Olmos says they might be material evidence. You were a cop, right? Olmos said you were. Can you have something that just *might* be material evidence? Doesn't it either have to be or not?"

"What do you want, Kinsey?"

"Pay this hospital bill, for one thing." He didn't laugh.

"Yeah, I'll get right on it."

"There's no way I can lay this on the driver. I was staggering in the middle of the street, drunk out of my skull. He was with the light."

"I think they've shot you up more than you think. Maybe I'll let you go to sleep and get the rest of the details from Olmos."

His head came off his pillows so fast I could feel the jab in my own head. "I can't use my insurance card! As soon as it goes into the computer, I'm advertising where I am! There're people I just don't want having that information." He subsided again. "And don't ask me who."

"No, I'll just take my finger out of my ass long enough to pay your bill. Good Night, Kinsey. Or, Good Morning. Whatever it is."

"I know what happened, Finley!"

"Happened where?"

"In Paris and around here. Both things."

He had a doubt; only a flicker of one, but stark enough even for that nanosecond to see how much he had been counting on me for something. If I didn't move, just stared back at him, I could have stopped his breathing until he had asphyxiated himself. "So tell Olmos. That's what he's getting paid to listen to."

"But he's not a JABPUNite like you."

"Look, slug. My client's dead and you obviously don't interest the cops, so so much for my good works. Why should I care what happened in Paris 25 years ago or anything else involving you?"

He heard the feeble undercurrent as much as I did, and his doubt was gone. His swathed head seemed to feel the pillow under it again. "Because of that old Chinese saying," he grinned. "Give somebody a gratuitous slap in the mouth and you're responsible for his life. At first, I thought that was for Ali. Some grievance you'd built up because you were no help to him. Then when your friend Olmos kept asking me about Mireille, I wondered if you weren't being the valiant avenger of dead damsels. But somewhere in the middle of my first drink tonight at Pete's Tavern, long before things started getting a little hazy, it occurred to me you hit me for yourself. I saw that look on your face. Something about a dead father or a dead brother or somebody dead under your Christmas tree during World War I or something. Nothing at all professional about it. Real personal. You really didn't like me! And after only 10 seconds of meeting me! Deep waters there, Finley. Rivers, oceans, seas. Sewers, too, right?"

I would have enjoyed it as another drunk's bluff much more if my mind didn't run off to a thought about how much exactly his bill might have been. "These people you don't want tracing you—your JABPUN friends?"

"I'm tired of being measured by clowns. That's what they are. Self-important, creepy, and all over the fucking place, but clowns. I need this favor, Finley. It'll cost you exactly two seconds of your time. Give me that bag there." There was a small traveling case on the floor against the wall next to an unused drip stand. "Give me the checkbook inside."

I was back to taking orders and not objecting to the three-second timeout they provided. It took a lot of clumsy pawing, but he finally got the checkbook opened to where he could show me he had $7,789.54 in a Minneapolis bank. "See? Almost eight thousand. You write me a check for the damage here and I'll give you a check right back. You want ten percent for your trouble, I'll throw it in. Even if they've got you red-flagged, I'll be out of here by the time they put two and two together. Inge and Servais can't give me that edge, Finley. They're being watched. Only you can help me."

That explained the absence of Matson and Servais but still shouldn't have left me the one wishing the emergency room *did* have a chair. "If your check didn't bounce and if you didn't cancel it after writing it out to me and if I wanted to."

"I didn't kill anybody, Finley. Not Mireille, not Sayyid. Ask your cop friend. I convinced him, didn't I? Why I need you to do this has nothing to do with either one of them."

Why *had* Olmos let him go on Sayyid? He'd seen the same damn movie I had. "With who, then? I'm running out of people, Kinsey. You're not afraid of the cops. You're not afraid of your JABPUN sponsors. So, who're we talking about?"

He seemed to have already conceded having to tell me. To save as much as he could, he tried to look defiant as he said, "Modred."

"Who?"

"Modred. The one who killed King Arthur."

CHAPTER 31

Yes, I agreed to write Kinsey his check. I told myself there was little risk involved. He wasn't going anywhere for a while without a pulley holding up his leg, giving me plenty of those famous "business days" for his check to clear in Minneapolis before putting my own signature to anything. The worst part of my bother would be some visit down the line from Seldes after he found out Kinsey had been writing checks to me. And so what? When I'd last looked, quitting as the webmaster for a sting website without a two-week notice wasn't a felony.

And all of this for what? Fulfilling my contract with Caporale? Satisfying whatever expectations the Professor had built up around me in his usual presumptuous way? Partly. But also in there somewhere was what Jake Klein had said to me about *accounting for* people. Even before Phil Caporale had handed over his retainer, there had been an awful lot of them slipping away from me without that accounting. The popular expression was dotting the *i*'s and crossing the *t*'s. But when you've developed the uneasy sensation that every letter of the alphabet was missing some little piece, it didn't seem like much of a gamble to seize an opening that might get me back to feeling whole about kindergarten fundamentals.

Not that Kinsey made it easy. Once he decided my agreement made me a captive audience, he had only so much largesse to spoon out at a time. He might have been crippled and on his back, but didn't that make him even more of a marvel worthy of patience and attention? Why shouldn't he draw out his revelations for greater impact? It was barfly sermonizing, it was self-contempt with a lot of proper names, it was egocentric delusions delivered as erudition. As he went on, it was also a Neil Kinsey whose drugs and injuries were beginning to kick in.

"So Modred, whether you believe he was Arthur's son or nephew, was a bad guy. A back-stabber. Evil. Slayer of kings."

"Why was it so important to get out of Minneapolis so fast?"

"Modred was coming."

"And that would be . . .?"

"*I'm* Modred. Haven't you figured that out yet, Finley? When I was younger, I created this wonderful world of knights in shining armor. But then Modred showed up, and I made sure all those nobles were tainted, polluted, tarred . . . Give me another word."

"When Pouchol called you, she wanted to talk about Visiv?"

"She wasn't Pouchol anymore. She was something called Jo-bert. That's not how I knew her. A quarter-century of knowing her as Mireille Pouchol, remembering her as Mireille Pouchol, but suddenly she shows up again as a real human being and she doesn't even have her name. That was a downer, Finley. Who had I been jerking off with all those years since I'd last seen her? Not somebody named Jo-bert."

"What did she want from you, Neil?"

"Not my life. She made it clear she had a better one. With this Jo-bert guy."

"How were you going to help her?"

"She really had a lot of gall when you think about it. Two-and-a-half decades, Finley. And there she is on the phone talking to me like we just rolled out of bed in our old hotel room. Her voice sounded harsher, older. I mean, I still heard that little whisper she could lay on when she wanted you to think she was *really* sincere and hurting, but there was an extra, deeper note. Know what I think? I think she aged the same number of years the rest of us did over those 25 years. I wouldn't swear to it, but I'm pretty sure."

"How did she find you, anyway?"

"Telephone. Little black thing they used before e-mail. You use the pad of your index finger like this and you punch . . ."

"If you weren't in contact all these years, how did she know you were in Minneapolis?"

"I'm in the book there. I don't have airs. Bet you didn't notice that."

"There're a lot of directories. How come she knew to get the Minneapolis one for you?"

"Peyrot, I suppose. The old guy that runs the studio. He always had his hand in a thousand things. Think after all these years he doesn't know who to call to find out who to call? That's what influential people do these days, Finley. They don't call the local cop on the take to cough up an address, they go into fucking optic fibers. Old Peyrot probably has every phone number and address in the world under his pillow. Minus one, of course. That's why he and Jo-bert fear this Visiv. Outfit like Visiv, it has one *more* optic fiber under its pillow . . . I'm getting a little tired here. They said they were going to send me upstairs to a room. The Jo-bert Room. Maybe you should ask them what happened to it."

"Okay, she finds you. Looking for what?"

"She betrayed me, Finley."

"I've heard."

"Yeah? What have you heard? Have you heard she was my Guinevere back in my Arthur days? That she found her Lancelot to go fucking behind my back?"

"So you beat her up."

"Fucking right I did. She had it coming. That one I could've justified even without drinking. I had my illusions, and she punctured them. If it wasn't for her and Lancelot, I wouldn't have turned into Modred."

"Okay, Mr. Kinsey. We're going to move you up to the fourth floor now. Your friend can come back later to visit you."

I hadn't heard Caterina come up behind me. That fit. I wasn't sure of anything I *had* heard, either.

CHAPTER 32

I dithered about going home, showering, getting fresh clothes, and then coming all the way back or hanging around in Manhattan until some fourth-floor Caterina awakened Kinsey with a scrumptious bowl of Corn Flakes. Leaning a little this way and a little that way, I ended up watching the sun come up from an old diner near the South Seaport. The place had lost most of its trade with the closing of the fish market, and seemed to be scraping by on the maintenance people from the new skyscrapers nearby. The morning light didn't look like it had much of a future, either: a quick shot of adrenalin to make me feel even grottier in my clothes, then a dreary gray sky with rain coming.

I knew the day was ruined before I finished my coffee and bacon sandwich. Whatever else I did would be an afterthought to getting back to listening to more of Kinsey's fable. It was a loose-ends feeling I'd once had regularly before Jenny and I had been married, when I'd gotten off morning tours out in Mineola at 1:30 and had to decide whether to go home for a nap or go directly to the city for picking her up at her 5:30 quitting time. My usual solution in those days had been any movie that started between 2:30 and 3:00. At six in the morning, though, the only movies going were the ones unspooling in my head. Most of them starred a dead Indian named Sayyid. And no matter what Kinsey had said, he had been Sayyid's co-star. I had seen it myself, hadn't I?

Hadn't I?

I dragged out the diner for two-and-a-half coffees, then found an ATM machine to send Kinsey's check on its way to the little town named Another Unsmooth Move by Finley. Movie houses weren't open so early, but there was one place that was (back uptown, of course). What exactly I had in mind to accomplish I didn't know, but I took it as a good sign that my ferrets didn't protest when I surrendered to a crook in an Eighth Avenue parking garage, then walked down a couple of blocks to the Milford Plaza.

Dana had called the place more mall than hotel. I would have said as much airport terminal as hotel. Escalators led up to a carpeted reception area where there were desks for everything and for too much. There was an army of uniformed clerks selling room keys rather than tickets. Concierges seemed to have concierges, the Security desk had a telephone console that looked like it had direct lines to the Madrid Plaza and Moscow Plaza. All around the vast floor, tour groups and families were clustered together within rings of suitcases ready for early morning flights. It seemed unnecessary for them first to have to board a bus or cab to go out to Kennedy or LaGuardia instead of just walking down one of the several corridors off the lobby and through a door to their planes.

I gave it my best knowing stride going over to the elevators. I needn't have bothered. Two kids not enthusiastic about having to go back upstairs for jackets before a trip to the Statue of Liberty were mimicking their mother's "It's not summer anymore, boys" in front of one of the cars, then whacking at each other with the sweaters from around their middles. The closest security man I saw, eyes vigilant on the escalators, didn't give them a second's notice. I made a note to report that detail to Seldes.

As soon as I got off on the 12th floor, I felt like a total idiot. What had felt like a tempting curiosity a half-hour ago was a typical high-rise hotel floor of wall arrows and numbers, identical anonymous doors, and the hum of an ice machine next to soda dispensers in an alcove called REFRESHING IDEAS. If nothing else, the alcove knew what I needed.

I had come too far not to walk the walk anyway. I didn't have the exact room number where Pouchol had been killed, but that didn't feel all that essential. One room was the same as another for accessibility—whether the killer had gotten off the elevator with a clear design or had simply happened upon her in one of the corridors. The naysayer in my soul sought to interject the thought that Olmos and his legions had undoubtedly done everything I was doing, and probably with the help of ultraviolet scopes of one kind or another, but I sent that demon back into his corner. What Olmos could not possibly have counted on was the third of those three intuitions I'd told my class revealed themselves during every investigation. My first had been about Roberta Weiss and Caporale, and that had been totally wrong. The second had been about Reynaud-Grevin being in the middle of the financial grab going on in Europe, and that had been totally right. So now it was rubber game time with the third intuition, and I knew, just knew (maybe knew, maybe hoped, maybe needed some sleep) that it had to spring out of the 12th floor of the Milford Plaza.

Halfway through my patrol of the odd-numbered wing, I was over any chance of Pouchol dying at the hands of somebody she hadn't known. Jewel thieves, druggies looking for credit cards, other kinds of hotel prowlers—there would have simply been no need to worry about witnesses to anything. Practically every minute of the day, people were closing doors, saying hello to passersby in the hall, and walking on to the elevators. Who remembered what anybody looked like 10 seconds later? The only possibility in that sense at all was that she had interrupted somebody in *her* room, and the odds against that seemed too high to take seriously. For sure, my third intuition didn't want to hear about it.

It didn't want to hear about Kinsey, either. Even without the bus ticket that had excluded him, there had been the way he had admitted beating up Pouchol in Paris. He had become too familiar with that loathsome prick to have spawned another. If anything, he had needed her alive to keep his daily excuses to himself feeding off some past that could never again be reached, let alone amended. Broken legs from running into cars aside, Kinsey didn't live in the present tense.

With Caporale also accounted for in Philadelphia, it was time to cast a wider net. I bought a Refreshing Idea with a Pepsi. As much as Caporale had, Matson and Servais had positions to protect. If Pouchol had truly been bent on digging up the Sayyid story for some reason, neither of them would have appreciated it. And Servais was a Frenchman, wasn't he? Who would have suffered more in the corridors of power in France about the Sayyid tale than an ambitious diplomat? And the guy had lied to me about more than one detail, hadn't he?

The first bubbles exploded in my chest. I still didn't like Servais for any of it. Professionally public people didn't do personally public things. He might have been a liar, but that was what seemed to rule him out. The bridge from Sayyid to Pouchol wasn't about lies, it was about deception, especially the self- kind. From the start, it had been people doing what I'd blurted out at Da Francesco in front of Dana and Olmos—turning around only when they hoped their shadows were gone. Caporale keeping movies he hadn't looked at in 25 years, as the Professor had said. Jake Klein wanting to believe in something about idiot pay stubs. Inge Matson rebuffing Pouchol on the phone to avoid any talk about their bad consciences, but then suddenly putting up the source of that bad conscience. And Kinsey, still with some tiny pathetic belief that if he looked back too quickly, he would see Avalon in flames. The out-and-out lies had all been misdemeanors, after the fact. They hadn't killed Mireille Pouchol, self-deception had. That was my third intuition. Take it to the bank.

Along with the check from Neil Kinsey.

A door opened at the end of the hall. A wheelchair came out into the corridor. It was an elderly, emaciated woman dressed in a garish cherry suit. Right behind her came a chubby husband in an orange jacket that looked left over from a Tropicana convention. He fussed over the door two, three times before satisfying himself it was locked, then started pushing the woman toward me. Her head was all over the place in a Parkinson's way; he was already working at the chair as though he had been maneuvering it up and down the Alps all day. "Morning, fella."

"How're you, sir?"

"You'd never believe she was my daughter, would you?"

She grumbled something under his booming laugh as they struggled on to the elevator. I wondered if I'd still be running after four a.m. calls from hospitals when I too was bones in a wheelchair. Why not? As the old joke went, it was better than the alternative.

CHAPTER 33

I had apparently settled a bet for Kinsey by walking into his room. He did all but gloat with his one eye. "I thought you'd just grab the check and have me chase after you for it."

"We do jury duty together, we'll be equals. Other than that . . ."

There was a groan from the second, curtained-off bed in the room. "I think it's something serious," he said, for a fraction of a second showing the same doubt as when he had been talking about calling Florence Caporale at Servais's. "Which one of us are they torturing, do you think? Him, so he can wish he had only a lot of broken bones? Or me, because I have to put up with all his moaning?"

"You were telling me about Pouchol's call."

"Was I? I was having more fun thinking of how I came here to get the fuck that killed her. That's why I know you're an avenger, Finley. I've had my moments, too. Just recently."

"You heard she was dead how?"

"The Internet. More dependable than the Minneapolis papers. They're still endorsing Hubert Humphrey."

"Changed your life, huh? You hear she's dead and suddenly you can't be bothered with JABPUN anymore."

He looked truly stung. "They were all losers except for Mireille."

"Which they are we talking about?"

"All of them. In Paris. The propaganda creep show here. I thought they deserved each other. Okay?"

"Took you a long time to connect the two."

"But connect them is what I did. Like I'd been walking around with two raggedy, exposed wires all these years. Then Mireille called and gave me the idea. Contact! Bzzzzz!"

"Dead Mireille. Your Guinevere."

"Right."

"The woman you beat up regularly."

"She got over it."

"Except the last time?"

"You can't tell me anything I don't know, Finley. Yeah, she found her Lancelot, and they fucked me over. If you want symmetry, I should've died of my wounds right then and there. But I didn't. I went on to the fruitful career I've had."

"From what I hear, your career wasn't exactly tearing down the speedway even before she found her Lancelot."

He aimed a single, flat laugh at the ceiling. "That is correct, sir."

"So why give all the credit to Mireille?"

"Don't be sarcastic," he said mildly, his eye fixed on the ceiling. "We should all have symbols of our degeneration. She was mine. She showed me what my limitations were. I could drink this much, but not that much. I could slap her this hard, but not that hard. I could make it up to her fucking her this much, but not that much. Buying these flowers, but not those. Nobody ever defined Neil Kinsey so clearly. And believe me, Finley, that was something to hold on to when I came back to rejoin the Wonderful World of Disney. But degeneration symbols are supposed to be only that. They're not supposed to give you ideas about dying altogether. That's why I like living in the Midwest. You're always hearing out there about a way of life *dying out*. It's not like LA or New York. Here nothing gets to die out. It just gets hit by a cab. Boom. Dead. Goodbye."

"A guess?"

"You're the one covering my check."

"She called you to warn you."

"Olmos didn't know that. You got better bugging equipment than the New York cops?"

"I think somebody over there put the Sayyid story on the negotiating table, and she tipped you off. Guinevere's last gesture."

"Why does it sound like shit coming out of your mouth?"

"But not just that. She also came here to find out how Visiv got its hands on such an awkward tale."

He kept his eye on his new friend in the ceiling. "No mystery. I told you. They have more optic fibers under their pillow than even Peyrot."

"Yeah, but there's that reputation you have for shooting your mouth off when you drink enough. Yes, she called you to warn you. But she also probably had a tiny, tiny suspicion the source was you yourself. One of those nights out there in the Minnesota snows, and to keep your buddies at the bar warm, you told them the Sayyid story. A passing crow overheard you, and before you know it, the crow's whispering into the ear of somebody at Visiv. Something along those lines, Neil?"

He finally came back down to me. He didn't look exactly mad, more like he was remembering what being mad had felt like. "I never talked about it," he said evenly. "Drunk or sober. And she believed me when I told her that. If somebody was using Sayyid against the studio, it didn't come from me. She knew that when she hung up."

Sitting down on the chair at the foot of the bed didn't seem like such a great commitment. I'd just heard what I'd been waiting to hear practically since Caporale had been in my living room, hadn't I? I had *earned* not having to stay so aloof with my King Arthur; the truth had made me loose. "That must've made you feel really noble."

"You don't get it, do you? It was over, Finley."

"I think it had been for a helluva long time."

"I'm not talking about Mireille. I'm talking about me. Sayyid was my invention, Finley. He gave Neil Kinsey dimension. Okay, only with a few people, but you take what you can get. They all fan out on their separate 'career paths,' as they say. Robby here, Inge there, Servais over here. And they all carry their little Neil Kinsey secret with them. They don't go a week of their entire lives without having to give me and Sayyid a thought. They can't think of me as a great director or even an especially nice guy, but they've got to think about me anyway. Maybe they even enjoy it in some grubby way. I wouldn't put it past Inge. She always hit me as waiting for somebody to invite her down into the swamp. Never ask for it herself, but she'd be there for it. I don't think Ali ever got that about her."

"So they should all be grateful to you. You compromised them with Sayyid's killing, enriching their fantasy lives."

"Exactly," he said, totally serious. "But that all ended when Mireille called. The truth was going to come out. I'd have no more hold over them."

"Rough."

If I hadn't been there, I wouldn't have believed it. He gave his encased head two drawn-out shakes, but he still couldn't prevent the glaze of tears building up in his eye. "You don't know how much. I had power over those people, Finley. A fabulous power. Stronger than any of the bullshit I ever saw in Hollywood or Washington. Those places made and destroyed a thousand lives a day with their crap, but they didn't remember names anymore. Nothing was personal. But ask Inge Matson. She knew it was me in her dreams. Neil Kinsey, nobody else, was her bad conscience."

"It's called megalomania."

He laughed; mostly to stop tearing. "Right. And look what it gets you. They want to MRI my ribs. Did I tell you that?"

"So one way or another, this great power you've had over these people was about to end. Either Visiv would drop your name in some friendly publication or Reynaud would give you up as being too high a price for staying in business. And they'd be lining up to say, yes, Neil Kinsey killed our man Sayyid because he was fucking around with his girlfriend."

"I could see that happening, yeah."

"They have a statute of limitations on murder in France?"

"I don't know. Do they?"

"Olmos has been talking to the Indians. I guess he's told you that."

There was another groan from the guy in the next bed. Once again, Kinsey looked over at the curtain as though unsure of what he should be doing about it. "He might have. So?"

So? It was the kind of indifference my ferrets would have thrown at me in response to some lame claim. It should have

been the last thing I was hearing from somebody who had confessed to a homicide.

"I suppose it was just more than I was ready for," he said.
"Fuck them all if they're not going to be useful to me at least as
wet dreams. So, I took care of them before they got a chance to go
at me. Didn't you like that nice twist—how we were anti-Indian
agents? Whores talking about whores talking about whores or
something. That sound you heard, ladies and gentlemen, were
those tight jaws dropping at all those foreign desks in the State
Department, Justice Department, and Department for Greater
Police Surveillance Affairs! Then up on my steed and to New York
for avenging Mireille. Well, a Greyhound bus, anyway."

"And right to Inge?"

"That's an Olmos question."

"Curiosity."

"Hell, no! I stayed in Bed-Stuy in Brooklyn for a couple of
weeks. Only white guy on the street. Friend of a friend of a friend
when I was doing campaign work in Chicago a couple of centuries
ago. No way Seldes was going to look for me there. See, one big
chunk of insight I picked up working for these people a long time
ago is, yes, they like to have every man, woman, dog, and fern on
their radar screens. But they also like to keep certain people off
their radar screens. Makes them look like they have an intelligent
policy of some kind. Unless Muslims or Haitians are involved,
black neighborhoods are usually left off. That's for the local cops."

"So why'd you leave Bed-Stuy?"

"It got pretty depressing. The only smells in the air were grass
and dead fish. That's when I gave Inge a call."

"But why stay around at all? It must've dawned even on you
the cops didn't need your help for Mireille."

"Because they already had enough from you, you mean? . . .
Whoa, low blow to the PI! But what was the rush? In case you
haven't noticed, I'm at a new crossroads. That odor you smell
is all the bridges I left burning in Washington and points north,
west, east, and south. I need a new career path. Can you suggest
something? Maybe in your line?"

"No ties at all in Minneapolis?"

"You mean like Debra?"

"I don't know the lady."

"That's right. Well, all you need to know about Debra is she likes sitcoms and she believes in surface things. She liked 'Friends' a lot because everybody knows apartments are hard to find so why shouldn't six 40-year-olds be living together? She could never understand all those gay whispers about 'Frasier' because, after all, Frasier and Niles were always chasing after women, weren't they? Debra doesn't believe in second layers. What's out there is the truth, and that's all there is to it. Since I'm a surface thing, she believes in me, too. And no, I've never swung at her."

I wondered how much I owed Olmos. He hadn't bothered to tell me about cutting Kinsey loose, and there was no guarantee Kinsey would repeat his hospital tales in an interrogation box. How much more aggravation did I need in the name of Phil Caporale and the Professor? I decided to let Dana tell me. *And* to call her as soon as I washed off the egomania in front of me.

"So, yeah, sorry, I guess I do have some airs."

"I don't remember thinking you didn't."

"Must've been your vibe," he smiled. "Think I should hold on to them for a little while more? For the widow?"

"What're you talking about?"

Suddenly, I was displeasing. "You don't listen, Finley. I told you from the start I didn't kill Sayyid. All I've had is the fun of having other people *think* I killed him. You know, the way people invent winning a war single-handed? I still don't think Inge and Servais believe me completely. They've had too much wrapped up in protecting me all these years. Makes them look a little like assholes, too."

My ferrets were back, and biting right through the shoulder of my jacket. "You're denying you killed Sayyid?"

"Hello, Earth! Good to talk to you again! Yes, that's what I'm saying. Lancelot killed Sayyid. Just like he fucked Mireille behind my back."

"Lancelot."

"Your client, Finley! Ali! What was his other name . . .?"

CHAPTER 34

I had seen it, of course—on the film in the projection booth of the Cameo. I just hadn't read the subtitles correctly. The lingering look between Caporale and Pouchol and Caporale's tell of poking his Adam's apple hadn't been over his fake inhaling of the joint, but over his awkwardness at their touching one another in public!

I stared at the leg cast in front of me. I saw the plaster congealing into ever harder bedrock even as I was gazing at it. I decided the cast was as impenetrable as my brain, that nothing could get into it, that it would resist the hardest blows from a hammer, that someday somebody would autograph it just before dropping it into a hole.

"I never saw it coming, Finley. I guess that's why it worked. He and Inge were the friendly next-door neighbors. They were just supposed to hold Mireille's hand whenever I went roaring off into the night. Except Inge got tired of our little melodramas. She always said Mireille exaggerated. If Mireille was suffering so much, why the hell didn't she just leave me or throw me out? Swedes lack the nuances, don't you think? So, Ali got to do the hand-holding on his own. He'd give Mireille an ice bag, then his dick. More than Mother Teresa could do. But Ali having his Phil Caporale side, he felt bad about all this charity work he was doing. So, of course, he had to tell me about it.

"We had dinner one night on Sayyid. Fancy Vietnamese restaurant. I got what they call obstreperous. Ali took me into the john to throw water on my face. I thought that was aggressive of him and

told him so. I took a swing at him and ended up whacking a hand
dryer. He got right in there. He'd been rehearsing for his terrorist
voiceovers more than he had to. I ended up on the goddamn floor
with his knee on my windpipe. I don't recommend that as a sexual
position. But it does help you listen, I'll say that. He was *so* con-
flicted, *so* confused. He didn't want anything that'd happened to
have happened. But what was a guy to do when he was putting an
ice cube on Mireille's beautiful swollen lips? He hoped everything
could go back to the way it had been. That I'd smarten up and see
I was destroying everything for everybody. He meant it.

"Smarten up? Me? Belly up, okay. Ante up every once in a
while. But smarten up? Who the fuck did he think he was talking to? I got out of there. I wanted to cry that night, Finley. I'm
not saying I made it, but the will was there. I walked around
Montmartre. Seemed like the perfect place to be. Everything was
a goddamn hill. I was Jesus Christ dragging my cross up and
down. Over here, ladies and gentlemen, Van Gogh! And to your
left, Stendhal's remains! And here come the Can Can dancers!
Dah-dah-de-dah-dah-de-dah! Who's that little man with the tiny
legs scampering along? Is it, could it be, the great artist Toulouse-
Lautrec himself? No, actually, it's the shit artist Neil Kinsey, cut
off at the fucking knees once again!

"Even you would've shed a tear for me, Finley. The movies
I was shooting were shit. The moll I had at home was playing
around behind my back. Even the first Seldes in my life, a suit
named Riordan, wasn't all that happy with the stuff I was passing
along to him about what Robby and Servais thought of General
Pinochet. There are times when you just can't please a goddamn
living soul. I might as well have been back in the States praying
with Jerry Falwell for the Rapture to get started.

"You make do. Mireille confirmed it all the next night. Said
it like she could barely remember it. 'Oh, yeah, Ali and I made it
while he was using a Q-Tip on the cut on the ear you gave me. Oh,
and did I also tell you I went back to the hotel with Sayyid after
the Vietnamese restaurant?' Last time I ever touched her, in any
way at all. Of course, that meant another crisis call to Emergency
Services Ali. I guess since he was Ali, he'd be the Red Crescent,

yeah? . . . Anyway, she then did something stupid, Finley. She told *him* about Sayyid. Me she could've told and I would've just used it as an excuse for what I was going to do anyway. But Ali wasn't like that. He liked people to be the way they were yesterday. He didn't want them turning into something different with the morning sun. He wanted me to be his friend who wouldn't hold anything against him for screwing Mireille. He wanted Mirielle to be his exclusive tryst, a secret from both me and Inge. He wanted himself to be the kid who'd just fallen into this little crew at the hotel along the way to a comfortable academic life. Contradictions, hypocrisies, none of that counted. The important thing was he wanted you in yesterday's box. Think that's why he wanted to teach history?

"How else to say it? He went off the deep end. Flipped. Went nuts. I guess there *are* a lot of ways to say it. A couple of nights after the restaurant scene with Sayyid, he called me. I was still in the hotel. Mireille had gone off to live with her sister for a few days. They didn't want me at the studio anymore, and I wasn't too popular at the hotel, either. When the phone rang, I was sure it was this Simone Signoret-type manager who wanted to tell me she preferred Mireille's money to mine, so make sure my bags were packed by the morning. But it wasn't her, it was Ali. He sounded like he'd just messed up assassinating the Indian prime minister and had to get back to Pakistan before the Indian Secret Service got him. I had to meet him right away, he said. Forget everything else between us. I didn't see any advantage in that, I'll tell you. I mean, he's the one fucking Mireille *and* Inge, with the job, with the hotel room, even with the satisfaction of getting me down in that john. It was easy for him to forget it all. He already had it all. But where was the profit for me in forgetting it all? . . . Sure, I went. Why the hell not? He owed me a Pernod or two for all the ways he'd proven to be a superior human being, didn't he?

"He was waiting for me at the Pont Saint-Michel. Pouring rain, not a soul on the street. When I walked up to him, he pulled his jacket around him like he was protecting some orphan from a monster. It was his camera. He was trying to keep it dry. I thought, fuck him, he could afford to buy another one, I should knock it out of his hand, break it in a hundred pieces. But then, that would've screwed up the drinks, wouldn't it?

"He started blubbering. I didn't make out much until he pointed over to Sayyid. I thought it was some trick of the rain. But sure enough, there was Sayyid sprawled out on his stomach like he'd decided to take a snooze. I'll tell you, Finley, my estimate of Phil Caporale went zooming into the clouds. He was better than Ali. Scarier, too. I didn't like the idea, on top of everything else, of having to venerate the guy, but there it was. I went around feeling sorry for myself, but old Phil, he just went to whatever he decided was the source of his problem and . . . What do the English say? *Coshed* it. He fucking coshed it, Finley!

"Banality, really. He'd gone out before the rain started—to clear his head, he said. I don't know how he could've managed that without a bulldozer, but that's what he said. How funny his feet should lead him to the hotel where Sayyid was! Would that make it premeditated in a courtroom? Do you always assume the feet operate as a co-conspirator with the mind? But Phil's no longer with us, so why fret about that nicety? The point is, Sayyid finally came out or went in or flew down from the roof or something, and Phil walked up to him and got him into a conversation. It must've been a friendly one. Why else would the Indian walk off with him? Maybe Phil was offering him the pleasures of Inge on top of Mireille. Our mutual friend wasn't too clear on that detail. Then again, I didn't ask him.

"What could he do? That's what he kept asking me in this pathetic whine. He made me feel like the most responsible guy on the street looking down at Sayyid's body. That was a novelty right there! And I rose to the occasion. I told him he couldn't do squat. I didn't know anything about dead and non-dead, but I didn't feel any pulse in Sayyid, and that part of your neck that's always throbbing, well, it wasn't doing anything. Guy felt like tepid fish. I told him he should tell the gendarmes it was an accident, something like that. I didn't know what the hell I was saying. It just seemed like the thing you say in that situation.

"Then Phil says, 'Maybe we can tell the cops we came across the body like this.' What's this *we, kemo sabe*? I'm just here because you called me. That knocked him out. He walked off a few yards, like I'd just dropped the last screen between him and reality. He was thinking of jumping in the Seine, no shit. That's why this thing a few days ago didn't completely surprise me. But fuck him. The one thing I *really* didn't need was him taking a one-way swim. Here're the two guys who've been screwing around with Mireille, both are corpses, and I'm on the scene for explaining how it all happened without me having anything to do with it. No, thanks. Not even Perry Mason saves me from the guillotine on that one. So, I prior-it-ized. Keep old Phil away from the river, remind him there was always another tomorrow and another losing lottery number. Why let a little thing like murder discourage him? A week at the outside, he'd forget the whole thing. Keep positive, that was the key.

"Damn, did he want to believe me! Looked at me like I'd done the loaves and the fishes! Started jabbering about how he'd cracked Sayyid over the head with his camera, like if he said it all to me, he wouldn't ever have to think about it again, he could get down to all that positive thinking I'd told him to concentrate on. They'd just been walking along, Phil steaming, the Indian bragging about how hot Mireille was in bed. Kaboom, cosh, and kaboom. I mean, that should've been *my* role. He's defending Mireille's honor from slimy locker room talk, but he shouldn't even be a member of the fucking club!

"What can I tell you? The guy was more of an original than I'd given him credit for. Then I had my epiphany. What greater *cinema verite* than someone you've just brained into the next world? Caporale looked at me like *I* was the whack job! To read his face, cameras are only for rapping over somebody's head! Like a century of directors had misused their invention by turning it on instead of just swinging it! Godard should've been out there crashing that Bell and Howell over the skull of the guy standing next to him on the street corner. Well, that was a little too *verite* for me. Call me a reactionary, but I thought a camera was for shooting what you got in the lens. I had to pull the thing out of his hands. He'd crowned somebody with it, but now it's like that security blanket in the comic strip. Of course, if you'd been there, you would've reminded me, because you're the kind of guy you are, that I was leaving fingerprints all over the camera. I didn't care. I needed Sayyid on film. It was the most original thing I'd ever shot. Maybe I already knew it was the most original thing I would *ever* shoot. The only other person able to shoot it was catatonic. It was up to me, and I wasn't going to blow it. A hand for Kinsey. And if you've got one of those Cannes Festival trophies, you can throw that in too!"

CHAPTER 35

He kept talking. I didn't want to hear any more. Whatever the name of the pathology in front of me, I was sure my attention to it was only making it thrive in bigger, newer directions. It was like one of the arguments at the Green Fox: Take any side around anything Miles Harkleroad or Johnny Yeager had to say and you were already making the mistake of conceding life to it. But I didn't get up and leave. The ball to keep my eye on, I reminded myself, was not Neil Kinsey or even Sayyid, whose killer was now apparently as dead as he was, it was Mireille Pouchol. She was the one who had yet to be accounted for.

"... And that was about it. I got my footage, we got out of there. They found the body the next morning. Robby called to say the studio was in a panic. But that's not why she called. Mostly, she wanted to hear my first reaction. I could feel her weighing my every word. By the time I got through flogging her with questions about the how, who, what, and where, she didn't know what to think. I was asking what anybody would've asked, but she also had to remember I was clever, so it was a mind-fuck and she hung up with a draw. People around the hotel acted the same way. It wasn't all bad, believe me. The hotel manager—she started looking at me with more respect. Begrudging, but respect. There was no way she was going to toss me out. There were only two ways I was ever going to go out her front door for the last time— because I'd found a better place to live or because the cops were dragging me off to jail.

"Inge I didn't see for a couple of days. Then I ran into her at the cafe across the street from the hotel. She was at the bar drinking coffee. I walked in, and she looked at me like some exotic animal at the zoo. It was only a second, but I could see she thought she knew. Obviously, Phil hadn't been spicing up their pillow talk with too much candor. Then she gave me this half-nod and went back to her coffee. It was up to me if I wanted to go stand next to her. Damn right I did. I wanted to see how far she could carry her I'm-not-uptight-at-the-very-sight-of-you pose. Know the first thing she said to me? She asked if I'd found 'something else.' What'd you have in mind, Inge? Somebody else I can waylay down at the river? Got any leads for me? It was funny as hell.

"Meanwhile, the cops said mugging by unidentified thugs and the prefect assured all foreigners Paris was a safe city and the usual crypt keepers wondered why Sayyid had been out in the dark rain by himself in a district Jean Genet was once known to have walked through. Servais's little troupe was told to go home while Peyrot consulted with somebody who was flying in from Delhi. Maybe there was a witness, maybe there was a suspect, maybe there was fucking Charles Laughton swinging from the bells of Notre Dame. It was wonderful. Nobody knew anything except what they'd just learned from another somebody who knew nothing.

"And you know who else knew nothing, Finley? Yours truly! I didn't drop a word about any of it to Riordan, my Embassy contact. He was fishing around, trying to sniff out what he couldn't get from the cops. *Moi?* How can I help you, Riordan? I don't know anything about that shit. My specialty is loose political talk. Want to know how many tears Robby Weiss shed because the American Ambassador to Lebanon was assassinated, I'm the guy who can tell you. But don't ask me about this Sayyid business. That's police blotter crap. Why didn't I just give him Caporale? Because I didn't want to, that's why. What am I, some bastard who betrays his best friends? . . . Okay, he was something even better than a best friend. He was *mine.* Where Phil Caporale was concerned, I was the CIA, FBI, NSA, and Mensa combined! I knew so much about him, had him under so much control, I redefined intelligence. He knew it, too. No more cracks about how I was always taking mental notes for Riordan. He belonged to me, Finley. I didn't have to blackmail him for a car or kidney transplant. I blackmailed him just by opening my eyes in the morning.

"Mireille was my big test. I was standing outside the hotel catching a smoke one afternoon when she came driving up with her sister. The sister was a fat blonde who'd never thought much of me. No accounting for taste. Mireille gets out of the passenger seat. She's still got a mouse and still looks pissed. But just like Inge, the first thing she does when she spots me is look me over like I'm some rare raccoon she didn't know had been included for the admission price. But there's a little extra thing, too. That's right! Guilt! And why not? Who else was responsible? She may not have been clear on all the details, on exactly when she'd made the mistake of opening her trap, but she was an accomplice. We must give her that, don't we?

"She wanted to ask me. She really did. But then big Sis got out from behind the wheel and told her to keep going inside for her stuff. Mireille was leaving the hotel. That sneaked up on me worse than Sayyid. What was I counting on? Getting back with her? Yeah, I suppose. The next 15 minutes lasted forever. I got tired of matching glares over the roof of the car with Sis and walked around the block. All the way around, I didn't know whether I wanted to find the car still there when I got back or not. Whatever I wanted, it wasn't there. Mireille was gone. She'd just grabbed a few things and told the manager she'd be back to settle up. When I got back to the entrance, the empty space there seemed to be for a lot more than a VW.

"I never really talked to her again until she called Minneapolis. Once she came by the hotel to pick up Inge and Caporale for a farewell dinner at Reynaud-Grevin. They didn't admit that, that would've been too awkward. 'Oh, we're just going to Jean-Claude's house,' Inge says. Subliminal message: And of course, you can't be expected to be invited *there*. Mireille stayed in the car, didn't come in. Since it was her sister's VW, I assumed she was still living there. A few weeks later, I saw her in a Metro station. She didn't see me. She looked really good. Got a full 10 from me on the Pang Meter. She got into the train, and I waited for the next one. I wasn't up for pain-and-ache talk that'd be cut off because one of us had to get off at our stop. As the train was pulling out, I imagined her mingling with a whole car of strangers, passing on to them the information I'd killed Sayyid in jealousy over her. I was a goddamn contagious disease, Finley! By the time she and the others got through spreading their assumptions around, all Paris would know I'd killed Sayyid!

"Now our friend Phil, that was really special. Outside a couple of times when I caught him giving me an extra look, he was Mr. Normalissimo. Some days he'd ask me if I'd lined up another job, sometimes he was in too much of a hurry to say anything at all. Then comes the big announcement one morning in the breakfast nook that he's going back to New York. The dubbing work is over, so there's nothing to keep him in Paris. I'm looking at him and I'm thinking, 'Yeah? And what else? Like how about for starters, where's that special movie I shot?' I catch him later at the front desk. He doesn't even want to hear the name Sayyid coming out of my mouth. Cuts me off right away, says he'll drop off the film— THE FILM, code in case the hotel cat's eavesdropping—as soon as he separates it from his stuff on the reel. And then he's off to check on his plane tickets or something. It wasn't just the Sayyid footage, either. He'd been promising forever to bring me the reel cans I'd left at the studio. No sweat, babe. Hey, all taken care of. Consider it done.

"Next morning I go down to the desk and find out he's already taken off for the airport! I ask Simone Signoret if he's left any package for me. She gives me this sad look like how at my age can I still expect anybody in the civilized world ever to leave anything for me? I go tear-assing upstairs to Inge. She's what you'd call melancholy. The bloom's long off the rose with Phil, but it's still the end of an era. No, he didn't leave anything for me. Would I mind leaving her alone? I stood there in the hallway listening to her sniffling for a few minutes. I wanted to strangle that son of a bitch Caporale. Then Robby comes up. She knows all about Phil leaving. I think the President of France knew about it! She wants to give Inge a shoulder to cry on. I ask her could she do me a favor, could she go down to the studio at some point and pick up my reels? She looks at me like I have two heads. All that stuff was cleared out days ago. She herself saw Phil wrapping it all up to be sent to New York. Not his stuff, I say, my stuff. That's funny, she says, meaning it's anything but funny. She'd asked Phil if we were going to hook up in New York because he was wrapping up my stuff, too. She hadn't realized I had plans to go to New York.

"It took me awhile to figure out why he'd grabbed my things, too. He was thinking ahead, that's why. If he ever got into a tight spot about our collected works, he wouldn't have to explain why the piece with Sayyid was the only one I was supposed to have shot. Throw everything together, and who remembered when I used his camera or he used mine? So much for having Phil Caporale under control.

"Anyway, that was it for almost two years. I bounced around. Nobody ever heard about Sayyid again. Until one night out in Chicago I got into this housecleaning frenzy. Too many garbage cans in my life with most of the garbage laying on the floor next to them because I was too lazy to aim. I wrote to Caporale, asked him for the films. I was a little surprised he even bothered to answer. But he did. Sorry you've been hoping all these years, Neil, but they were destroyed in a fire. My stuff, your stuff—all kaput. And when you think about it, it's probably just as well since anybody seeing some of it could come to a lot of false conclusions about some of the things you were up to in Paris. Nothing right out explicit, but it was there between every line. That footage was the evidence *I'd* been the one to kill Sayyid. I mean, it sure wasn't *his* hand trying to reposition the body. And *he* sure wasn't the one who got into snarling with Sayyid at the Vietnamese restaurant. And it wasn't *his* girlfriend who made it with Sayyid. Talk about positive thinking!

"There were whole minutes every year I actually believed the fire story. But what could I do about it? Our friend Phil was pretty snarly. You should be proud he chose to hire you instead of somebody else. What he was telling me, of course, was that I should have *wanted* to believe in a fire. I should have *wanted* to erase that whole part of my past with him. Getting right down to it, maybe I should have *wanted* less of my existence all around since it sure had been wasting a lot of oxygen without giving back much in return. Ruthless outlook, wouldn't you say? It makes me sorry I didn't sit in on one of his classes. But what he hadn't counted on was I could be just as perverse as he was, that I could get off on the others thinking naughty things about me.

"That's where it all was when Mireille called. She didn't know what to say after I told her I hadn't killed Sayyid and I hadn't gone around bragging I did. She thought she'd had it all in one package. And what I was telling her was, no, dear, you're going to have to go elsewhere for both your questions. I didn't tell her the truth about Caporale. She'd been believing what she'd been believing for so long. Suddenly I'm going to let her think of her Lancelot as having done Sayyid, too? No, thanks. I still had a little pride. I wanted her to keep at least one fond memory of me. See? Arthur or Modred, I guess I'll always be a romantic."

"Why you telling me all this?"

"You're helping me with my bill here."

"Why, Kinsey?"

"You thought I was a shit before you even met me. You're not entitled to that point of view, Finley. I've worked hard at who I am. Come back tomorrow and I'll tell you all about JABPUN. You'll be proud of what we've been doing to keep you safe in your bed every night."

CHAPTER 36

I belonged to the rain walking from the hospital to the garage, to my clammy pants driving home. Wannabe movie directors waterskied ahead of me along the Belt Parkway. Back in the apartment, I took a shower at sauna degrees, then finished a bottle of San Pellegrino's purest in two gulps. All I was missing was Helen Reddy belting out "I Am Water."

I owed the Professor a call, so I phoned Dana instead. She wanted to relay a message from Olmos, but I didn't want more third-party bulletins. I cut her off to say I'd liked that veal piccata at Da Francesco and wouldn't mind doing it again that night. Would she be pleased to consider it a date? Good, because that was what I was proposing. "What's the matter?" she asked, not sounding half as flattered as I'd hoped.

"I need to see human beings. Please tell me you're not just wearing a latex mask over some kind of Casper the Ghost head."

She laughed; suspiciously, but still laughed.

I still owed the Professor a call, so called Olmos instead. The woman who answered had heard of me and seemed to be speaking for all of Midtown South in expelling air at a volume of pained tolerance. She said she'd be sure to tell Olmos I called, making it sound as though he could return any year soon. I told myself I no longer owed the Professor a call, at least until Olmos got back to me. If I had to talk to the old man about Neil Kinsey, I was going to give it to him in one shot, and that meant first hearing from Olmos there was absolutely no way Caporale could have taken a break from his Philadelphia conference to shoot up to New York to drop in on Pouchol at the Milford Plaza.

I tried to busy myself in the doings of Walter Ochs, the vet who had apparently been supplying a dog mill. The American Veterinary Association said he was a member in good standing, but the American Veterinary Medical Law Association agreed his fatality rate was "exceptionally high." A desk sergeant at Ochs's precinct wanted to know who was so interested in the number of complaints filed against him and wasn't impressed when I told him. By then, I wasn't, either. It started with a vague sensation I wasn't alone in the apartment, that whoever was operating a sanding machine on the floor over my head was annoying somebody besides me. While the Vet Law guy was measuring out percentages in my ear, I realized where the feeling came from—my burglars. The apartment had been violated, and I still hadn't dealt with it. I hadn't even bothered with a police report. Why? Because nobody gave a damn about 25-year-old home movies? Because I'd already turned the things over to Olmos?

I didn't like those answers. I got up from my desk and opened every window in the place into the spitting rain. Feeling chilled and surrounded was better than feeling infested. From the bedroom to the living room to the bathroom to the kitchen, I ushered every burglar spirit out into the noon air. Some of them looked like Seldes and Cicut, others like Kinsey and Caporale, still others like Mireille Pouchol and Robby Klein, whom I'd never seen except on a 25-year-old movie. And why stop there? Cynthia, Miles Harkleroad, and Johnny Yeager—they followed. And there went the vet Walter Ochs, the Klaus clan, and Sarah Harrah—wafting out into the gray, losing their traction in the ether, and dropping down into the street. Finally, there were even Joe Carroll, Jenny, and Susan—all caught up in the suction and dragged outside. I waited an extra five minutes in case there was someone lurking from school days or the Police Academy or the job on Long Island, then went around closing the windows again. Then I flopped down on the couch and took a nap.

CHAPTER 37

I had forgotten my Trilbys. They went out Dana's bedroom window. She watched me watch after them. They had none of her strawberry sweat scent, were too transparent to hold the street lamp as she did in the center of her eyes. They left nothing, reflected nothing. "But that doesn't make it any easier to let them go."

"No," she agreed. "And maybe you shouldn't be in such a hurry to send them on their way. You might need them again."

"Thank you."

"No problem."

Olmos had said she had tall eyes; what she also had was a top lip that seemed to hold all the ironies and glibness while the lower one waited for more direct things. I didn't want to lose either one, and kissing her felt like the only way to bring her completely together.

"Why'd you do that?"

"Seemed like a good idea."

She nodded, then immediately looked as if she regretted it. "Slow, right? We don't take out a nightly subscription to Da Francesco."

"I couldn't afford it."

"What I'm saying. Either can I right now."

"If we were pirates, you'd have me signing articles of spoils."

"Take the honor where you find it."

"Yes, Ma'am."

"Nostalgia's right in there with booze, gambling, and shopping. It can be an addictive substance. It holds out a promise of security. But what it really does . . ."

I knew that one. "Tempts you with less."

"Correct, sir. I want orange juice. Want some orange juice?"

I wanted an orange juice, I wanted to see her get up and pad naked out into the kitchen, and I wanted to believe I was more than 24 hours better than I had been the same time a day before. The only thing that felt in the way of all these gifts was her relayed message from Olmos that Caporale's time in Philadelphia had been locked in practically to the hour. Somebody out there was still mocking my striving for moral renewal.

She came back with two glasses that looked like they each held a container of juice. "All the burglars gone?"

"Except one."

"It's not your job," she said, standing a pillow against the headboard. "Alex is having a tough enough time believing it's his."

"Screw Alex. He's just pissed because he got a breeze from the foul wind known as Neil Kinsey."

"No, what he's pissed at is having his squad detoured for a couple of days. Not counting all the time for screening those movies."

"Ah, gee! I guess Midtown South's just used to being handed possible leads and following them straight to a happy ending."

"He's just stressed. You know that."

I remembered what Olmos had said to me standing outside Servais's building. "But not *that* much. He said it himself. The French haven't been bugging him the way governments usually do when something lousy happens to one of their nationals."

"Maybe he's got a good boss who keeps that stuff out of his Inbox."

"That would be a first."

"What're you saying—this diplomat Servais?" I hadn't realized I was saying anything. "Any day now we'll hear about him being called home pending some new assignment?"

I still didn't like it. "It's occurred to me and it's not bad. He'd have a lot to lose, maybe more than anybody, by having the Sayyid business blow up after all this time. But how does killing Pouchol keep the lid on that? The cat was already peeking out of the bag. She was here trying to find out who loosened the strings. Kinsey confirmed that much."

"If you believe him."

"I never believed anybody so much in my life. Kinsey doesn't lie, he makes the truth a lie."

She observed me patiently. "I'd want more," she said, taking a big swallow. "Servais explains why the French have stayed low-key."

"Servais just doesn't scan, Dana. He lets himself get talked into playing host to Kinsey, and that sure as hell isn't going to do much for his career. He makes an embarrassing show of coming on to Robby Klein at some opening. He tells me some oafish lie about not knowing who Pouchol was until days after her body was discovered, acts like he doesn't know who this Jobert is. It's all too out there."

"So the French need better diplomats."

"No, I'll bet he's Mister Subtlety most of the time—when it has nothing to do with the Reynaud-Grevin dubbing days. But that period was different for him. I could hear it the first time he talked about it. Telling these Americans and Scandinavians how to curse the Indians and Pakistanis through their headsets was a highlight of his life. I'd bet you in some ways he's been Kinsey's greatest triumph for a bad conscience. But just like Kinsey, he's all in the past. And Mireille Pouchol, the reason she was killed, has to do with the here and now."

She slid her foot up and down the back of my calf. "Sure you're not just trying to keep the rest of the world up to your speed?" she smiled.

As nice thoughts went, it ranked up there. Right next to the two small folds setting off her belly button.

CHAPTER 38

I invited the Professor to lunch before and after passing along Kinsey's tale. The before invitation got me a clipped "That bad, heh?" the after one a "I'm not all that hungry right now." The in-between was a lot of silence in my ear. Then I made the mistake of trying to sign off on some neutral note. "How's Mr. Fix-It in the workshop going?"

"Sometimes being a wiseass isn't all that funny, Finley. Thanks for the information."

I pondered that one until even the receiver in my hand asked to return to its cradle. In the old man's place, what would I have told Florence Caporale? The quickest answer was nothing. There was no certainty anything about Sayyid would ever come out or that, even if it did, it would come out the way Kinsey had told it. For all anybody knew, it would take just another few million euro from Visiv to persuade Reynaud-Grevin to sell out amicably, making all the blackmail and defensiveness over Sayyid, threatened or imagined, academic. Why chip away at the widow's memories of Caporale when nobody else figured to? Joe Carroll's disillusionments over his disciple didn't have to be Florence's. Would the old man see that?

Just as I was deciding he would, the doorbell rang; not the downstairs bell, but the floor bell. I wouldn't have been too hot on that even if I'd had a client scheduled to drop by. Visitors were always supposed to give you time to hide the grass, porno mags, or week-old peach pits—that was why they made downstairs bells. Since nobody was due by, my first unpleasant thought ran to the

Brows brothers, who must have known by now about the photos I'd sent the Canarsie lawyer. My .38 was still in my bureau, but I felt closer to it as I went to the peephole.

"Trick or treat," Olmos said.

He liked seeing my surprise, but made a half-hearted effort to hide it as he strolled in. "Now I know the decor for a fashionable PI," he said, glancing around. "Looks like my uncle Felix's living room. He could never figure out what furniture was for, either."

"I know! You've come all the way out here to tell me you're not holding Kinsey anymore."

"No. I've come all the way out here to tell you St. Clare's isn't holding him anymore. Got a beer?"

He didn't waste my lead-legged trip to the refrigerator. When I came back with the last two bottles I kept for clients, I found him swinging lazily on my desk chair and surveying the tabs on the folders strewn all around. "A vet? Let me guess. Some pit bull has bitten a four-year-old and your job is to find out if the four-year-old and her parents have been working this con against other pit bull owners."

"You got it. How did he get out of the hospital? Last time I saw him, he couldn't stand up."

"He didn't have to. An ambulance drove up, some very able looking people wheeled him into it, and drove off with him."

"Seldes?" His shrug and sip from the bottle were supposed to mean something. "Well, what do you care? You didn't want him for anything."

"He told you the Caporale-Sayyid story? That what all those sessions in his room were about?"

I was sorry I'd opened the second bottle; his edginess was even less sociable than his impatience outside Servais's building. "Okay, so you kept your eye on him after you sent him on his way. You didn't help him very much with that driver." Another shrug. "And goodbye to all that."

"You believe his story about Caporale?"

"As a matter of fact. You haven't done anything about it?"

He thought that was funny in a weary way. "I had my intentions. At least to alert the Indians and French they could stamp their files CLOSED or MAYBE CLOSED. But that all depended on our favorite movie, didn't it? And when I went to take another peek at it, it wasn't where it should have been. Before they picked up Kinsey, they picked up the reels. Federal warrant. That annoyed me, Finley."

"I don't care about Kinsey anymore, Alex. He's told me all he's ever going to tell me."

He didn't doubt it—or think it relevant. "I didn't come here to drink your beer. We've got to take a ride. How's that for Jimmy Cagney?"

"Where?"

"Over to see Seldes. I don't like it any more than you do, but they're my orders. I show up with you, we listen for a few minutes, and I walk out with the name of Pouchol's killer."

"Just like that."

"They want guarantees you stop rolling around the deck like a drunken sailor. My people want Pouchol wrapped up and they swallowed all the thorns before calling me in. I'm just a good soldier and I'm recruiting you to be one."

Sometimes I could really appreciate my *Calm* print. The hotter the seething, the more important to call it the opposite. "And you'll just accept whatever name they give you."

"I said I'd listen to whatever they had to say. If they've got the evidence and can convince . . ."

"Let's save ourselves the trip. How about Phil Caporale? They've got pictures of him climbing out his hotel window in Philadelphia and renting a car to get to New York."

"Beats Kinsey, right?"

"Go without me."

"I can't. You're part of the deal. You don't want to hear about Kinsey anymore? Well, they don't want to hear about you anymore, either, and they want to make that official in front of me. The old political woodshed. In and out and it's over. You wanted to do me a favor, do this one."

"I don't like the personal payback tone."

"Not intended. Sorry. Kinsey looked good to me, too."

"Now who does?"

"Let's listen first, okay? Want to shove off?"

He didn't leave me much choice. But then I did something so paranoid and obvious while getting my jacket I was surprised that he waited until he was pulling away from the curb to smile at it. "Who you think you're going to need that against?"

The Smith & Wesson felt heavy in my jacket pocket, but then so did the feeling that I couldn't automatically exclude him from the list. "I have an appointment later."

"Oh, yeah. Those pit bulls."

The ride down to the Battery Tunnel took a year and a day, and he didn't force the conversation. Only when we came up out into Manhattan did he say: "So you really believe Kinsey's story?"

"So do you or you wouldn't have let him go."

"Not having the evidence to hold him isn't the same thing."

"So we'll pretend it is."

"I felt like fumigating myself after talking to him."

"Don't say it too loud. He'll hear you and be happy."

Another block of silence. "I don't think they're going to try to hand us Caporale."

"It's the Frenchman. Foreigner and all that."

"More likely," he nodded. "And they'll wrap that up by saying it's Federal jurisdiction, they'll handle it. 'Thanks, Sergeant. We must do this cooperation thing again real soon.'"

"Dana thinks your bosses have been running interference for you with the State Department and that crowd."

"She drinking a lot lately?"

"What I said. But the fact remains . . ."

Clearly, he had already been over that ground. "Servais doesn't have that kind of clout. He's a 50-something playing out the string at the UN. If I had to worry more about him or French papers screaming the government isn't doing enough for Pouchol, I'd worry more about the papers."

"Well, *something* seems to have slowed down all the usual diplomatic notes to the State Department."

"You get that feeling, don't you?"

His tight smile made me think of the Professor's outburst about wiseasses not always being funny. The old man had a point.

CHAPTER 39

Seldes was waiting in front of the fourth-floor elevator, this time in a
green turtleneck that matched the color of the triangle hanging
in the Klein living room. He couldn't have been brisker leading
the way past the bullpen cubbyholes to his office; there were a
few more voices coming from the headsets in the work areas and
nobody at all clack-clacking. Cicut and an olive-skinned woman
with bangs introduced as "Mary" were already standing at the
Seventh Avenue window; they seemed to need only togas to be
Coliseum fans eager to see how long we'd last against the lions.

"Okay, we all want to get paper off our desks, so let's cut
right to the chase," Seldes said, going behind his desk and not
caring who took the single visitors chair. "We've had a situation
here that's generated too many costly surveillances and time-
consuming memos and that, unfortunately, has lapped over and
doubtlessly complicated your investigation, Sergeant. The good
news, though, is that our crossed paths have allowed us to gain
information I think is relevant to your case."

Olmos muttered something, but didn't move for the chair, so I
did. Seldes seemed to have expected both of us to keep standing
at attention. "And why is it so important I'm here?"

"Because there are also national security concerns here," he
said, recovering, "and I don't want it said later you didn't understand the big picture. All of us in this room will be able to attest
you didn't leave until you understood perfectly."

"Like the warning on Marlboros. Ignorance won't be a defense."

"More consequential than that, actually."

"In other words, you're giving the police Servais."

"Finley . . ."

"It's all right, Sergeant. Animals scent trees, Mr. Finley likes scenting wherever he is, too."

"It took me a while to get your smell out of my apartment."

Every time I was with Seldes or Cicut, I seemed to get the most profound look of admiration; or contempt, whatever it was. "I think it would be your final obligation to your client, Mr. Finley, to accept the results of what we've turned up. For his sake and that of his widow, most of all. There's no need to bring in 25-year-old events or his tragic response to them when they threatened to be revealed. We should all be able to agree that the only important detail from what happened in Paris is the intimacy Mireille Pouchol enjoyed with the prime suspect."

"Where'd you get that from?"

"Where do you imagine?"

"If that's supposed to mean Kinsey, try again. He's too indebted to his Lancelot to believe she was sleeping with Servais."

He made a bad effort at looking bewildered and having to settle for Story B. "Did I say Kinsey? I was referring to other information sources. Servais and Pouchol continued working at Reynaud-Grevin at close quarters long after he broke up with the future Mrs. Klein. We have films indicating a *ménage à trois* relationship with them and Klein. We have other evidence he never quite outgrew that triangular infatuation. Among other things, he apparently made a fool of himself at some art show of Klein's and had to be asked to leave. We have phone records indicating Pouchol called the French Consulate the very day she was killed. We have testimony from hotel personnel that somebody with flawed English and answering Servais's description went up to Pouchol's room shortly before she was killed. We have collaboration from Servais's doorman that he returned home that evening looking the worse for wear. I'd like to say we also have recordings of what took place in Pouchol's room, but we don't. But given the murder weapon and other circumstances, the inescapable conclusion is that there was an argument, perhaps about relighting old romantic candles, Servais lost his head, and . . . did what he did."

It took me a second to realize I was mainly disappointed by the lack of subtlety. *Flawed English?* Servais spoke more fluently than Seldes! After listening to Miles Harkleroad at the Green Fox so long, I suppose I'd come to expect finer things from people not named Miles Harkleroad.

"So where's the national security?" Olmos piped up. "You're giving me a spat between old lovers."

Seldes was at the hard part. "As a matter of fact, Sergeant," he said, clearing his throat and playing nervously with a pen, "all I'm giving you, all I'm empowered to give you, is deep background. We've already filed papers requesting the lifting of Servais's diplomatic immunity so he can be prosecuted under our laws. But I wouldn't be candid with you if I didn't admit we view that only as an opening gambit. Honestly, we don't give a rat's ass about Jean-Claude Servais. What we care much more about is the French owing us one."

"And suppose the French don't give a rat's ass about him, either?"

"Then we proceed normally, and Servais will be tried for murder. It's a win-win situation."

I thought Olmos was wasting all his jaw flexing. Giddy toon creatures should have been parading around the room. What we were listening to wouldn't even have been enough for a kangaroo court. "So if you had your druthers, you'd really prefer the French not giving him up."

"I don't make policy, Sergeant."

"But if you did . . ."

"We try to steer clear of hypotheticals."

"But if you did . . ."

"If it makes you happy, I'd take the long view, yes. Our relations with certain countries lately need every edge we can find."

"And even if that got spoiled, if you had to go trial . . ."

"This really isn't productive, Sergeant," Cicut put in from the window. Mary immediately shook her head in agreement.

"Even if you had to go to trial . . ."

Seldes raised his hand to the two at the window as though reassuring the keepers with the nets there was no immediate danger. That seemed worth another laugh until I looked back at Olmos again: His eyes had shrunk to brown dots.

"Yes, there would probably be jurisdiction questions," Seldes said.

"I don't see how. It happened in a hotel, not in some embassy."

"We're really getting ahead of ourselves, don't you think, Sergeant?"

"Oh, right. First we're just going to try to nail this on Servais for national security reasons. Whisk him out of the country after midnight. And then what? We get the Eiffel Tower back in exchange?"

I was starting to agree with Seldes: Nothing was going the way it should have gone. If anybody should have been acting like Olmos, it ought to have been me. And I would have been the first to swear—as recently as coming up on the elevator—that Olmos had resigned himself to the bullshit he was about to hear, that he had learned to play the game.

"Well, guess what?" he said, jutting his face across the desk. "It's not going to play out that way. A, because it's our case. B, because I've yet to see the evidence chain for what you're talking about. C, because Servais is just a little bit too easy for my taste."

Seldes sat frozen, but Mary grabbed a file folder from the window sill behind her and quickly shoved it into Olmos's chest. "Then maybe you better look at this before you compromise your position further."

Olmos let the folder fall into his hand, seemed to wonder where she had come from, and nodded reluctantly. As he walked over to the window with the folder, Cicut cut a nimble angle to get out of his way and Seldes seemed to restart his lungs without losing his rigid position. "Temperamental," Dana had said about as passingly as you could say it. It would have been nice to remember she had been just as offhand about saying she loved and adored me more than anybody else she had ever met, but I couldn't quite recall that.

"Where's Kinsey?" I asked, to ease the quiet. "You people went to an awful lot of trouble for a free-lancer."

"Getting better," Cicut volunteered tightly.

"So I can look forward to seeing him on Diane Sawyer?"

Seldes kept his eyes glued on Olmos at the window. "Nothing final has been decided," Cicut said dully.

"At least more JABPUN, for Christ sake."

"If that's deemed a priority."

"Right. Main thing is, keep him busy. You don't come across mental gifts like that every day of the week."

Seldes didn't even realize we were ping-ponging around him, he was so intent on watching Olmos. For someone who had started off announcing a *fait accompli*, he suddenly looked unsure of himself. I didn't like that in bureaucrats. It usually meant they were waiting for you to supply the coffin as well as the rope for the hanging.

Olmos finally read the last notation. I thought I was ready for all the possibilities—a shrug that Seldes had made his case at least superficially, a cynical non-commitment, even a ringing "Bullshit!" The one I'd overlooked was Olmos Frisbeeing the file across the room at Seldes, Mary and Cicut making belated reaches for it, and Seldes turning scarlet as it fell just short of him. "I don't think so."

"This meeting is over."

Maybe if Cicut hadn't said it so belligerently and maybe if he hadn't thrust himself up against Olmos as some kind of human shield for Seldes, it might very well have been. But the physical move was too much. Olmos's hard fingers into Cicut's breastplate sent him stumbling back a few steps, where he crossed his feet clumsily and started flailing to regain his balance. Seldes jumped up from his chair as Cicut helplessly splattered the photos and everything else around the desk and on to the floor. None of it should have been happening, I told myself; what shouldn't have been happening was that I was on the wrong team in jumping up to grab Olmos from behind. It was like trying to pin a moving rock, and I almost yanked a couple of fingers out of their sockets trying to lace them behind his bull head. Mary still wasn't encouraged. She ran to the door for stronger arms to come to the rescue.

The pressure eased only when he remembered I wasn't his chief enemy of the moment.

"You pull this shit in Washington or Dallas, Seldes! You don't do it here! You don't do it on one of my cases!"

Seldes had regained some of his nerve on his feet. "I seriously doubt it's going to be yours much longer, Sergeant."

"Then a lot of people are going to know why, aren't they?"

"Cool it, Alex."

"No, I wouldn't expect so," Seldes said, becoming more imperturbable by the second. "I'm sure you'll be given your instructions. Goodbye, Sergeant. Pleasure working with you."

I gave that snide crack another few seconds to settle before loosening my hold. Mary's distress call had brought a skyline of heights jammed into the doorway—tall ones, small ones, fat ones, skinny ones. They all looked relieved to be able to step out of the way as I nudged Olmos through them. Mary looked at both of us severely. The good part was that at least I'd gotten a look at one of the photos on the desk after it had tumbled to the floor: not mating aardvarks at all, but two gawky teenage boys waiting for Dad to put down the camera so they could go back to shooting hoops. If the gods were kind, I thought, the kids would soon open a major coke ring in the garage behind them.

CHAPTER 40

Why hadn't I seen it coming? There seemed to be a lot of reasons. I hadn't taken Dana all that seriously. I'd taken Olmos for a professional who wouldn't jeopardize his job. I didn't know him. Etcetera, etcetera. And somewhere in there, too, was the importance of turf wars only for those directly involved in them. Maybe I'd just been away from the job too long. Maybe I'd become as indifferent to other people's territorial problems as Caporale, Kinsey, and the others had once been to those of Indians and Pakistanis; at best, they were for entertainment and a paycheck. For sure, I was out of condition. At least Cicut and Mary had been spry enough to reach for the whizzing file folder. The damn thing could have decapitated me before I'd woken up to not being the only martyr on the scene.

"Look at the bright side," I told Olmos in the car. "You not only predicted they'd go for Servais, you were right about them thanking you for your cooperation."

He kept kneading the steering wheel until his knuckles were white. "Know what the last line on that report was? 'The chief investigator for the New York Police Department, Sergeant Alex Olmos, has probably impeded the investigation with erratic personal behavioral traits that have been a source of disciplinary action in the past.'" He smiled at me bleakly. "They played me, Finley. That's the only line they wanted me to read, so I'd do what I did. They didn't want you there so you could be put on notice with me as a witness, they wanted you there as a witness for what *I* did!"

"For what? The case was already out of your hands."

"Was it?"

"Okay, so you've put a bow on their package. It would've ended up that way anyway. Now your captain has one less argument when the State Department calls to tell him the lay of the land."

He shook his head, stared down the street a moment, then shook it again. "I just don't feel the usual drill here," he said. "Look out the window. They could be selling storm windows out of that office."

I looked at the same dowdy building I'd been unimpressed by the first visit. "They're not Feds?"

"Oh, they're Feds, all right. That much I checked. But why do you move them out of headquarters altogether? Can't they be doing their special bag jobs for Homeland Security in the west wing of the 14th floor behind some broom closet at Federal Plaza?"

I knew where he was going, but still didn't know the name of the destination. "Distance."

"Deniable distance," he nodded. "We're not talking about affairs of state here, Finley. We're talking about the telephone companies opening their little Mom and Pop stores to sell beepers. We're talking big subsidized business. We're talking about this Visiv outfit."

"That's a helluva leap. Visiv's in Europe."

"Not altogether it isn't. It's got a couple of TV stations in New England, a newspaper in Ohio, a few other things scattered around. But even if it was, so what? Where's Europe? Between Saturn and Jupiter?"

"Somebody's been doing a little homework."

"Yeah, but now the dog's eaten it." He laughed bitterly at the sight of a woman several cars down shrieking as the bottom of her supermarket bag gave out and groceries tumbled onto the sidewalk. "There you go! Welcome to the club, lady."

"So what're you going to do?"

"If I'm lucky, I'll turn my attention to the gripping adventures of Jose Paradiso, a dealer blown away on Tenth Avenue last night. If I'm not, I'm going to blow the Christmas vacation I put in for sitting around the house watching television and waiting for the

kids to come home from school. You must know daytime TV. Anything good on?"

"And they'd be interested in Visiv because . . .?"

"Who the fuck knows! Maybe the Attorney-General's on the
board of directors. Or Visiv was an election contributor to the
genius in the White House. Or Visiv and ESPN have a deal to
bring Major League Baseball to the Congo every Tuesday night.
What difference does it make? But that's the ballpark, Finley. I'd
bet the house on it. They move against Servais, they don't move
against him—who knows? With the kind of shit 'evidence' they
were shoveling at us; my guess is you can call him at his apartment two weeks from now and he'll answer the phone. He may
never get to hear word one about any of this. That's not what it
was about today. It was about laughing the competition off the
field. Pouchol? She's just somebody who stumbled in front of our
global village bus. Fuck it. Run right over her."

When he dropped me off at the subway, I made the same mistake I'd made with the Professor earlier: I thought it was important to say something. "For what it's worth, I'll deny whatever
they claim."

He couldn't manage more than a snicker. "You better straight-
en that out first with whatever camera or recorder they had going
in there."

It was another reminder of how many steps I'd lost and it
discouraged wallowing in my usual reflections on the R train on
the way home. The .38 in my pocket felt like an unused umbrella
at the end of a relentlessly sunny day. I couldn't even move it
to some place more comfortable without raising an alarm in the
subway car. I'd been prepared, just not for the right things.

CHAPTER 41

Olmos was right about Servais. After a week of nothing in the papers about Pouchol except a passing reference in a *Times* Op-ed piece about big city violence, I called the French Consulate to see who had taken over his desk. Per the switchboard operator, Jean-Claude Servais's replacement just happened to have the exact same name and would I please hold on while she transferred me to him. No, I wouldn't.

I also let another Wednesday slide by without going to the Professor's soiree. I could have cooked my first steak for Dana as easily on Thursday as Wednesday, or even taken her to Garden City with me, but I liked him thinking I was sulking as much as I was afraid he still was. It seemed a better solution all around to sit on the couch with Dana and laugh like know-it-alls at Peter Falk reruns.

"You know why *Columbo*'s bullshit, right?"

"Tell me."

"Because his logic is great, but what starts it ticking in the first place? Intuitions he couldn't possibly have because he wasn't around when we saw what the killer did. *We're* the ones giving him credibility. We know why the killer emptied out the ashtray, but there's no reason in hell he should be looking at the ashtray and rubbing his chin. We give him the benefit of the doubt by assuming he knows as much as us."

"Gee, Finley. You should be a detective."

It was the second-best idea of the night. I was still considering it listening to Dana breathing in her sleep. The Chelsea Follies, it dawned on me, had included one skit too many—the one where Seldes had added Servais's bad behavior at Robby Klein's art show to the so-called evidence against the Frenchman. Where had *that* come from? According to Jake Klein, only his daughter had been home when Seldes had visited Hoboken, and that was hardly something she would have shared with strangers, even if she had known about it. Had Seldes been back to New Jersey since? It seemed like a detail Lieutenant Columbo would have nailed down before he gave over the rest of his life to the Brows brothers and killer mastiffs.

CHAPTER 42

FIND THE FUCK, FINLEY.

As spam went, it didn't exactly have me rushing for my credit card. What could you buy at the Madison, Wisconsin Public Library, anyway? Still, it got my attention more than the cyber casino ads and come-ons to Florida that usually greeted me when I checked in with my e-mail every day or so. And it was gratifying to know Neil Kinsey was back in the Midwest liking his sense of alliteration and probably also liking the way he had sneaked a message through his keepers to me.

The rest of it was harder. He might have truly still felt something for his Guinevere or he might have just liked spitting in the Servais gruel Seldes had whipped up. I didn't have a clue. What I did have, on the other hand, per my latest bank statement, was the check he had never canceled after his health plan or Seldes had taken care of the hospital bill. In other words, what I had, if I wanted it, was not Phil Caporale or the Professor, but Neil Kinsey, as a client.

I wanted it.

At least for a couple of calls.

I figured the late afternoon was a good time to catch a teacher who lived only a couple of blocks away from where he taught. I was half-right. Jake Klein was home, but it was one of the girls I'd wanted to avoid who answered. She sounded lively and polite, didn't declare NOT in every sentence the way I sometimes imagined Susan growing up to say. By the time she passed the phone to her father, I'd decided we could have had very reasonable conversations about the grungy tattoo artists she was hanging around with instead of studying for her SATs.

Klein was less lively, but also polite. He hadn't expected to hear my voice again and had liked it that way, but he also had to say he was interested when I told him I wanted to update him on what I'd discovered about Pouchol's killing. I gave him something about Visiv being involved in some way; he said "Really?" I told him both Caporale and Kinsey had been contacted the way Robby had, but neither had been particularly helpful; he said he was sorry about that. Had I talked to Inge, he wondered, mainly to keep up a second end to the conversation. I told him she was next, then sprang my question.

"Why would they come back again?" he asked predictably.

"I don't know. In case they wanted to talk to you instead of your daughters. You weren't there the first time, right?"

"I saw this Sergeant . . ."

"No, not Olmos. The second visit."

His reasonableness had limits. "I told you," he said, more strained, "only Rachel was here that day and she finally had to ask them to leave."

"That's what I thought. Yeah, okay."

"Why's this so important?"

"I'm not sure it is. Just something somebody said."

"What? What did they say?"

"It was a reference to that scene Servais made at Robby's art show. I couldn't imagine your daughters mentioning that."

There was the briefest pause, as though he were looking around to make sure the girl who'd answered the phone wasn't eavesdropping. "No, either can I. And I don't remember any cops at the exhibition. If you think it'd be helpful, I suppose the gallery has a guestbook . . ."

"No, no, that won't be necessary. I just couldn't figure out . . . never mind. I guess I'm just clutching at straws."

"Yeah. That I can understand. And I appreciate your calling."

He didn't, but I liked him for saying it. More to the point, though, if Seldes hadn't made a second visit to Hoboken, that raised Inge Matson to the top of the list as the source for the art show story. The trouble with that was I couldn't picture her hearing I was calling and immediately clearing her office so she could talk to her good friend Finley. In fact, the only thing I could picture was her shouting something like "Tell him I'm dead!"

I let it ride for a couple of days. I didn't have to invent things to keep occupied. Within three hours I picked up jobs for background checks on two juries, one in Brooklyn and one in Queens, and a third assignment for locating a husband who had skipped alimony and child support payments. Then there were the Brows brothers and Walter Ochs, miraculous healer of dead animals. I was feeling pretty good about all this action when I dropped in for an afternoon coffee at Roger's candy store—or, as an old sign on the window advertised it, HOT MEALS AND TOYS. Roger was an Indian from Guyana who had been adding about a thousand gray hairs and a forehead wrinkle a day since he'd taken over the store two years before. His first few weeks behind the counter, he had acted as if he had taken personal possession of the American Dream. Everybody had gotten a smile, extra books of matches had been thrown in with the cigars and cigarettes, lottery players had received a hearty "Good Luck to you!" The road from there to a constant grouch had been a little painful to watch, running through too many losing horses, too many monthly losses on the Snickers bars, and too many tickets for not shoveling the snow on his sidewalks fast enough. When he wasn't snapping at customers for giving him twenty-dollar bills for a morning paper, he was banging his Lotto machine for breaking down. The bottom line was that Roger had become indifferent to any conversation that wasn't about how the wholesalers had screwed him and how he, in turn, had to screw his customers. But then, it occurred to me, not everybody could offer him the kind of conversation I could.

"When you were a kid in Guyana, Roger, go the movies much?"

Since there was nobody else at the counter and he had nothing better to do than wash cups, he conceded a shrug. "Movies? Sure. Clint Eastwood. Steve McQueen."

"No, I mean Indian movies."

Did I work for Immigration? "That Bollywood crap? Dancing around with all the bracelets?"

"Spy things. Cops and robbers. Mad scientists."

The transformation was immediate. He still didn't completely trust my interest, but, as long as the water was drumming the aluminum basin, he could laugh at the cup he was scrubbing. "The Buxton! That was the name of the place near where we lived. Every Sunday morning, my father walked me and my brother down to the Buxton Cinema. You saw two films for what would be . . . what? Seven cents! We were in there for three, four hours!"

"And the bad guys were always Pakistanis, right?"

He hated showing it, but he was too curious not to turn off the faucet and wipe his hands on his apron. "How do you know that?"

"I've never seen them, but I've heard about them. From a friend."

He nodded—to me, but also to something far more distant. "Always the Pakistanis," he nodded. "They were going to destroy the world. Until our super agents captured them, yes?" He laughed more spontaneously than at any time since I'd first congratulated him for buying the store. "Ali and Fatima, they were always the villains. Evil schemers, yes?"

"And these things were dubbed?"

He had forgotten that detail, but only for a second. "How do you know that? Yes! In English, but with the strangest accents. Americans, French, Germans, I don't know. Everything but Indian. The Hindu wiseman talked like he was from Milwaukee!"

It wasn't hard to laugh with him, not after my e-mail from Wisconsin. But maybe I would have felt just as giddy if he had said Atlanta instead of Milwaukee. When all was said and done, Roger was my first reliable witness that the Reynaud-Grevin dubbers had ever existed!

"The Buxton had these old seats," he said, more enthusiasm coming with every thought. "The leather was worn through, they hadn't fixed them in years, and there was straw inside. When Ali and Fatima came on, we would scoop out great handfuls of straw from the seats and throw it at the screen. Oh, that caused trouble, Mister! There was an usher. A very big man. We called him Soma because he was big like a bull, looked like a wrestler. Soma would come down the aisle with his flashlight. We were misbehaving, yes? We were destroying property! Oh, but it was fun to throw that straw. Always it would end the same way, almost every Sunday."

"How?"

"With me and my brother begging Soma not to tell my father what trouble we had been causing! Happy for us, he was a nice man. He looked like a wrestler, but he was a nice man . . ."

I'd seen Mireille Pouchol in the Caporale-Kinsey archives, and she hadn't looked at all like a bull. But I doubted she had been as nice as Soma the night somebody had been begging her to keep her mouth shut.

CHAPTER 43

Inge Matson blamed herself. It wasn't her fault that I'd invaded her Fifth Avenue building or had waited her out for more than a half-hour in her overly lighted reception area, or even that she had finally given in with a curt "You've got one minute, Finley" in front of her receptionist and led me into her private sanctum. But what she couldn't forgive herself for was accepting the slip from Roger's check pad and reading the same sentence on the back twice. "Who is this?" she demanded.

"An old fan of yours. Used to listen to your voice every Sunday morning in Georgetown. That's in Guyana. In South America."

She couldn't have cared if it was on Neptune. "This is another one of your cheap tricks to . . ."

"The guy's asking Fatima for an autograph! Is that such a hard thing? How many other people ever asked you for one?"

She brought as much distrust as she could to fingering the silver bow at her throat and rereading yet again "My name is Roger Patel and I enjoyed very much all your films that I saw in my homeland. I would be honored to have your autograph." But she was losing resistance with every letter of Roger's crabbed handwriting. "You're a ridiculous person, Finley. You wrote this yourself."

"No, I didn't."

"Roger Patel!"

"That's the name he was born with. What can he do?"

She sat down with the slip at her conference table of a desk, and that seemed concession enough for taking the armrest of the blue settee against the nearest wall. I almost missed it because of the sun streaming through the window: In the center of the main wall's magazine covers with spidery looking models was a Robby Klein special—an emerald green triangle flanked by the kind of two cream squares I'd seen at the Pandora Galleries.

"And this is going to cost me what, this autograph for Roger Patel?"

"A question. Did you attend an art opening of Robby Klein where Servais made a fool of himself?"

Her squint went behind my shoulder to the triangle, then she spat a laugh. "Jake's told even you about that? No, I wasn't there. But I know it mortified Robby. She told me about it."

"And you, who did you tell?"

"How the hell do I know? Why would I tell anybody?"

"Nobody official ever asked you about it?"

"If you have a question, Finley, why not just ask it?"

"When the people looking for Kinsey came to see you . . ."

"Another exhilarating day," she said tartly. "They walked in outside more arrogantly than you did. I had exactly a half-hour to prep eight people for a trip to Milan. I told them that if they weren't from Immigration or the Internal Revenue, they'd have to wait. They were offended. They mentioned Neil's name, as though that should freeze my blood. I told them I hadn't seen him in 25 years, which was then true. So, either come to Milan with us or leave at once. Fortunately, they didn't choose Milan."

"You made an impression. They thought you were odd."

"A common reaction when people aren't treated as self-importantly as they would like. Okay, now? We finished?"

"So it wasn't you who told them about the scene between Servais and Robby at this art show?"

"Should I say it in Swedish for you?"

Her answer was more deflating than I'd expected. I'd wanted to give the benefit of the doubt to Jake Klein. We were fellow souls on Widower Walk, weren't we? "When Kinsey ran to you, you took him in. I wouldn't have bet on that kind of hospitality. Why'd you do it?"

She cocked her chin over Roger's check; it was as close as she had ever admitted I could ask a reasonable question. "I felt sorry for him. I'd misjudged him."

"Because Robby told you he hadn't killed Sayyid." She shrugged. "And Robby knew because Mireille'd told her after speaking with Kinsey." Another shrug. "You'd all wasted your bad consciences."

"Are they ever really wasted? If not for one thing, there's sure to be something else. My Lutheran upbringing."

As long as she was collecting odd pieces of paper, I gave her Robby Klein's old pay stubs, too. "What are these?" she asked, hesitating about even touching them. "From Reynaud-Grevin?"

"Klein said that was why Mireille came to talk to Robby. Something about money you were all still owed."

She handed them right back to me. "Some of them were, not me. And believe me, Mireille wasn't owed it, either. Every shopkeeper in Paris knew better than to trifle with her. A centime was a centime."

"No chance at all this was why Mireille went to see Robby?"

"Mireille went to see Robby because Robby was dying and Mireille knew it would be her last visit! Shouldn't that be obvious even to you? Talking about idiot pay stubs . . . Only Jake could believe that." She preferred Roger's company. "If this isn't a joke of yours, I'd be happy to give an autograph to your Roger Patel. Who is he? What does he do?"

"High finance," I thought aloud.

"What does that mean—a bookie?"

"Play a game with me for a second."

"I've done nothing else since I've met you."

"And it's been fabulous. But answer me this: If Mireille had been an artist and she had a show, might Klein make the same kind of scene with her as Servais did with Robby?"

She signed her name, then wrote something under it. "You mean, did he have an affair with her? Not that I'm aware of or that

Robby suspected. Jake's problem was that he was too protective where Robby was concerned. Wife, mother, or artist, she was his golden trust."

"All the more reason to suspect an affair."

"You're trying to be cynical, Finley, but no, you're wrong. Jake was all fantasy, and I would guess many of them were about the threesomes Jean-Claude had with Robby and Mireille . . . You didn't know? I'm surprised at you, Finley. I thought by now you'd have figured out their brand of mouthwash 25 years ago. It was a pretty open thing before Kinsey came on the scene. Then everybody seemed to drift off into more traditional habits. Maybe they got bored, maybe they didn't need to experiment anymore. I don't know. Maybe it was even Kinsey's wholesome influence. But as for Jake, I always sensed he felt left out of something."

"These old threesomes?"

"More than that. The *life* Robby had in Paris."

"So she definitely told him about Mireille and Servais."

"Aren't those the things husbands and wives confess in their candid moments? I don't know. I've never been married. Here, for your Mr. Patel. And tell him I would've been even greater on the screen than behind it."

On the back of the blank check, she had written: "Thank you, Roger, for reminding me I had an audience," signing it "Fatima."

"Why don't you sign your own name?"

"Why? He doesn't know who I am. I'm not even all those bad actresses he saw. His evil Fatima is just a voice in bodies. Who else can I be for the poor man?"

"Now that you mention it . . ."

"Good. So, are we finished now? Can we get back to our lives?"

"You haven't asked me about Kinsey."

She glanced at an appointment calendar at her elbow. "I didn't realize you were his travel agent. In any case, I'm not all that interested in his whereabouts. I'm sure wherever he is, he'll continue being a credit to his kind, whatever that is. As for me, I think a couple of nights on my couch liquidates my exaggerated opinion of him. Thanks to you, Jean-Claude got off even easier. He too sends you his goodbyes."

I almost opened the door before I gave in. "You were never involved in this ménage à trois thing?"

"You mean because I'm Swedish?"

"I mean because you're here, Jean-Claude's here, and I bet there's a third person living somewhere in New York."

She gave a shake to the thin bracelet on her wrist and dropped her head back into her calendar. "We're not married, Finley. Find a justice of the peace and then I'll tell you all kinds of scintillating things you missed out on. Have a nice day. Goodbye. *Adieu. Addio. Adios.*"

CHAPTER 44

I listened to *Calm* too much. First, it told me to slow down, to sit on my thoughts until they sprouted a few more buds. Then it kept rolling waves of anxiety through my chest, warning me that if I didn't act immediately, I'd get another fit like the one at the Cameo. What I mainly felt like doing immediately was ripping the damn print off the wall and trashing it. Instead, I decided to do the mature thing: throw the problem in somebody else's lap.

Dana strolled up to Carvel's like a gunslinger entering a saloon. Maybe it was her boots and her neck strings, maybe it was the occasional wind gusts that made ice cream less inviting than a couple of weeks earlier, but she came over to my picnic table as more cop than friend and lover. It didn't dawn on me until she sat down with a tentative smile that she suspected all three things might have been up for testing. "The ice cream isn't that good here."

"I think I know who killed Mireille Pouchol."

It seemed to take her forever to hear me. Then she stuck both fists in the pockets of her navy-blue jacket and let go with a longer sigh than I was supposed to notice. "Is that all?"

It was another of those moments when I should have understood I wasn't the only fragile soul on earth—and, at the same time, that this wasn't a cause for rejoicing. "I'm not that whimsical, Dana."

She took the chocolate cone out of my hand for a quick lick. "Maybe I was wondering if I was," she smiled, giving me the ice cream right back. "So who is it?"

"Jake Klein."

I ran through it in a race with the Union Turnpike traffic light. If I got it all out before engines started zooming past us again, I thought, it would be more tenable. I almost made it, though the only real noise unleashed by the green light was the loud exhaust from the city bus's air brakes. She was intrigued enough not even to wince. When I'd finished, she studied the chip marks on the plastic table a moment, nodded, then sat up. "Certainly sounds like enough to ask some questions."

"Right."

"'Right?'"

"I mean you're right. I should call Olmos and bring more grief to his life. He should then start World War III with his bosses and they'll tell him he's not only suspended; he's being deported to a weather satellite. You're right. That's what I should do like a good citizen and forget about it. Who knows? It may even all be true."

She took it in deliberately, then shivered. "It's too cold out here. C'mon, I want a coffee inside."

I followed her inside and listened to her banter with the kid behind the counter while he filled a Styrofoam cup with coffee. He was showing he was pals with the neighborhood lieutenant with the ID tag around her neck and I was trying to do the same thing. "So what's the problem?" she asked sharply when we had moved over to the end stools at the window. "This is a nice guy with two daughters who've already lost their mother and really don't need losing their father, too?"

"That sums it up."

"Does it? How about Pouchol? Did she have kids?"

"I never heard of any."

"Then that makes killing her okay?"

"You know I'm not saying that."

She slurped her coffee as if wanting to offend some of the invisible eavesdroppers outside the window. "No, you're not saying that," she said after a moment. "But what you are saying is that you're not on the job anymore, so you can play hide-and-seek with it. You can think straight up and talk straight up, but you're not really obligated to act straight up. In this particular case, even your client's dead."

"Actually, he isn't. Caporale is, not Kinsey."

"Better yet! You're even playing hide-and-seek with that! That's a helluva no man's land you're in there, Paul. Looks like it can be convenient. But I bet in the long run it isn't."

I'd predicted several responses, including the one she had given. But even though it had come out practically word for word as I had imagined, it was different because it was her voice instead of mine. "I figured on giving it to Olmos. I just had to play it out for somebody first."

She didn't relent; there was still something weekday afternoon gray, banal, and deceiving out on the Turnpike. "But you don't want to turn it over to him just like that," she said. "You want to know. You think you've earned it. You think Jake Klein owes *you* an explanation. Why should he be the one to still have some family left even though he's more of a bastard than you've ever been? Yeah, I think Alex might understand that. So, ask him. He's a good guy. Plus, he's not in a very strong bargaining position. I'm sure he'll give you first shot."

That response I hadn't predicted. In any voice. "Dana?"

She took another sip, more quietly, still trying to recognize somebody among the ghosts walking along the Turnpike. "You're really good at it," she said. "You even make your work work for your work. Or something."

CHAPTER 45

I had no argument against Olmos and the Hoboken cop named Puglia. I'd intended using my own tape recorder anyway; being wired even seemed to lower the hypocrisy quotient a little. Puglia, a cue ball heavyweight with Dentyne breath, detested the whole setup but was bent on protecting what was left of his jurisdiction. "You don't make any sudden movements," he lectured for the second time in the car around the corner from Klein's. "I want a complete record, every word. Got that?"

Olmos threw me something like an encouraging nod as I got out of the car and headed down to Bloomfield Street. I couldn't figure out how many times I had cost, saved, or simply endangered his job, or whether I had done any of those things. I was sure he had an accurate scoreboard somewhere. I pictured the scoreboard having a huge Visiv logo.

Jake Klein answered the bell as soon as I rang it. If he hadn't seen me coming from the window, he had been pacing around in the vestibule waiting for the bell to ring. And looking the more harried for it. His yellow dress shirt was half-hanging out over the belt of his jeans, the belt itself wasn't totally notched around his big waist, and what was left of his hair seemed to have gone halfway through a carwash. I could have been there with the Chinese takeout. "Got me in a parent moment," he said, taking a second to decide conversation was called for. "You just missed my daughter Rachel storming out. Come in."

I stepped inside to a bad movie memory: of *The House of Wax*, where people walked in from perfectly lighted streets to completely shrouded horror chambers. I'd come the last time as a phony dubber; this time I was a spy. As a House of Finley's Wax, the Klein place wasn't bad. "Suddenly she doesn't want to hear about college!" he said, banging the door closed, then flinching with the sound. "Like all she has to do is go to some computer institute for the fatally jobless, get a worthless piece of paper, and she'll be happy ever after! And in the meantime, there's Emily's house for this and Emily's house for that! Where's goddamn Emily going to be when she wakes up and realizes she's screwed up her whole life for a lousy joint?"

"Takes a little more than that, doesn't it?"

He finally seemed to remember I had no reason for being there, but he was in so much disarray he tried to invent one. "You want more of those pay stubs?" he asked, leading me into the over-stuffed living room. "I'm not sure I have any more. But I can look."

"No, I don't need any more stubs. But there were a couple of things I wanted to go over with you again."

It was a line I should have handed in with my badge on the Island, but he didn't seem to notice. He dropped his too many pounds down on one of the couches as though determined to send it through the floor. The plate of candies was still on the coffee table, but only one piece was left and it looked stuck to the dish. "It's like you have two minds when you're talking to them. One mind keeps trotting out all the warnings, commandments, and laws of the land. The other keeps whispering how you heard the same shit when you were their age and why should they listen any more than you ever did? Maybe I'd even think *less* of her if she did what I said! What the hell kind of way is that to fly the plane?"

I didn't want to hear more about Rachel Klein; it was enough to know talking SATs with her *wouldn't* have been so easy. "This financial consulting you told me you did in Europe, Jake—any of that for Visiv?"

He sniffled a smile to himself and turned his gaze to the points of his loafers. "That's blunt. What kind of cop are you anyway, Paul? I know you told me you weren't, but I think you are."

He looked proud to have asked the question. "Private."

"And the first time you were here, you distrusted me so much you had to make up that dubbing story?"

"My priority was a client. I didn't know whether to trust you or not."

"And now?"

"You tell me."

"All for Mireille."

"Let's say that."

He flicked at the bottom of his glasses with a nervous pinkie; he wasn't sure he had satisfied anything, but he wanted to think he had. "What the hell? In for a penny. What was your question?"

"Visiv. Ever work for them?"

"No."

I imagined Olmos groaning and Puglia scowling—and me running for the PATH train back to New York before either one of them could get his hands around my throat. "How about one of its subsidiaries?"

"What's any of this got to do with the price of pork rinds?"

"I'm not sure yet."

"Visual Arts International," he shrugged. "In Amsterdam and Paris. Satellite production and distribution. They weren't a subsidiary when I was there. I was already back here when that happened."

High fives in Olmos's car or was I still running for the PATH? I didn't know. Klein's face didn't help. He still looked preoccupied with Rachel. "You must've kept up some friendships with the people there, right? With the people who went into Visiv with the merger?"

"A couple."

"Any you've seen recently? Maybe talked to by phone or e-mail?"

"Not for months."

"You haven't been curious about Visiv?"

"Curious, sure. I read the *Times* stories on the Business page."

"Maybe give your students an extra insight into corporate tactics?"

"I don't have to cross the ocean to find examples of that. You want to tell me where we're going here?"

If I hadn't been wired, I would have gladly taken off my jacket; the wet on my chest was sweat, not the glop Puglia's assistant had put there for the mike. It was the kind of interrogation I'd conducted at a refresher course in the academy—not just of a guinea pig suspect, but for the monitors sitting behind a window and making their checkmarks. I had to get through to *all* of them. "We're there. Thanks."

He looked baffled, the way he was supposed to. "That's it?"

"Yeah. It was a timeline detail I couldn't see."

"Oh . . . Well, whatever. Who you working for, anyway?"

"He prefers I don't say."

He smiled, but looked on his way back to Rachel. "And you don't."

"Just one more thing, as Lieutenant Columbo always says. You told me that when you walked into Robby's room at the hospital, she was being grilled by Mireille on a tape recorder."

An anger line tightened in his cheek. "So?"

"About these pay stubs."

"If you can believe it. Her closest friend, but all that mattered to Mireille was that old debt."

"You're sure that's what they were talking about."

"I heard it myself."

"Oh? I thought you said it was Robby who told you afterward what they'd been discussing."

"I don't remember all the specifics. I think it was both. I stood there for a few seconds before they saw me and heard what they were saying. Robby filled in the details later."

"But Mireille was acting like 'Sixty Minutes,' like you said? She was asking a lot of questions?"

"Why else would she have a tape recorder?"

"I don't know. Maybe just to play something."

I thought he must have been a good swimmer: the more he realized he was being dragged under, the calmer he became. "Like what?"

"If I had to guess, I'd say a phone conversation Mireille had recorded with Neil Kinsey. I know it exists. She'd taped it hoping to get an admission from him—something she could use to plug Visiv's guns about the killing of an Indian gentleman named Sayyid. You've heard of him, right?" He stared through me. "Maybe the idea was that the studio could be the first to publicize it in France, blame this ancient dark deed on this American screwball and embarrass Visiv in the bargain for trying to use the whole thing for boardroom extortion. But then a funny thing happened, Jake. Kinsey persuaded Mireille of two things. First, that he wasn't the one who killed Sayyid. Second, that he wasn't the little bird who chirped all this into the ear of somebody connected to Visiv."

He took off his glasses to clean them on his shirt. I wanted to believe it was a tell and that it had come just in time. "But I told you what I heard them saying when I walked in."

"You could've been mistaken, though, right?"

"And that's what Robby told me."

"Sure, she did. You heard an ambiguous phrase and you immediately flew east instead of west. Happens all the time. And Robby, she knew you had a lot on your mind and she just agreed with whatever you misheard."

He refused to see the lifebelt I'd thrown him—at least until he put the glasses back on. "Seems like a century ago now."

"What I think is, Mireille wanted to tell Robby what she'd heard from Kinsey. Tell her that they'd both been wrong about him half their lives. It would be a nice thing for Mireille to do, Jake. Kind of relieve Robby of all the queasy feelings she'd been carrying around for so long."

"Their forbidden memory!"

"What?"

He didn't need my lifebelt; he could come ashore on his own and I could make of it whatever I wanted. "I used to say to Robby that if they didn't have that between them, they wouldn't have had anything, just an old job once upon a time in France. But thinking that about Kinsey, that made them co-conspirators in this secret society of theirs. All of them. Robby, Mireille, Inge, Servais. I don't know about Caporale, but Kinsey kept the others together. And everybody else—husbands, children, family pets— well, I suppose we were all the Pakistanis."

I tried to keep my eyes off the green triangle hanging behind him. "But that's normal, isn't it? You meet up with old school buddies, people you knew in the service. Whoever's with you is going to feel a little left out while you rehash old times."

"It isn't what they talked about, Finley," he said, spelling it out for the dunce of the class. "The studio hardly came up most of the time. It's who they *were* together. Do you understand?"

I didn't want to understand. Even with what Inge Matson had said and the green triangle painting, I wasn't ready to cash out everything on some 25-year-old *ménage à trois* and a sexually inadequate economics teacher. The last time that had explained anything, Sigmund Freud was still trying to adjust his pince-nez on the bridge of his nose.

"Anyway, you'll notice that as soon as they lost that secret, as soon as Kinsey wasn't their killer anymore, they all started dying off. All the bonds came loose. They had to deal with things on their own. You think that's a coincidence? I don't."

I saw Olmos doing the scowling this time: Jake Klein talking himself into a straitjacket instead of hard time. "I don't think Mireille got much of a chance to deal with anything."

He looked instantly regretful. "No. Sorry. That was glib."

It seemed time to go back to Track One. "When's the last time you saw one of your old colleagues from . . . what was it? International . . .?"

"Visual Arts International," he said, a last thought for Pouchol. "Viktor von Praag. He was here the spring before last. He looks at me lately like I'm quaint. There he is on the board of Visiv and here I am getting chalk on my sleeves. He doesn't approve of my career choice."

"He's the one you told about Sayyid? What Robby told you?"

He laughed. "You could've just asked me that straight out."

"Was he?"

"You mean am I the one who gave Visiv the ace in their dealings with Reynaud? You believe in the devil, too, Paul? Some red guy with a pitchfork and a tail?"

"Somebody had to tip them off."

"I'm sure. How about a few dozen people roaming around Europe over the last 25 years who've heard third-hand and thirty-third hand stories? How about the old studio head Peyrot having too many cognacs one night after a board meeting? Or better yet, Jobert whispering the dark secret to his mistress while Mireille was skiing in the Alps with *her* lover of the week? You really have nobody better to point at than me?"

I shouldn't have still been missing something. I'd already wrapped and tied all the bundles together. Even Dana and Olmos had said so. "You haven't answered my question, Jake. Did you tell this Viktor about Sayyid?"

"Me??!! *Robby* did! As soon as she told me, she was telling him, wasn't she? That's how communication works. Haven't you heard?"

He jumped up from the couch so abruptly I might as well have been unarmed. By the time I got my hand anywhere near my pocket, he was charging past me out into the hall and into the interior of the house. "We need a drink!" he called.

I told the heat in my lungs I would've already been dead if he had been coming at me. Then I told it he wouldn't be taking off with his belt half-open and without telling his daughters; the weather alone would have forced him to grab a jacket first. Robby Klein's green triangle agreed with me. Neither one of us needed a shattering of glass from inside. It sounded far too loud for a dropped liquor bottle.

Puglia had said not to make jerky movements, and I didn't, mainly so he and Olmos wouldn't come breaking down the front door too soon. The hallway outside went through a dining room and into a big kitchen. The air smelled of a scoured frying pan. Klein was sitting at the table cradling a bleeding hand. He had taken out the lower pane of a kitchen window and was staring up at the hole he had made. He looked stunned, as if he'd just discovered the laws of fists going through windows.

I grabbed a dish towel from the sink, wetted it down, and looked at his hand. He opened it, then let me turn it over without resistance; too much had dammed up behind his glasses since he'd jumped off the couch. A chubby sliver of glass between his second and third knuckle came out as soon as I pinched it between my fingers. The bigger problem, where most of the blood was coming from, was the heel of the hand; it looked to have been ripped up as he had pulled it back in after his swing.

"Just this Viktor? He's the only one you told?"

He didn't need the extra second to remind himself what we had been talking about, but he took it anyway. "Who else?"

"I don't know, Jake. I'm just trying to keep up."

"This client of yours. Servais?"

"Why him?"

"A feeling."

"No, it isn't Servais."

He looked genuinely surprised. "Really?"

"Really. You were talking about Viktor."

He sighed; he had to stop making bets with himself. "It had to be at least two years ago. He was here on business. We went to dinner, then back to the bar at his hotel. All night he's telling me these stories about Visiv. The Croatians and the Germans and the Dutch and the rest of Europe climbing over one another. Transmission rights, industrial secrets, who controls what bank account. I suppose I should've been interested in it, but I wasn't. That's what I thought I was getting away from when I went into teaching. An illusion, but at least the corridors where I work now don't have beige carpets and the stuff on the walls isn't some abstraction crap called PRODUCTION PRODUCTION. Anyway, I couldn't take in all the countries, let alone all the manipulations he said were going on. I guess I had one umbrella drink too many. Just to shut him up for a couple of minutes, I told him about Sayyid. To show him I'd had my brush with more than Gresham's Law, too. He wasn't very impressed. Went right on to talk about how they were about to grab some Swiss outfit."

"Mention Kinsey?"

"Never. I was tempted, I'll say that. Break up Robby's secret society, get her back to earth where killers weren't the most interesting people you could meet. But that would've been hypocritical. Even I thought it was interesting, that's the whole reason I told Viktor in the first place. But I never mentioned Kinsey by name. If they found out, it was on their own."

I finished dabbing away whatever glass I could see in his heel and handed him the towel to finish the job. "There's scotch above the sink," he said, standing up. "Pour me one."

"If you're going for a band-aid, leave the bathroom window alone."

He didn't answer, just trudged out, then went clomping up the stairs. That was twice in five minutes I'd let a murder suspect out of my sight. But it was the first time I wouldn't have minded if he kept going—up the stairs, up to the roof, up to the first airliner flying by. I'd nailed what *I* had wanted. Dana was right. The rest was law and order, throwing him into the system, mug shots and trials—secondary things. Why be there for the shrieking of Rachel when old Dad was led away in handcuffs for the last time? Why be there when it dawned on Mireille that old Dad had murdered her favorite aunt, the one she'd been named after? I had mine, and, for all I cared, Olmos and Puglia could have sat outside for the rest of the week.

I found a three-quarters-filled bottle of Vat above the sink, took a nice taste, then a bigger swig, then poured doubles for both of us. When he came back down, he was checking a sloppy criss-cross he'd made of the band-aids around the heel of his hand; the things would last an hour, at most. But so what? They'd be replaced by a doctor in the New York prison system.

"If it wasn't over pay stubs, why the scene at the hospital? Why'd you throw Mireille out of Robby's room?"

A 10-year-old sneaking his first sip couldn't have grimaced more with his swallow of half the glass. "You don't give me an umbrella in the glass, I'm in unchartered territory," he said, seeing my reaction. "How much you charge for what you do?"

"Not enough."

"Then change the system, shut off your self-esteem, or become a plumber. My parting advice to my students every year."

"Original?"

"Mine." He pulled out a chair and sat down; the hard screeching across the floor somehow made me think he was using Robby's chair for the first time since she had died. "When I walked in on them, the recorder was on the edge of the bed. Mireille was staring at it like she could've listened to it a hundred times without believing what she was hearing. Neil Kinsey hadn't killed for her, after all! How many nights had that thought comforted her vanity? How many others had it made her skin crawl? Now, though, nothing. Phsst! All over, gone, kaput. It'd all been a mirage. Robby, she was just gazing up at the ceiling. As white as the pillows, the goddamn drip in her arm, but to see her face, Kinsey was the one ruining her life! Not fucking cancer, fucking Neil Kinsey! It was grotesque. Like they'd both depended on the worst you can think about somebody else for their own lives! What kind of crap is that, Finley? How do you get to that point?"

I didn't know, but the old guy in the Panama hat and Yankees jacket at the Pandora Galleries had known. Had he been Jake Klein in disguise? Or had Robby Klein and her triangles just brought that thought out in all the people she'd encountered?

"Robby didn't need that. She had the girls. She had her art. And believe me, there's a lot worse than me running around out there, too. Weren't we worth more than this slug sounding like he was half in the bag? Kinsey had made them believe in the worst parts of themselves."

"That's why you blew up at Mireille?"

He looked over to where the hole in the window was beginning to let in too much cold. "It wasn't right they were both in a trance over this asshole. She'd come to see Robby because . . . Well, why waste their last time together . . .? Too much mortality to think about, I guess. After Mireille left, Robby started in. She knew Viktor, and suddenly she's adding up two and two. Since it hadn't been Kinsey with the big mouth, it had to be me. I told her the same thing I told you—they could've gotten that from a hundred people. But not according to Robby. She'd made up her mind, and that was it. I'd betrayed them all with Viktor. Do you understand how funny that was? First, she's more worried about who the hell's going around talking about things than the fact that there's this dead guy that somebody killed! I mean, what the hell is that? It's okay to leave a corpse here and there, but don't start blabbing about it? If you shut up about it, it'll just be our secret? Then it's how I betrayed them! *Betray* them? I never even belonged to their club! Anyway, that's when the nurse threw me out. I was the one getting Robby excited. I ought to get some cardboard for that window."

I sat down. I wasn't going anywhere: Did he need me to say it in digital neon? "What did you think you were going to accomplish by going to see Mireille at the hotel?"

"You say that like it's a fact."

"Apologize to her?"

He got up with his glass and started looking for something in the closets. "I'm not a drinker. Or have I already made that obvious? One sip of something and I get this craving for pretzels or popcorn. Before you know it, they're all gone and I've still got the drink in my glass."

He was talking; I didn't see any reason why I shouldn't be, Olmos and Puglia be damned. "There're lots of variations on the last meal. You know, the last steak the guy on Death Row gets? You don't always have to be on Death Row."

"No?" Not interested.

"I've seen guys arrested in bars having a beer. Then they get sent away for life and that turns out to be the last beer they ever had."

"Yeah?" Not understanding a word.

"Just a fact."

He finally stopped opening and closing the little wooden doors. "We ate all the pretzels last night and I haven't been to the store yet."

If he didn't want to hear, I told myself, it was his problem. "Why'd you think I was working for Servais?"

"Just a feeling."

"Let me guess why. Because Brian Seldes came here asking about him recently. A second visit."

He thought I was funny. "Goddamn it, Finley, if I ever need . . . what do they call it? A shamus? . . ."

"He came to ask you about Robby and Servais."

The pulse line returned to his cheek, but without the anger. Instead, he chugged what was left in his glass, exhaled loudly, and looked happy with himself. "I know this," I heard myself telling him, "because I have intuitions on every case. More than three of them, in fact."

"How do you manage that?"

"Innate."

He nodded. "His name wasn't Seldes. There were two of them. John and Mary, they called themselves. I was supposed to respect that, so I did." "Why didn't you just throw them out?"

"Because they had golden references. My friend Viktor. They didn't take two steps into the vestibule before they mentioned him. Just an hello from across the ocean, that kind of thing."

I remembered what Olmos had said about ESPN bringing games to the Congo. "They ask about Pouchol?"

He decided his glass was too empty, so came back to the bottle on the table. "No, and I thought that was weird. They sure as hell suspected me of something, and what was hotter than who killed Mireille? That I was glad to get Robby's funeral over with? That I don't like Rachel's friend Emily? But the only thing they wanted to know about Mireille was about France back when. When—history will bear me out on this—she was still alive. Mireille and Robby and Servais. Wink, wink. They couldn't hear enough about that even after I told them I hadn't been on the scene then. They were ready to take my fantasies for facts. Robby dead? A husband and daughters in mourning? Oh, yes, it must be a hard period for you. But let's move on to what we consider the greater good. And you know something, Paul? It *was* good for me. They let me feel my numbness. It was like when the Novocain starts wearing off and you can start feeling where it's still working. They made me feel like a thing, just so many *parts*. Some were working better than others, but forget about that. Just function. Stop looking annoyed and just answer our questions."

"They give you any idea why they were asking what they were?"

"All I could make out was something about some home movie they'd seen. Something of Kinsey's, I think. I asked them when it was going to be available at my video store."

"They didn't laugh."

"You know them?"

"I've met John and Mary, yeah."

"You work with them?"

"No."

"I should take that as the truth?"

"Yeah."

"Okay, that's what I'll do. Why not? So, I told them what they asked. I didn't want a single thing about Robby not being part of the official record. If I hadn't given away her dresses and bras, I would've given them to John and Mary. I mean, you don't like being under-papered in Washington these days. Especially with some foreign diplomat who used to stick his dick into your wife. You want all those details in the files. Never can tell when that'll come in handy for a world trade conference."

I didn't resist when he dropped the bottle over my glass even though I still had half a drink left. As Dana might have said, toast myself. I'd just given Olmos enough to take to his bosses about Seldes, hadn't I? And what could I have done about the wire at that point? I'd tried to warn Klein, but he had been too dense to hear it. And if I tried to pull off the mike, Olmos would have come running. Somehow I'd maneuvered myself into the nicest of all places—responsibility for nobody. "Did you apologize to Mireille?"

He shrugged himself back down into Robby's chair. "It seemed like a good excuse to see her."

"Just an excuse?"

"Maybe you're not the shamus I thought. It wasn't about apologies, my friend. What I needed her to do was to call Robby, back me up that I wasn't the one who'd started the Sayyid business with Visiv. I sure as hell wasn't about to go through those last days having Robby look up at me like I'd taken more away from her than her fucking tumors had!"

"Mireille turned you down?"

"Hell, no. She promised she'd do it the next morning."

"What?"

"She promised she'd do it the next morning."

I played it back a third time: '*She promised she'd do it the next morning.*' And that was it, wasn't it? Not only didn't he not have a motive for killing Pouchol, he'd had the best of all motives for keeping her alive. "So you thanked her and left."

"Is that what I did, Paul?"

He took as long to look up from his glass as I'd taken to reach for my weapon in the living room. I hadn't noticed before that the broken window overlooked a backyard with a gazebo. I wanted to notice things like gazebos before the mike started hearing other things. "Your only problem—if it ever comes up—would be to convince people she was still alive when you left her," I told whatever face he was giving me. "As soon as they put you in that hotel room, it's not going to take them too long to find out about the hospital scene, too."

"That sounds like professional advice."

I could hear the roar from Olmos and Puglia. "That's exactly what it's not. You're sure she agreed to help you get off the hook with Robby?"

"I just said so."

So what? Didn't I have a third time coming, like Julius Caesar with the laurel? Or, was I trying to remember somebody else, somebody more in the dipshit class, some other *shamus* who didn't know what the hell he wanted and kept asking the same question in the hope that the Vat sloshing around inside him would let him believe the answer? "Okay, then." He was waiting for me when I got tired of the gazebo and the lovely bare tops of two backyard trees that existed only in Hoboken, New Jersey. His big face said he had seen the digital neon and heard the warnings—and that they somehow mattered to him about as much as guys drinking their last beers before going to Attica on a life sentence. "What?"

"Nothing."

"I should get a move on . . ."

"I want to give you the rest of those stubs."

"I don't need them."

For somebody used only to *piña* coladas, he stood up too in charge of things. "You don't take them; I'm going to throw them away."

"Then throw them away."

"C'mon."

I didn't like the way he kept his glass as he went off to the hallway again. Suddenly, he was a flitting party host going from room to room to act sociable. I hadn't told him he had beaten a charge. The son of a bitch was taking far too much for granted.

"The funny thing," he said, weaving just a little on the stair-case, "was when Mireille was killed . . ."

"I don't think that was funny."

"No, in another way. With Robby. She was devastated. But how much can you take after a while? She was all out of energy for anything but trying to make it easy on the girls. My point is that Mireille never got to call her about the leak to Visiv. But I didn't see all that blame in her eyes I was worried about, either." He stopped at the top of the stairs and looked back down at me with a sway. "Know why?"

"Why, Jake?"

"Because somewhere in some scary little corner of her mind she suspected I killed Mireille . . . Don't you get it?"

"Get what?"

"*I'd replaced Kinsey for her!* She could think the worst of people again! Now it was me who was so fascinating! I gave her back a reason to live even those last hours!"

A car beeped in the street outside, and he broke his terrified gaze to look at it. Only when he seemed persuaded it wasn't Rachel coming back with Emily did he pivot off his foot and resume his plodding walk toward where he was going.

His destination was a bedroom at the end of the hall. Except for the bathroom, the other rooms on both sides of the corridor were closed. Maybe all second floors look the same, but, minus one or two doors and the Robby Klein triangles on the walls, I could have been steering myself through my last place in Valley Stream with Jenny and Susan. No matter how lived in everything below them looked, second-floor ceilings were always slapdash, as if they'd just been clamped down on some gaping hole facing the sky.

Klein was sitting on the edge of the bed in his bedroom, going through an attaché case on his lap. The bed was unmade, the business suit and tie he'd worn to work thrown over it. There were two vials of pills and a glass of old water next to the scotch on the night table. The room not only needed an airing but an ironing. "I don't want the stubs, Jake."

"Sure, you do. You come this far, you put in this much effort, you should have them. Like a trophy."

"I don't want any fucking trophy."

"I was thinking of putting something appropriate in the coffin with Robby," he said, oblivious. "Her sister and brother-in-law were really in favor of that. But what the hell? What could be more appropriate than Robby herself? That seemed more than enough."

I hadn't had a discussion like that with the Professor. I had just given Jenny my ring and Susan her favorite stuffed alpaca. What the hell had there been to discuss? It had been none of Joe Carroll's business. Killing them hadn't been enough for him? He was also supposed to have had a say in what was buried with them?

"But that doesn't mean I should get to keep what was important to her, either. Like what you were saying downstairs."

"What was I saying downstairs?"

He found what he was looking for, put it next to him on the bed, and closed the case. "If some official people ever connect me to the hotel where Mireille was staying," he said, reaching over for his drink. "What a nightmare that'd be! Who has to have an alibi for every step he takes? What the hell kind of world would that be?"

"Support your local police and let them carry the burden."

"That's easy for you to say. But take a worst-case scenario. Suppose Mireille had said, okay, Jake, I'll call Robby for you, but you don't deserve it because you shouldn't have said anything to your Visiv friend. I'll do it just because Robby's dying and we don't want to make that harder than it should be. And suppose I said to her, you're missing the point, Mireille. You won't be lying to her. It *wasn't* because of me. I have nothing to do with Neil Kinsey or dead Indians or all these big business manipulations. I'm Jake Klein. I carry 12 hours of teaching a week, and if that makes for a couple of more MBAs every year, that's the extent of my responsibility for anything in this world. And suppose she just nodded in this very condescending, hard-ass way she could have sometimes, sort of like, okay, anything you say, Jake. She'd lived with this Kinsey lie for so long—they all had—that they couldn't recognize the truth anymore when they heard it! And suppose this tiny, little smirk of hers, you wouldn't have seen it if you weren't watching closely, suppose it reminded me of their fucking secret club attitude . . . You see what I mean?"

One more shot for Rachel and Mireille. "Things you'd think about if you're in a situation like yours."

"Some things are more credible than others."

"Imagination."

"Imagination."

I'd gone as far as I could—with the scotch, with Alex Olmos's patience, with what Neil Kinsey's money had bought. "Give me the stubs so I can get out of here, Jake."

He plucked them out from under him. "Just as long as there's nothing I could've taken from her room she wouldn't have given me on her own, right? Isn't that what'd you call evidence? The smoking gun?"

I didn't like the way he extended his hand to me fist closed—or the feeling that I was still lagging miles behind him in something. Then the stubs were in my palm. But they weren't old French paper, they were a new French mini-cassette. And the penned words on the cassette were KINSEY TELEFON. "Why put that stuff in with Robby?" he was saying. "It wasn't important to her anymore. Everything must stop somewhere. Why not with you, Paul Finley, dubber, investigator, solver of problems?"

My body seemed to have deserted me. It had taken much less at the Cameo for my breathing fits to kick in, but now they were just lolling around wondering why I wanted to be excited. "Because I don't want it!"

"You said you wanted to clear up at least Mireille. In fact, that's what you promised the first time you were here. Or you telling me your promises aren't all that important?"

"Why you doing this, Jake?"

He smiled tiredly. "Hoping you'll stick to your guns . . . I know, I know. *Which* guns? You get so bogged down sometimes thinking this and then its opposite and then its counter-opposite. You get too many guns to stick to. Suicide by brain. Sometimes it's a godsend to be able to say, no, you over there, you with so many axes to grind you don't have any, you make the call. You're the umpire in the ninth inning of the seventh game of the World Series. Safe or out?"

"It's not up to me to make the call."

"One on one, Finley. I don't have the energy for any more triangles. They've taken over this house, haven't you noticed?"

I watched him polish off his drink. My very first intuition about Robby Klein, back when she had been Roberta Weiss, had been right, after all, I thought: She *had* been the key to everything. All I'd missed was the door, the building, the street, the city, the country, and the planet. But he was right, too: At least I could make up my mind. So, I put the cassette and my empty glass on the bureau next to me and walked out. I heard his weight shift off the bed spring, but he didn't call out after me. The wind on Bloomfield Street seemed to have been rushed down from the Arctic, knowing I was about to appear. I recognized Olmos's car turning the corner. I turned the other way, toward the PATH train at the end of Washington Street. I got a few doors down before I heard Olmos brake, then Puglia and him get out of the car and go up to Klein's front door. I wouldn't have looked back in any case, but I had an extra reason not to in the two teenagers with the backpacks coming toward me. One was a thin black girl being criticized by the other as "Natalie." The girl criticizing Natalie had her mother's round, chunky face and the blonde bangs of the French woman she had been named after. I didn't see Jake Klein anywhere in it.

CHAPTER 46

Jake Klein was taken back to New York for questioning. But Olmos never found the cassette and nobody at the Milford Plaza could remember having seen Klein on the premises. The *News* and local TV channels briefly made it sound like a break was imminent on the Mireille Pouchol case, then beat a quick retreat when Olmos could say for the record only that he had "interrogatives" about Klein's statements to his office. The media went back to worrying about the clothes of rockers and language of rappers, and Jake Klein went back to Hoboken. This time, when I could have done without it, Olmos called to thank me. He said I'd done as much as I could have done, that he agreed with me that Klein was the one and that even his bosses agreed enough not to go ballistic against him when Seldes had called them in a fury and with a warning to release Klein right away. "The teacher has more friends than he used to have or maybe even wants," he told me. "Who knows how he'll pay it off to them?" Sometimes, I rationalized to myself that, as soon as Rachel and Mireille had graduated from school and gone off to their own lives, Jake Klein would walk into Olmos's office with the cassette. Other times, I pictured him unspooling KINSEY TELEFON and dropping it into the toilet between the time I'd left and Olmos had rung his doorbell. Most often, I tried not to think about it one way or the other.

Where Dana was concerned, of course, this was near impossible. On the one hand, I couldn't presume to make her an accomplice after the fact by telling her about the cassette (and leaving on her the choice of whether to tell Olmos). On the other hand, Mireille Pouchol's phone call to Neil Kinsey took up residence with us like a spider hanging down from a ceiling corner: It should have been swatted away for good housekeeping, but what else could that lead to but eons of bad luck? Best stay out of that room so that the spider had its space and we had ours. Why worry about what we were giving up? We still had plenty of room, didn't we? And those odd sounds behind the door? Forget about them until the growing freak wasn't satisfied with what it had inside, broke down the door, and crawled out looking to munch on bigger game.

Arbitrary as it might have seemed on some levels, the Finley Code became more stringent after that day in Hoboken. Since I couldn't open up to Dana about everything, I decided it would have been an added insult to her to share those confidences with anybody else, including the Professor or Cynthia. Cynthia blamed what she called my "new aloofness" on Dana, and I didn't correct her. I cut down my club sodas at the Green Fox to about one session a week and kept my attention on the Quick Draw numbers whenever Johnny Yeager or Blanche Walsh started telling tales about the weirdness that had died with Miles Harkleroad. I hadn't been comfortable with the man while he had been alive, so didn't feel entitled to raising him to the level of colorful neighborhood legend while he was in his grave. I also cut down on caffeine intake, knocking off the afternoon coffees at Roger's. When I gave him his autograph from Inge Matson, he tried to look pleased with having built some bridge back to Georgetown, then stuck it in his shirt pocket and yelled at two kids for keeping the door of the soda freezer open too long.

I made sure to spend every dime of Neil Kinsey's money on office improvements; among other things, that meant ditching *Calm* and bringing in Mrs. Chalian's teenage son to help me computerize my files. Finley Investigations wasn't automatically more profitable, but the programs installed by Jeffrey Chalian offered the illusion it was a little less dog-eared. To replace *Calm*, I found a framed color photo of Mookie Wilson hitting the first base bag after the Buckner error in the sixth game of the 1986

World Series and a print of Cezanne's Card Players. Past glories, I wanted the clients who looked at my wall to know, wouldn't prevent me from dealing with their present problems with the deepest concentration.

A squiggly day was the one I picked up the *Times* to read that Visiv had completed its takeover of Reynaud-Grevin but that the studio's executives would stay at their jobs; Charles Jobert was a slight, crewcut 50ish and he smiled for the cameras as he shook hands with some Visiv honcho. If he believed what they were telling him, I thought, he probably also believed everybody had done as much as they could have in New York to solve his wife's murder. A happy day was when I went to court with the Canarsie lawyer and the tenants in their suit against the Klaus family. First, the judge studied my photos as though reviewing a Robby Klein show for the *Times*, got no acceptable explanation for them from the Klaus attorney, then set a 30-day deadline for "dramatic improvements" or jail time for the Klauses. Then, on the way out, big Brows ducked into a john, and I ducked in after him. It didn't totally satisfy as a Thug Moment (the stall door did more damage to him than my left hand), but it balanced an open account.

There was no way I could have missed the Professor's next soiree without making it a declaration of war, and I wasn't *that* pigheaded. Dana had been up for it, too, but an hour before knocking off, she had been hit with a burglary gone very wrong. An elderly couple had returned home early to find two morons rifling their place, the woman had been stabbed to death, and the man had collapsed of a heart attack. It was the lead story on my radio all the way out to Garden City. I could have done without it, but the image flashed before me anyway: The morons doing their next job on Bloomfield Street in Hoboken, Jake Klein showing up unexpectedly and dropping dead of shock, and the spirit of Mireille Pouchol resting more comfortably despite Paul Finley's best efforts at obstructing justice.

The Professor's house was a Mardi Gras. I had never seen so many at one of his gatherings—a good 25 or 30 people, bursting out of the living room into the hallway and stairs, pocket groups even in the kitchen. The old man himself was in his usual recliner, hemmed in by acolytes on the floor and not needing the table lamp in his eyes to look dazzled. "Running for office?" I shouted across to him. He looked happy to see me but cupped his ear for me to repeat what I'd said. Instead, I noticed the music box back on the shelf where I'd always seen it, its hinges and latch no longer quite as rusty. I wondered if he'd also fixed it to play a tune.

The attraction turned out not to be the chance to hear the Professor hold forth on the sinking of the Spanish Armada, but the engagement of two of his middle-aged hires for the History department. Since the couple insisted on playing up his role in their meeting, showing up on his doorstep with a few bottles of champagne and their own friends had seemed a natural idea for celebrating. If I knew Joe Carroll, they had been smart not to announce their intentions ahead of time. Given the opportunity, he would have been quite capable of telling them to rent the back room of a restaurant for another evening and leave him with his Wednesdays. It wasn't that he would have been less happy for them than he looked preening in his recliner, it was his increasing dependence over the last few years on his routines, and no routine was more carved into his calendar than his weekly talk gatherings. I was even surprised to see him presiding so effortlessly over so many separate, cocktail party-like clusters of conversation. It was almost as though he had felt as much need as I had to open a few windows and air out some encrusted habits.

I drifted around for a couple of hours, meeting the bride-to-be as an American history expert and the groom-to-be as the Professor's successor in European history. Both told me how much of an ogre the old man had been during their job interviews and how he had come close to terrifying even their references with questions about their credentials for referring anybody. I could believe it since I'd practically had to go through the same interview when Jenny had introduced us, but there was also a clinker of a note in what they said I couldn't identify. My longest conversation was with a computer lab guy from the university who was determined to advise me on how to elaborate on Jeffrey Chalian's programs. The more he told me how "easy" it would be to do this or that to end up with NATO secrets, the more I wondered if I'd been too hasty about clearing my paper files out of my bookshelf.

The Professor caught up with me as I was thinking of calling it a night. He steered me out into the kitchen, didn't like the sight of the two couples drinking beer there, and kept going down to the basement. I didn't like the purposeful way he snapped on the light and closed the door behind us. That mood usually meant he felt he had something due him, and I had nothing to tell him about Jake Klein.

Naturally, I was wrong. "You haven't been burning up my phone lines lately," he said, easing himself down into the captain's chair, "and I don't blame you. I wouldn't have called me, either."

"It's been a bad . . ."

"Shut up and sit down. When I'm apologizing, I want to apologize." I didn't have much alternative to the staircase step he had usually commandeered during our conversations, and he liked that. "There, see? You can just listen to the pathos for a change."

"I'm not hearing it yet."

"All right. But one question: Anything you find out contradict Kinsey's story about Caporale and the Indian?"

"No."

"Or the French woman . . .?"

"Did Caporale kill her? No. What happened, I think, is he got too many shocks in too short a time. First, there was Pouchol's call out of the blue. Then she's dead. Next, Seldes comes rapping on his door looking for Kinsey. Caporale gets panicky, can't believe this is all coincidence. But he's still got the movies in his cellar and needs to remind Kinsey they won't make him look too good even 25 years later. So, he comes to me to find Kinsey. He had no intention of returning the movies, he just wanted me to find the guy. What we were good for was keeping the extortion going."

"Lovely."

"But then Florence blew everything by sending me the movies. He didn't have his weapons of mass destruction in the cellar anymore. Worse, he could be made out to look like at least an accomplice in Sayyid's killing. No one on the planet was going to believe he'd never seen what was on them. From there, all the worms in his gut became pythons."

He took it in stonily, then shook his head. "And I was so sure he couldn't kill anybody. But he ends up killing two people."

"That's not what you're apologizing for."

"What do you think it is?"

Maybe I wouldn't have known if I hadn't taken his seat of wisdom on the staircase, forcing me to look directly over at the worktable where I'd last seen him fixing the music box. And maybe I still wouldn't have known even then if the couple upstairs hadn't reminded me of how brutal Doctor Carroll could be when interviewing people for positions as teachers or sons-in-law. But I thought I had one more intuition—my forty-ninth—coming to me on the Phil Caporale case. "Not telling me about you and Florence Caporale. Something along those lines?"

His middle finger wanted to tap an armrest, but the captain's chair didn't provide one as long as his arms. "What makes you say that? Because she wanted me to sit in the front pew with her for the funeral?"

"Not just that. Hiring Caporale for something he wasn't qualified for. The music box. Suddenly needing to fix a symbol of your marriage after all these years. When? Right after Caporale departs the scene. When Florence surprises you by 'acting human.' Like you were finally free to get things to work the way they should. What tune does that thing play anyway?"

"It did. I didn't fix it that much. 'Tea for Two.'"

"You're kidding! When was there a demand for that?"

He nodded; he appreciated the stupid tangent, but he didn't need it. "I hired Caporale because Florence asked me to," he said. "Only time she ever asked me for anything. I couldn't say no."

"A student of yours?"

"She had been. Florence Russo. Bright, but hardly brilliant. Always so solemn and withdrawn, almost cold. I suppose that was the attraction."

"Got it."

"What have you *got*? You haven't *got* a goddamn thing!" He sank into a volley of laughter from the kitchen to regain his composure. "It was the only time I cheated on Ruth. Seemed over before it began. A few years went by, and one day here's Caporale in my office looking for a job. He's not only got a résumé; he's got a note from Florence. The son of a bitch knew about us but didn't know. He lived his whole life that way."

"With one exception."

It took him a moment to understand. "Yeah, right. You're sure of that? You believe Kinsey?"

"Everybody asks me that."

"He doesn't sound like somebody you'd go to the bank with, Paul."

"He's one-for-one on that score."

"Seriously."

"I am serious. If he'd ever bloodied his hands personally on anything, there would've been a lot less Neil Kinsey in everybody's life. Probably not even a JABPUN. But the fact is, he's the only one in this whole mess who's never been bothered by a bad conscience. Even this guy who owns a candy store near me thinks about how he used to wreck property when he went to see these old movies as a kid. Not Kinsey. He *is* bad conscience, and somehow that comes out to making him innocence on parade."

"So they're never going to get this woman's killer."

"I didn't say that."

"No, there's an awful lot you're not saying."

This time he didn't pay attention to the hilarity upstairs. We were at the *quid pro quo* he thought he had coming for Florence Caporale. And maybe I owed him even more than the story of the Pouchol cassette. That had been me, hadn't it, who had accused him of killing Jenny and Susan while I'd been drinking with Klein? "An agreement I made with my phantoms, Joe. Maybe someday."

He relaxed his curiosity but not his disappointment. "Just as long as you don't end up like this Paris crowd," he said, reaching under him to slap at the armrests and lift himself. "That's why Pouchol's dead, isn't it? People who took their voices too seriously?"

"What did you think you owed Florence Caporale, Joe? For all those years of someone you didn't want, you didn't like, and you didn't respect?"

That much he had made his peace with. "My fear. What else?"

"And that's why you owe me an apology?"

He laughed; sadly. "One of the perks from dedicating your-self to fear is exaggerating its powers, making it a source of vanity. I worried I was interfering with your investigation by not telling you Phil Caporale went into his bathtub because, after all these years, he couldn't deal anymore knowing about me and his wife. Funny?"

"Sort of."

"Well, then you've lost your sense of humor with this little secret you're keeping. My last piece of advice and then we'll go to this goddamn party I seem to be throwing."

"What?"

"Whatever it is, make sure it's about something you've done or not done, not about what you think you know about others."

He took the stairs up to the kitchen slowly. The creaking could have been from him as much as from the steps. I thought of my impression with Servais—that he had just shaved a mus-tache or had had a physical mark of some kind removed from his face. It had nothing to do with people shouting into micro-phones in Paris or even with others lecturing students in Long Island classrooms, but I knew I was still missing something.

And then the old man snapped off the basement light for the fluorescent glare from the kitchen.

www.ingramcontent.com/pod-product-compliance
Lightning Source LLC
Chambersburg PA
CBHW030413020726
47493CB00003B/1058